FROM THE DEPTHS

And Other Strange Tales of the Sea

edited by

MIKE ASHLEY

First published 2018 by
The British Library
96 Euston Road
London NW1 2DB

Cataloguing in Publication Data
A catalogue record for this book is available from the British Library

ISBN 978 0 7123 5236 9

Frontispiece illustration by Harry Clarke from
The Year's at the Spring, compiled by Lettice D'Oyley Walters

Text design and typesetting by Tetragon, London
Printed and bound by CPI Group (UK) Ltd, Croydon, CR0 4YY

CONTENTS

INTRODUCTION

"As if it were too great, too mighty for common virtues, the ocean has no compassion, no faith, no law, no memory..."

So wrote Joseph Conrad in *The Mirror of the Sea* in 1906, highlighting why we both love and fear the sea. There is much that is both frightening and awesome about the oceans of the world. They cover over 70% of the planet's surface and on average are about 3.5 kilometres (or over 12,000 feet) deep, with the greatest depth at around 11 kilometres (over 35,000 feet). And we know so very little about what's down there. Little wonder that over the years there have been stories of monsters, ghost ships, and the plain inexplicable at sea.

And that's what this volume contains—fifteen stories of mystery, horror and the uncanny.

There are an abundance of mysterious sea stories, dating back to Edgar Allan Poe's "Ms. Found in a Bottle" (1833) and Samuel Taylor Coleridge's magisterial "Rime of the Ancient Mariner" (1798) and arguably the travels of Sinbad the Sailor in the *Arabian Nights*. All these and more are easily available on the internet and in other anthologies.

For this volume, I have tried to select lesser known stories, covering the whole range of the mysteries of the sea. Legends such as the *Mary Celeste* and the *Flying Dutchman* have inspired many stories and you will find their influence here in "Ship of Silence". There was the legend of the Sargasso Sea which was believed to be so wracked with seaweed that ships caught there could never escape. Both "Sargasso" and "Held by the Sargasso" draw upon this but in wholly different

ways. "Sargasso" also considers a deadly sea monster and another of
a very different kind appears in "From the Darkness and the Depths".

Derelict ships and hulks also haunt the seas and investigating
them leads to unusual problems in "The Mystery of the Water-
logged Ship" and "The Floating Forest". There are stories of revenge,
whether by ghosts ("The Black Bell Buoy") or by ships themselves
("The Murdered Ships" and "The Ship That Died"), psychic research
("Tracked") and haunted ships ("Devereux's Last Smoke"). Then
there are the stories of the inexplicable or bizarre, "The High Seas",
"The Soul-Saver" and in particular "No Ships Pass", all of which show
that the sea is another world and one of which we should be wary.

Probably best not to read these stories before going on a cruise—
but then, why not? As you stare out into the dark night from your
cabin it will help you populate the world beyond with every possible
horror.

THE SHIP OF SILENCE

Albert R. Wetjen

Albert Richard Wetjen (1900–1948), who was always known as Dick or Dickie, was born in South London of German descent. Young Dickie had a wanderlust and ran away to sea when he was fourteen as a merchant seaman and served during the War though did not sign up formally to the army until 1918. He could not cope with civvy street after the War and emigrated to Canada in 1921, smuggling himself into the United States and settling in Oregon. He took out American naturalization papers in 1925. By then he was selling regularly to the American pulps and rapidly established himself. He was almost a dual personality. In person he was belligerent, rude, offensive and a heavy drinker, but in print he was literate, clever and imaginative. His story 'Command' won the O. Henry Memorial Prize for the best short-short story of 1926, the Awards Committee going so far as to say that he was in "direct line of succession to Joseph Conrad." Amongst his books he was applauded for Way for a Sailor! *(1928), which tells of a sailor's life in language surprisingly frank for its day, and* Fiddlers' Green *(1931) where a sailor experiences many of the legends of the sea. But his best known character was undoubtedly Shark Gotch, a ruthless, amoral seaman and mercenary who will go to extremes to avenge wrongs. Scores of stories were collected in several volumes starting with* The Chronicles of Shark Gotch *(1937). Wetjen's lifestyle cut short his life and he died, suddenly, aged only 47. The following story, from 1932, shows the power of his writing.*

B ECAUSE THIS IS A TRUE STORY, THERE IS NO ENDING... IT WAS early in the night and very hot, the sticky tropical darkness pressing all about us, seeming to muffle the lights of the city ashore and rendering to a soft velvet the waters of the harbour as they rippled through the anchor chains and along the hull of the little coffee freighter that had brought me to Santos, Brazil. I had been sitting with Captain Massey and old Billings under the awning of the afterdeck, drinking long, cold gin *tonicas* and talking of the sea in general and of ships that had vanished into its mysterious immensity. Old Billings never romanced, let it be said. He was a dignified man, red of face and with silvery hair, in his eightieth year and at that time the Lloyds surveyor and agent at Santos. He had followed the sea for some forty years before leaving it to take his present position, and so he spoke as a sailor.

"It's not so hard perhaps to account for the foundering of most ships," he said. "They get into bad weather and have their hatches burst in; or they're built or loaded top-heavy and capsize. That's all in the run of the game. What isn't so easy to explain is how they can sometimes drop out of sight without leaving a trace, especially in these days of wireless and with the regular sealanes all well travelled. But we know they do. And we know too that it's hard to sink a vessel without something floating clear—a boat, lifebuoys, hatches, oars and what-not. Of course the sea's big and it's not hard to believe that searching vessels can overlook such small things. You've only a visibility of from ten to fifteen miles on the clearest of days from a ship's deck, and hatches and lifebuoys and even bodies are level with the water, easily hidden behind the swells.

"Yet even at that it seems curious that nothing comes to light. Take the *Waratah* now. You'll remember her—a modern liner of over fifteen thousand tons, newly built and on her second voyage. Carrying over two hundred souls, what with passengers and crew, and running on a regular route, down the coast from Durban to Capetown in South Africa. Of course she carried no wireless. That was before the day it became compulsory for liners to carry it, and it hadn't come into general use.

"But there she was, on a thickly travelled run. Soon after leaving Durban she speaks to the freighter *Clan McIntyre*, drops her astern and then proceeds to disappear. Of course there was a heavy gale reported soon after and it seems reasonable to suppose she foundered. But a new ship, remember—absolutely vanished! They sent out searching vessels, of course, when she was reported overdue. For months Government and private craft patrolled the coast waters. One vessel searched for over ninety days and covered close to twenty thousand miles of sea, and there was even a vessel sent to follow the normal current-drift far to the south. But nothing was ever found. Not a body, not a hatch, not a plank!

"Then there was that American transport the *Cyclops* that dropped out of sight—and she *did* have wireless. Then only this year there was that Danish training-ship the *Kobenhaven*, clearing from Buenos Aires for Australia. Been overdue for months and nothing found; must have gone down—and she's taken the flower of Danish youth with her, sons of the best families. My personal opinion is that she got too far southerly, into the Antarctic ice, struck a berg and crumpled. You know.

"But that isn't really what I started out to tell you. You can set up some sort of reasonable explanation for ships that just vanish. It's the other vessels that make the real mystery—the ships that don't drop out of sight, but turn up like a lot of wandering ghosts, sound above and below but without a soul on board. In '23 or '24, I forget which, there was a schooner picked up off Diamond Shoals, to the north. Sails set, boats in place, no unreasonable amount of water below. But never a sign of her men… *Why*? Foundering doesn't cover that—for there's the ship!

"Somewhere in the records too you'll find notice of a Japanese steamer discovered drifting in the South Atlantic. Carried a crew of forty-odd and all they found were eight dead men on the main deck, and nothing to show how they had died. Boats all in place there too. No sign of heavy weather. No sign of fire or disease… Queer, isn't it? And then of course there was the *Mary Celeste* in the '70's; I suppose she's the classic of what I am trying to say.

"They found her in mid-Atlantic in calm weather, you'll remember, with all the usual signs of mystery. Everything in order. Hull and spars sound. Fair-weather sails set; not a lifeboat missing. Everything as it should be, except she had no crew. What makes her case a classic are the number of altogether peculiar features.

"There were the men's clothes hung on a line to dry. Breakfast, half eaten, was on the fo'c'stle and the main cabin tables; and the food was still good, proving she had not long been abandoned. Under the needle of a sewing-machine in the Captain's room was a child's dress, half-finished, where the Captain's wife had obviously hurriedly left it. Then they found a cutlass in its scabbard, with stains like blood on the blade, and on the rail in the starboard bow they found a deep new cut with stains about it also. Cut into the bow itself, a little above the water-line, were two deep grooves, gouged out each side, as it were, and quite fresh. Most curious of all, the only thing missing on board was the chronometer. But again—why?… Why?

"Where had everyone gone? There was no sign of mutiny or of a raid, shall we say, by pirates. How had the men left the ship—and why had they left, it, obviously in haste, in the middle of breakfast? We don't know. There have been a lot of theories put forward, but for one reason or another they can be discounted. If it were only the *Mary Celeste* we might let the matter go, just write it off. But there are all those other ships, not only those that drop out of sight, without trace, but those that are found, abandoned for no earthly reason. New cases still turn up too, once every decade or so—and there you are.

"I think I'm a hard-headed man. I've had lot of experience one way and the other. I don't take much stock in ghosts and I believe everything has a reasonable explanation if we could locate what it is. And yet sometimes—well, I don't know. The sea is pretty big and we haven't learned much about it and what's in it. Remember the land only covers one-fifth, or is it a quarter, of the earth's surface—and we haven't fully explored the land yet. As for the sea, we have only gone down a few hundred feet—a few hundred feet in five miles of depth, remember. Ships stick to narrow and clearly defined lanes as a rule. There are tremendous areas where I suppose vessels only wander once in fifty years, or perhaps never go into at all and never have been.

"Is it something in the sea that comes out and loots these abandoned ships of their men? I know and you know that there are queer things in the sea. There're the giant squids on which the sperm whales feed; I've heard they sometimes are a hundred feet from the tip of one arm to the other. Then there's the sea-serpent. Yes, I know landsmen laugh at us for believing in that. But why shouldn't we believe in it? It's been known from ancient times. It's been seen more than once, even if we acknowledge that a length of kelp, a barnacle-covered log or a school of porpoises in line might often have been mistaken for it. But how can you argue away the report of the *Daedalus*?

"Here is a British warship, certainly in command of a reliable man, certainly officered by some few gentlemen whose integrity cannot be questioned. They sight a long snakelike animal, observe it for some time and are even able to sketch it. The scientists and public may laugh, but you can't argue away the testimony of a whole ship's crew. Nor is it only the crew of the *Daedalus* you have to figure on. Captain Hope of another British war vessel, the *Fly*, saw a large animal with the body of a crocodile, a long neck and four paddlelike arms, in the Gulf of California. A Lieutenant Hayne, in command of the yacht *Osborne*, sighted something as queer, but I forget where. There are two other men who filed a joint report also, and they were members of the Zoological Society cruising in a yacht off the coast of Brazil. They saw a creature with a neck seven or eight feet long alone and as thick around as a man's body. I say you can't laugh away all this, and you can read the full accounts yourself if you doubt me. I've gone into the matter pretty thoroughly because—well, you'll understand in a minute.

"I don't say, mind, that any sort of animal such as the giant squid or the sea-serpent can account for these mysterious and deserted ships, nor for the actual complete disappearances. I don't know. No one knows, and we can only wonder. I do hear that some scientists have recently suggested the survival in deep waters of some of those gigantic animals that occupied the world in ancient times, before man came. It doesn't seem unreasonable to me.

"But we'll let that pass. What I wanted to tell you when I started out was of an experience that came to me. I shall never forget it. No man could. It was one of those nightmarish things that remain with a man all his life, and I suppose everyone goes through something as ghastly at least once before he dies, if he follows the sea... Yes, I'll take another drink!

"It all happened a long time ago. I was just a young third mate then, around twenty, serving my first voyage as an officer on the bark *Doyon* out of Sydney for Callao. We had good sailing weather, as I remember, and we were coming up to the South American coast after a couple of weeks out, when we sighted just such a ship as I have been talking of.

"I don't want to exaggerate or to imagine things after all these years, but I'll swear there was something eerie about her from the moment we first saw her. It was early in the morning, as I recall, and I had just come up from breakfast to take over from the mate—a decent sort of chap named Mathews, tall and well-built, not many years older than I was myself but very highly strung, as I afterwards discovered.

"'That's a queer-looking packet ahead of us,' he remarked when I joined him on the poop. He had been staring through the glasses and now he handed them to me. 'Looks like she's not under control,' he said. I stared through the glasses myself and saw a small barkentine some distance ahead of us and apparently crossing our bow. She was under plain sail but her after-booms were jarring crazily and it was obvious that she was yawing all over the sea. I could discover no sign of life on her decks, nor could I locate anyone at her wheel and I suggested to Mathews that he'd better call the skipper.

"'I've sent for him,' he observed and so we both continued to inspect the strange ship until the skipper came on deck. The morning was very calm, with a gentle wind from the south. There was no sea, just a long oily swell almost a bottle-green in colour, and the sky was a clear blue dotted with a few clouds on the weather horizon. It was warm, too, but I remember I felt uneasy and a little chilled, just as if I had a presentiment of what was to come. The skipper came on the poop rubbing his eyes, for he always slept late, and he took the glasses from the mate with considerable impatience.

"'What is it now?' he said bad-temperedly, and he stared through the glasses for some time. Then he said, 'By George, it looks like she's abandoned!' and I knew from the sound of his voice he was feeling pleased, thinking of the salvage.

"Well, to cut a long story short, we hove the *Doyon* to and the skipper sent the mate and myself away in our longboat, together with four of the men. We came up under the barkentine's counter and read her name, painted in white letters, '*Robert Sutter*—SAN FRANCISCO,' and it didn't need a second look to tell she was abandoned all right. One of the men got aboard over her midship rail when she rolled down, and he threw us a line so the rest of us could swing up. We left two men in the boat and proceeded to inspect our prize, telling the two men who had boarded with us to look over the fo'c'stle while Mathews and myself went aft.

"It is a curious thing—but I swear I had gooseflesh all over from the first moment I put foot on the *Robert Sutter's* main deck. There was something so lonely about her, so—how shall I say?—*uncanny!* You could feel by the swing of her she was not water-logged. There was no sign of fire that a first casual inspection brought to light, and she was clean and had evidently been newly painted. Every rope and line was in place and her two boats were secure in their chocks on top of the galley house. We searched her from stem to stern and found no hint of life, save that in a large iron cage, suspended from a hook outside the galley 'midships, there was a parrot.

"The bird seemed in a bad way. It was crouched down on the bottom of the cage, lying half on its side and sort of pulsing all over, its eyes glazed and half closed. From the look of it—it was all but bald—it was a very old bird and it made no move when we approached it. 'It needs some water,' said Mathews, a fact which was obvious, and after we had brought it water, which it eagerly dragged itself up to, we went on with our search.

"Near the break of the poop, on the starboard side, we discovered what must have once been a cat. The creature had been smashed flat—as flat as a pancake, I tell you! It was just a thin sheet of black fur and dried flesh, literally sticking to the planking. But there was nothing to show how it had been killed, and at the time we did not pause to ask ourselves about it. We had to complete our searching and get back to the *Doyon* to make our report, you understand.

"Well, in the scuppers right opposite the port galley door we found a revolver, a bright nickel affair somewhat rusted and with every shell fired. And that was all, except that over the whole vessel there hovered a curious sort of smell, dried-up, if you know what I mean, like the stale, weedy, fishy smell you get from mud-flats when the tide runs out. But even that we didn't particularly notice at the time.

"Anyway, that was all, as I said. The ship's cargo was cut lumber, which we ascertained by lifting the hatches, and when we sounded the well we found only the usual amount of bilge water which every healthy wooden ship will take through her seams. It was all very mysterious, though, and if you can picture us staggering about the swaying deck with the spars jarring above us, the canvas thundering and slatting, the wheel and rudder creaking, every block and line making its own individual noise, and not a soul to be found, you can understand how we felt. Mathews was getting the jumps even before we were through with the inspection and I noticed he wiped the sweat from his face repeatedly.

"We went back to the *Doyon* at last and made our report, and the skipper didn't take much stock in what we had to say. 'She must have had a third boat,' he observed carelessly. 'They probably thought she was foundering or something and just left her. I've known whole crews to panic before. You say there's no sign of disease, and no bodies? Well, there's nothing to be afraid of, then!' He did admit it was queer that we had found her hull sound and that none of her navigation instruments appeared to be missing. Even in a panic the master and the officers of a vessel are not liable to forget their working-tools. And then in the log-book we'd discovered and brought back there was no hint of anything amiss. It was written up to within four days previously and reported only fair weather. I remember I pointed out to the skipper that no crew would be likely to abandon a vessel and leave the logbook and ship's papers behind, but he brushed all that aside. He was a man almost completely without imagination, and all he could think of was salvage.

"'I'll give you six men,' he said to Mathews, 'and you can take the third mate along with you. Bring her to Callao and we can go into the whole matter there with the port officials.'

"Mathews wasn't a bit pleased with the prospect, though most mates would have jumped at the opportunity of making themselves a nest-egg and enjoying a first command, even if it would be only for a short time. 'I don't like the idea at all, sir,' he said. 'There's something queer about the whole business!'

"The skipper waved all that away. 'Nonsense!' he said. 'You ought to thank your stars for the chance!' But then, you see, he hadn't been on board the *Robert Sutter*, and we had to admit—now we were back on the *Doyon*, surrounded by the curious crew—that our feelings did seem rather silly. So the long and short of it was we picked out six men, or rather the skipper appointed the six most useless we had on board, and we pulled back to the deserted barkentine, four other men coming with us in the longboat to take it back. The *Doyon* squared away on her course again and I can remember that Mathews and I

stood on the *Robert Sutter's* poop and watched her with something
of the feeling of being deserted to our fate.

"There wasn't any use of our worrying about that, however. There
we were with a perfectly sound and well-built ship, amply found with
water and provisions, rolling at will on a bottle-green sea and with a
fair wind blowing for Callao. Mathews pulled himself together and
we got the vessel on a course, set watches, wound up the rundown
chronometers, setting them from a spare one we had brought from
the *Doyon*, and so prepared to make port.

"It was somewhat uncanny to clear out two of the cabins below
ready for our occupancy, for the gear of the previous inhabitants was
scattered about, and in the room I chose, which had been the mate's,
there was even the imprint of his head still on the pillow and a half-
whittled plug of chewing-tobacco tossed on the blankets, together with
an open clasp-knife. I shook off my feelings however, before very long.
I was young, healthy, usually in good spirits and it was not long before
I was whistling to myself. Mathews came and stood in the doorway
while I was fixing my bunk and his face was very serious, more serious
than I had ever seen it. I think I have said he was a highly strung man.

"'I don't see how the devil you can whistle!' he burst out irritably.
'Good God, man, doesn't it bother you? The crew—fourteen men,
according to the articles—all gone!'

"I stopped whistling and looked at him. 'It is queer,' I agreed. 'But
it doesn't do us any good to worry about it.'

"Mathews shivered and looked over his shoulder. 'But where did
they go?' he said, his voice dropping. '*Where and why?* It's all right for
the skipper to talk of a third boat, but this ship carried no third boat.
I've been over her again. There isn't a sign of one.' He went away
and I could hear him muttering to himself as he straightened up the
room that had been the Captain's.

"A fine sort of business, wasn't it? Yet we could have probably carried on all right and accepted things as we found them, if it hadn't been for Mathews and—something else. When I went on deck I found Mathews staring down at the splotch of black fur and dried flesh that must have once been a cat.

"'You can figure it out,' he told me in a strained voice. 'That poor little devil was running away from something and then it was killed. Think how fast it must have been, whatever it was killed it. You know how a frightened cat can run.'

"'What makes you think it was frightened?' I asked him. But he only shook his head. Since that time I have seen a python smash flat a running dog with a blow of its snout—and that was quick work. Yet a dog isn't as agile as a cat. You see what I mean? And that python's snout only caught the dog in the small of the back. This, that was stuck to the deck, was *all* flattened, head, body and tail, and all about it there was a faint but perceptible depression in the hard teak planking, a sort of circle about four feet across.

"'Then there's this gun,' said Mathews later on, coming back to the subject. He held in his hand the nickel-plated revolver we had found in the scuppers. 'Every shot fired. What at? Why?'

"I tried to talk him out of his sombre mood, but each time I did so he would only shake his head and ask further questions—until I swear he had the whole crew of us completely jumpy when we might easily have forgotten the matter, or at least relegated it to the back of our minds... Until, of course, the next thing occurred.

"This was late that same afternoon, or rather close to evening. The men had gone for'ard, all except the helmsman, of course, and Mathews and I were pacing up and down the poop waiting for the seaman we had delegated as cook, to serve supper. The day was still fair, the sea calm and smooth. We were under full sail and making about six knots before a freshening wind which was coming up with the approach of nightfall. And then, all of a sudden, there came the most terrible scream and quite distinctly some one shouted, '*My God, Collins!*'

"I can't describe the electrifying effect of the thing. That scream sent all our spines cold, froze the very blood in our veins. And that voice! There was everything in it that told of utter terror. More than that, it was a strange voice—it belonged to no one of the men we had with us.

"Mathews and I had stopped pacing the poop and were riveted to the planking. 'Good heavens!' said Mathews in a strained voice at last. 'What—who was that?'

"Before I could even venture a reply there came a whole series of screams, splitting our very ear-drums. And then we heard another voice, a different voice from the first: '*It's coming aft. It's coming aft!*' And if ever there was sheer, pitiful and desperate horror in any man's tones there was in these. The crew had come running up from the fo'c'stle. The cook had come out his galley and was standing open-mouthed, looking dazedly around, one hand clutching his apron and the other holding a cleaver.

"Mathews let out an oath and dropped down the poop companion to the main deck. He was badly shaken, and he ran 'midships toward the men. I was close behind him too!

"'Who the hell's making that racket?' he shouted hysterically.

"No one answered him. The men had stopped and were looking uneasily about. Again came those awful screams, ringing all over the ship, and the strange voice thick and hoarse with utter fear: '*It's coming aft! It's coming aft!*'

"Mathews stopped short and stared about him. 'My God!' he whispered to me. 'Am I going mad?' And then we both saw the men were pointing at something and after a moment the cook exclaimed in a relieved voice, 'Why, it's only the parrot, sir!'

"I can remember the vast flood of relief that came over me. I stopped shaking and let out a big sigh, and I could see that Mathews visibly relaxed. 'I'd forgotten the parrot,' he said with a queer laugh, and he walked round to the forepart of the galley where the bird's cage hung. The men gathered about too and some of them laughed, though there was nothing of mirth in the sound and not much of reassurance. Mathews looked into the cage and I peered over his shoulder. Since we had given the bird some water that morning it had apparently recovered, for now it was sitting on its swing perch—but sort of crouched down. And I tell you it acted like no parrot I have ever seen, before or since.

"Every one of its tattered remaining feathers was erect. Its eyes were fixed and staring and did not blink. It shivered the whole length of its body at regular intervals and did not move when Mathews shoved a tentative finger through the bars and spoke to it in a soothing voice. Even as we watched it the bird crouched lower, opened its beak and gave vent to one of those horrible screams. And this time it was the sound of a man in awful pain, wave on wave, abruptly cut off. There was an aching silence for a second and then the parrot croaked distinctly, with a queer tremulous catch in its voice: '*You can't shoot it! You can't shoot a thing like that!*' And the voice was again strange, the third we had heard, distinct in *timbre* and pitch. The voices of three separate men!

"I can remember that for at least a minute there was a tense and frozen silence. I could hear my heart thumping and the cold sweat was running down my throat. Mathews had pulled his finger back from the cage as if it burned him and he was the first to speak. 'I never thought of it,' he said, his words flat and strangely without expression. 'I never thought of it, but it's simple enough… He knows what it's all about! He knows what happened. He *saw!*' He spoke like a man half asleep, staring wide-eyed and ashen-faced at the crouching, shivering parrot. The men began to stir uneasily and one or two of them looked hastily over their shoulders.

"I nudged Mathews in the back. 'Pull yourself together,' I whispered. 'We can't have the men getting all jumpy.'

"But you couldn't get him away. You couldn't get the men away either; they all seemed riveted to the spot, watching that poor devil of a parrot. It mumbled to itself nearly all the time. Then it would chatter out some words we could not understand—not English words. Nor did it always use the same language. Mathews had a little command of Spanish and swore the bird often talked in that tongue. I am certain I caught German words and once or twice certain phrases in Polynesian which I'd picked up while on a trading-schooner through the Islands.

"You understand that the parrot was certainly old, incredibly old, I would say. It was almost featherless; it must have had many masters in its time. You know they say those birds live for a century or longer. And God knows where this bird had been and what it had seen. The things it muttered must have come from its ancient memory of many masters of many nationalities. And between its mutters it would let out those awful screams, exquisitely different screams—the screams of different men in agony and terror. And immediately after each scream it would choke out some phrase, not always in English, as I've said, but in other languages too.

"I don't know if a bird can go insane, but if one can that parrot was very close to it. There was only one thing we could deduce from its actions. It had been frightened almost out of its life, and the screams it gave and the words it shouted had been hammered into its head by some awful happening. The words it muttered half-mechanically were from long ago; the words it shouted were of recent memorizing. It was horrifying. It seemed trying to tell us something. From behind its fixed, unwinking eyes there seemed to hover a shadow; I even felt there was an uncanny flicker of pleading. It wanted to make us understand that it had seen something no living thing had seen before, something so monstrous and ghastly it had penetrated at once and indelibly even into its own cynical and calloused brain.

"How long we all remained about that cage, silent and shuddering, I do not know. But it was the night chill coming into the wind that roused us, that and the smell of the supper burning on the galley stove. We had all insensibly crowded together, as if each man feared to stand alone. The man at the wheel began to shout, his voice frightened. He wanted to know what was the matter and he wanted to be relieved. I told one of the other men to go aft and he went, but only with the greatest reluctance, his hand on the haft of his sheath-knife and his head continually turning to glance over his shoulder or at the darkening sea. And still at irregular intervals that crazy parrot let out its blood-curdling screams and shouted blindly at us: 'It's coming aft. It's coming aft!' or that desperate, 'My God, Collins!' or that flat, despairing, 'You can't shoot it. You can't shoot a thing like that!'

"I shook Mathews finally and told him we ought to be getting back to the poop. We hadn't eaten yet, and it was getting dark. 'Eaten?' he said, literally staggering as he went aft with me. 'Eaten? How can you talk of eating?' He stumbled up on the poop and leaned against the main cabin skylight, mopping his wet forehead. 'What was it that came aft?' He whispered hard, shivered and tried to straighten himself. 'The mate of this ship, was named Collins, according to the articles we found,' he said. 'And only the Captain would be likely to call him Collins. So it was the Captain who called out, "My God, Collins!" And what was it that came aft?'

"'You're acting like a damned fool!' I told him bluntly, though I was all but unnerved myself. You would have been too, to hear those terrible screams ringing through the ship every minute or so, and those strange voices of vanished men repeating those terror-stricken words! But I still had enough sense to face the fact it was only a parrot talking and that we had to get the *Robert Sutter* into port. I got Mathews below at last and we had a stiff drink together, after which we ate some canned beef and sea biscuit, the supper that had been preparing in the galley being hopelessly ruined. We knew for certain now there had been no third boat!

"Well, that night we faced another complication, for none of the men would remain for'ard, but insisted on bringing their mattresses aft and crouching down by the break of the poop. The helmsmen refused to be left alone and we had to let two men steer through the dark hours. Neither Mathews nor myself could sleep, with those screams ringing out, and we paced the night away together. It was uncanny to be on deck. We all had the feeling that at any moment something would loom up out of the sea and come toward us.

"You'd have thought that parrot would have grown tired, or that its throat would have worn out. But it never ceased its clamour. Hour after hour there was that terrible screaming, exquisitely depicting everything that vanished crew must have suffered in that last hour or those last minutes. And between the screaming, the voices and words of dead men shouted across the noises of the flying ship! Can you wonder we all had the same terrors a child has in the dark, a darkness it peoples with dragons and burning-eyed bogies? I have always considered myself a moderately courageous man, but I tell you that on the *Robert Sutter* I really knew fear, the sort of utter fear that gets you by the throat and turns your stomach and knees to water.

"As for Mathews, he was half insane, and he kept going below for a drink until he finally brought the bottle on deck with him. 'We ought to kill the damned thing!' he kept saying over and over. 'We ought to kill it!' But no one would go 'midships and kill it. I would not have gone 'midships myself that night for all the money in the world. And by the time the dawn came the sheer panic of the night had subsided enough to give Mathews some element of reason, Perhaps it was the whisky he had consumed, but he certainly evidenced more control with the coming of the tropical sun all red and gold along the horizon. And still, remember, that parrot was screaming and shouting, with never a let-up! I would never have thought any creature could survive such exhaustion as must have sapped its body.

"'No, you're right, we can't kill the damned thing,' Mathews agreed after we'd talked it over. 'It's the only clue we have. We've got to turn it over to the authorities and let them see what they can make of it.' He swore thickly to himself. 'But I'll go mad if it doesn't stop!' He plugged up his ears with some oakum, but he did not seem able to shut out the noise. He looked exhausted, drained out by the light of dawn. I think we were all drained out and I gave the men a tot of whisky apiece and made them go for'ard.

"We tried every means to make that confounded parrot shut up. We covered its cage with a cloth, which only seemed to drive it into new frenzies; and we tried lowering it in the hold on top of the cargo, but that had an even worse effect. It would not eat but occasionally would dip its beak in water. And nearly all the time, pulsing and rising and falling, the ship was wracked with screaming and the voices of those dead men. Mathews went below, half drunk and with a false bravado at last, and with his ears still stuffed up he managed to fall asleep. With the coming of full morning and the continued repetition of that parrot's noise I recovered some of my nerve.

"I drew some comfort from the fact that we were fully a hundred miles from the spot where we had picked up the *Robert Sutter*, and whatever it was that had made her a crewless derelict, was far away. I went 'midships, shuddering, to listen to the bird with the same morbidness that draws you to the scene of a murderer's crime, and tried to count the different remarks it kept making. There were, as I have said, only three in English but there were several in frenzied Spanish and one of the seamen who had been on German vessels assured me there were at least a dozen words shouted in that tongue. I thought I caught snatches of French too, but I was not sure. I am speaking now only of those words obviously registered on the bird's memory in that time of recent horror.

"I got hold of a copy of the ship's original articles and discovered that to judge from the names she must have carried a mixed crew all right, as most vessels do. There had been a cook named Jose Alvarez, obviously Spanish. There had been two men with Teutonic names, and one with a French-sounding name. I judged the officers had been Americans and it seemed reasonable to suppose that each man, in the moment of stress, would have reverted to his native tongue.

"The more I thought of the matter, under the comforting bright sun of day, the more I began to see the possibilities, and to grow curious. Somewhere in all that jargon the mad parrot kept giving forth there must be a clue, must be some word that would tell what it was that had come aft. It was not unreasonable to suppose that while the men were running madly about the deck some one of them must have shouted out a word, a sentence or a fragment giving a hint as to its appearance. And if that were so such a sentence or fragment might have registered on the quivering parrot's brain to be eventually spewed forth. I thought to myself: 'If once we get that damned bird to Callao alive there'll be linguists to take down everything it's shouting out. Then we might know!'

"You see, it really was intriguing, apart from all the terror and horror those wracking words and screams provided—coming, as it were, out of nothing. We were on the track of a genuine mystery. We might have in our grasp the clue that would account for those other ships that had been found as we'd found the *Robert Sutter*. We might even be able to understand why ships had totally disappeared, without trace. We might catch a glimpse of Something that should have died in the youth of the world. The parrot knew! Why had those men vanished? What was it that had come on them out of the calm sea, sending them into stark convulsive terror, causing one of them, undoubtedly the Captain, to empty a nickel-plated revolver at Something which someone else had declared you could not shoot? The parrot knew—and it was trying to tell us.

"Mathews came on deck soon after noon, quite drunk, his whole body shaking and his eyes burning in his face. The parrot had not fallen silent at all, and it kept up its incredible screaming and shouting all through the day. I could hear Mathews grinding his teeth together as he paced up and down, his fingers twitching, and he kept saying to himself, 'If it would only shut up until we get to port! If it would only shut up!' But it didn't shut up and I began to find myself twitching and grinding my teeth too. I knew that Mathews would never stand the strain. Nor could he… About three bells in the first dog-watch he stopped pacing and gave a terrific oath. 'I can't stand this!' he jerked out suddenly—and he took a running jump down the poop companion to the main deck and raced 'midships. *'It's coming aft. It's coming aft!'* screamed the parrot and then I saw Mathews rip one of the fire-axes from its metal holder on the bulkhead of the galley house. He disappeared round the house and there came the furious sound of metal on metal. The screaming rose continuously: 'It's coming aft! It's coming aft!—and then sudden new words, words in English we had not heard before, thick, choking, horribly sickening and despairing, 'Collins! Collins! It's got me!' What else there was, was drowned out by the high-pitched hysterical swearing of Mathews and the vicious noise of the swung axe. And then there was silence— sudden, almost ominous—and Mathews staggered back into view, rocking as if hardly able to keep his feet, and backing right to the rail against which he leaned, breathing hard, the fire-axe limp in one shaking hand. 'Throw the damned thing overboard!' he said viciously and I saw one of the men go reluctantly forward, very slowly, to drag to the side a mangled iron cage in which, bloody and limp, was what was left of the parrot.

"We all watched in utter silence as the cage curved up in the air and fell into the sea. And it seemed as if with the splash there was something oppressive lifted from the ship. She seemed to pick up, grow more buoyant.

"Probably I was the only one on board the *Robert Sutter* who had even a faint tinge of regret, and that mine was perhaps morbid I must admit. But I could not help reflecting that we might have found some clue, a clue to the mysteries of the sea, if we could only have brought that parrot into Callao and before men who knew languages. But there you are. The bird was gone—and we took that barkentine into port without further mishap.

"I remember I told the story to the consul there, told him what I had wondered and hoped, and he laughed at me for a fool. Mathews did not even mention the matter. He was, I fancy, rather ashamed of it. He wanted to forget it. And so whatever it was that befell the

Robert Sutter remains unknown to this day. I cannot even guess. I have given up trying to guess… Nobody knows. But that parrot knew, and there are times when I wake up at night, in a cold sweat, and can hear its clamour, and see its crouching, palpitating body, and feel ringing in my ears those wild, mad words of men who had been dead for days, screaming while *It* came aft—and trying to shoot Something which could not be shot!"

FROM THE DARKNESS AND THE DEPTHS

Morgan Robertson

Morgan Robertson (1861–1915) was a prolific writer of sea stories yet today he's remembered for just one novella, Futility: The Wreck of the Titan *(1898) which tells a story that so presages the fate of the* Titanic, *fourteen years later, as to seem prescient. It wasn't his only story that some felt forecast the future: 'The Submarine Destroyer' (1905) predicted submarine warfare whilst 'Beyond the Spectrum' (1914) tells of a war erupting between the United States and Japan following Japan's attacks on shipping in Hawaii. There are those who have claimed Robertson must have been psychic. Certainly, he was interested in the occult and a fair proportion of his 200 or so stories have elements of the strange and supernatural.*

Born in Oswego, New York, Robertson was the son of a Scottish ship's captain on the Great Lakes and he often accompanied his father in his youth. He entered the Merchant Marine in 1877 serving first on the Great Lakes before enlisting in the US Navy in 1881. He served until 1886, travelling the world before settling down, first as a jeweller, until poor eyesight made this difficult, and then as a writer. It is unfortunate that Robertson is remembered only for Futility *as many of his other collections are worth checking, especially* Where Angels Fear to Tread *(1899),* Over the Border *(1914) and* The Grain Ship *(1914). Robertson's death led to much speculation as he was found standing up leaning against a dresser on which was a bottle of tablets, yet the cause was recorded as heart failure.*

I HAD KNOWN HIM FOR A PAINTER OF RENOWN—A MASTER OF his art, whose pictures, which sold for high prices, adorned museums, the parlours of the rich, and, when on exhibition, were hung low and conspicuous. Also, I knew him for an expert photographer—an "art photographer," as they say, one who dealt with this branch of industry as a fad, an amusement, and who produced pictures that in composition, lights, and shades rivalled his productions with the brush.

His cameras were the best that the market could supply, yet he was able, from his knowledge of optics and chemistry, to improve them for his own uses far beyond the ability of the makers. His studio was filled with examples of his work, and his mind was stocked with information and opinions on all subjects ranging from international policies to the servant-girl problem.

He was a man of the world, gentlemanly and successful, about sixty years old, kindly and gracious of manner, and out of this kindliness and graciousness had granted me the compliment of his friendship, and access to his studio whenever I felt like calling upon him.

Yet it never occurred to me that the wonderful and technically correct marines hanging on his walls were due to anything but the artist's conscientious study of his subject, and only his casual mispronunciation of the word "leeward," which landsmen pronounce as spelled, but which rolls off the tongue of a sailor, be he former dock rat or naval officer, as "looward," and his giving the long sounds to the vowels of the words "patent" and "tackle," that induced me to ask if he had ever been to sea.

"Why, yes," he answered. "Until I was thirty I had no higher ambition than to become a skipper of some craft; but I never achieved it. The best I did was to sign first mate for one voyage—and that one was my last. It was on that voyage that I learned something of the mysterious properties of light, and it made me a photographer, then an artist. You are wrong when you say that a searchlight cannot penetrate fog."

"But it has been tried," I remonstrated.

"With ordinary light. Yes, of course, subject to refraction, reflection, and absorption by the millions of minute globules of water it encounters."

We had been discussing the wreck of the *Titanic*, the most terrible marine disaster of history, the blunders of construction and management, and the later proposed improvements as to the lowering of boats and the location of ice in a fog.

Among these considerations was also the plan of carrying a powerful searchlight whose beam would illumine the path of a twenty-knot liner and render objects visible in time to avoid them. In regard to this I had contended that a searchlight could not penetrate fog, and if it could, would do as much harm as good by blinding and confusing the watch officers and lookouts on other craft.

"But what other kind of light can be used?" I asked, in answer to his mention of ordinary light.

"Invisible light," he answered. "I do not mean the Röntgen ray, nor the emanation from radium, both of which are invisible, but neither of which is light, in that neither can be reflected nor refracted. Both will penetrate many different kinds of matter, but it needs reflection or refraction to make visible an object on which it impinges. Understand?"

"Hardly," I answered dubiously. "What kind of visible light is there, if not radium or the Röntgen ray? You can photograph with either, can't you?"

"Yes, but to see what you have photographed you must develop the film. And there is no time for that aboard a fast steamer running through the ice and the fog. No, it is mere theory, but I have an idea that the ultraviolet light—the actinic rays beyond the violet end of the spectrum, you know—will penetrate fog to a great distance, and in spite of its higher refractive power, which would distort and magnify an object, it is better than nothing."

"But what makes you think that it will penetrate fog?" I queried. "And if it is invisible itself, how will it illumine an object?"

"As to your first question," he answered, with a smile, "it is well known to surgeons that ultraviolet light will penetrate the human body to the depth of an inch, while the visible rays are reflected at the surface. And it has been known to photographers for fifty years that this light—easily isolated by dispersion through prisms—will act on a sensitized plate in an utterly dark room."

"Granted," I said. "But how about the second question? How can you see by this light?"

"There you have me," he answered. "It will need a quicker development than any now known to photography—a travelling film, for instance, that will show the picture of an iceberg or a ship before it is too late to avoid it—a travelling film sensitized by a quicker acting chemical than any now used."

"Why not puzzle it out?" I asked. "It would be a wonderful invention."

"I am too old," he answered dreamily. "My life work is about done. But other and younger men will take it up. We have made great strides in optics. The moving picture is a fact. Coloured photographs are possible. The ultraviolet microscope shows us objects hitherto invisible because smaller than the wave length of visible light. We shall ultimately use this light to see through opaque objects. We shall see colours never imagined by the human mind, but which have existed since the beginning of light.

"We shall see new hues in the sunset, in the rainbow, in the flowers and foliage of forest and field. We may possibly see creatures in the air above never seen before.

"We shall certainly see creatures from the depths of the sea, where visible light cannot reach—creatures whose substance is of such a nature that it will not respond to the light it has never been exposed to—a substance which is absolutely transparent because it will not absorb, and appear black; will not reflect, and show a colour of some kind; and will not refract, and distort objects seen through it."

"What!" I exclaimed. "Do you think there are invisible creatures?"

He looked gravely at me for a moment, then said: "You know that there are sounds that are inaudible to the human ear because of their too rapid vibration, others that are audible to some, but not to all. There are men who cannot hear the chirp of a cricket, the tweet of a bird, or the creaking of a wagon wheel.

"You know that there are electric currents much stronger in voltage than is necessary to kill us, but of wave frequency so rapid that the human tissue will not respond, and we can receive such currents without a shock. And I *know*"—he spoke with vehemence—"that there are creatures in the deep sea of colour invisible to the human eye, for I have not only felt such a creature, but seen its photograph taken by the ultraviolet light."

"Tell me," I asked breathlessly. "Creatures solid, but invisible?"

"Creatures solid, and invisible because absolutely transparent. It is long since I have told the yarn. People would not believe me, and it was so horrible an experience that I have tried to forget it. However, if you care for it, and are willing to lose your sleep to-night, I'll give it to you."

He reached for a pipe, filled it, and began to smoke; and as he smoked and talked, some of the glamour and polish of the successful artist and clubman left him. He was an old sailor, spinning a yarn.

"It was about thirty years ago," he began, "or, to be explicit, twenty-nine years this coming August, at the time of the great Java earthquake. You've heard of it—how it killed seventy thousand people, thirty thousand of whom were drowned by the tidal wave.

"It was a curious phenomenon; Krakatoa Island, a huge conical mountain rising from the bottom of Sunda Strait, went out of existence, while in Java a mountain chain was levelled, and up from the bowels of the earth came an iceberg—as you might call it—that floated a hundred miles on a stream of molten lava before melting.

"I was not there; I was two hundred miles to the sou'west, first mate of one of those old-fashioned, soft-pine, centreboard barkentines—three sticks the same length, you know—with the mainmast stepped on the port side of the keel to make room for the centreboard—a craft that would neither stay, nor wear, nor scud, nor heave to, like a decent vessel.

"But she had several advantages; she was new, and well painted, deck, top-sides, and bottom. Hence her light timbers and planking were not water-soaked. She was fastened with 'trunnels,' not spikes and bolts, and hemp rigged.

"Perhaps there was not a hundredweight of iron aboard of her, while her hemp rigging, though heavier than water, was lighter than wire rope, and so, when we were hit by the back wash of that tidal wave, we did not sink, even though butts were started from one end to the other of the flimsy hull, and all hatches were ripped off.

"I have called it the back wash, yet we may have had a tidal wave of our own; for, though we had no knowledge of the frightful catastrophe at Java, still there had been for days several submarine earthquakes all about us, sending fountains of water, steam bubbles, and mud from the sea bed into the air.

"As the soundings were over two thousand fathoms in that neighbourhood, you can imagine the seismic forces at work beneath us. There had been no wind for days, and no sea, except the agitation caused by the upheavals. The sky was a dull mud colour, and the sun looked like nothing but a dark, red ball, rising day by day in the east, to move overhead and set in the west. The air was hot, sultry, and stifling, and I had difficulty in keeping the men—a big crew—at work.

"The conditions would try anybody's temper, and I had my own troubles. There was a passenger on board, a big, fat, highly educated German—a scientist and explorer—whom we had taken aboard at some little town on the West Australian coast, and who was to leave us at Batavia, where he could catch a steamer for Germany.

"He had a whole laboratory with him, with scientific instruments that I didn't know the names of, with maps he had made, stuffed beasts and birds he had killed, and a few live ones which he kept in cages and attended to himself in the empty hold; for we were flying light, you know, without even ballast aboard, and bound to Batavia for a cargo.

"It was after a few eruptions from the bottom of the sea that he got to be a nuisance; he was keenly interested in the strange dead fish and nondescript creatures that had been thrown up. He declared them new, unknown to science, and wore out my patience with entreaties to haul them aboard for examination and classification.

"I obliged him for a time, until the decks stank with dead fish, and the men got mutinous. Then I refused to advance the interests of science any farther, and, in spite of his excitement and pleadings, refused to litter the decks any more. But he got all he wanted of the unclassified and unknown before long.

"Tidal wave, you know, is a name we give to any big wave, and it has no necessary connection with the tides. It may be the big third wave of a series—just a little bigger than usual; it may be the ninth, tenth, and eleventh waves merged into one huge comber by uneven wind pressure; it may be the back wash from an earthquake that depresses the nearest coast, and it may be—as I think it was in our case—a wave sent out by an upheaval from the sea bed. At any rate, we got it, and we got it just after a tremendous spouting of water and mud, and a thick cloud of steam on the northern horizon.

"We saw a seeming rise to the horizon, as though caused by refraction, but which soon eliminated refraction as a cause by its becoming visible in its details—its streaks of water and mud, its irregular upper edge, the occasional combers that appeared on this edge, and the terrific speed of its approach. It was a wave, nothing else, and coming at forty knots at least.

"There was little that we could do; there was no wind, and we headed about west, showing our broadside; yet I got the men at the downhauls, clewlines, and stripping lines of the lighter kites; but before a man could leave the deck to furl, that moving mountain hit us, and buried us on our beam ends just as I had time to sing out: 'Lash yourselves, every man.'

"Then I needed to think of my own safety and passed a turn of the mizzen gaff-topsail downhaul about me, belaying to a pin as the cataclysm hit us. For the next two minutes—although it seemed an hour, I did not speak, nor breathe, nor think, unless my instinctive grip on the turns of the downhaul on the pin may have been an index of thought. I was under water; there was roaring in my ears, pain in my lungs, and terror in my heart.

"Then there came a lessening of the turmoil, a momentary quiet, and I roused up, to find the craft floating on her side, about a third out of water, but apt to turn bottom up at any moment from the weight of the water-soaked gear and canvas, which will sink, you know, when wet.

"I was hanging in my bight of rope from a belaying pin, my feet clear of the perpendicular deck, and my ears tortured by the sound of men overboard crying for help—men who had not lashed themselves. Among them I knew was the skipper, a mild-mannered little fellow, and the second mate, an incompetent tough from Portsmouth, who had caused me lots of trouble by his abuse of the men and his depending upon me to stand by him.

"Nothing could be done for them; they were adrift on the back wall of a moving mountain that towered thirty degrees above the horizon to port; and another moving mountain, as big as the first, was coming on from starboard—caused by the tumble into the sea of the uplifted water.

"Did you ever fall overboard in a full suit of clothes? If you did, you know the mighty exercise of strength required to climb out. I was a strong, healthy man at the time, but never in my life was I so tested. I finally got a grip on the belaying pin and rested; then, with an effort that caused me physical pain, I got my right foot up to the pinrail and rested again; then, perhaps more by mental strength than physical—for I loved life and wanted to live—I hooked my right foot over the rail, reached higher on the rope, rested again, and finally hove myself up to the mizzen rigging, where I sat for a few moments to get my breath, and think, and look around.

"Forward, I saw men who had lashed themselves to the starboard rail, and they were struggling, as I had struggled, to get up to the horizontal side of the vessel. They succeeded, but at the time I had no use for them. Sailors will obey orders, if they understand the orders, but this was an exigency outside the realm of mere seamanship.

"Men were drowning off to port; men, like myself, were climbing up to temporary safety afforded by the topsides of a craft on her beam ends; and aft, in the alleyway, was the German professor, unlashed, but safe and secure in his narrow confines, one leg through a cabin window, and both hands gripping the rail, while he bellowed like a bull, not for himself, however—but for his menagerie in the empty hold.

"There was small chance for the brutes—smaller than for ourselves, left on the upper rail of an over-turned craft, and still smaller than the chance of the poor devils off to port, some of whom had gripped the half-submerged top-hamper, and were calling for help.

"We could not help them; she was a Yankee craft, and there was not a life buoy or belt on board; and who, with another big wave coming, would swim down to looward with a line?

"Landsmen, especially women and boys, have often asked me why a wooden ship, filled with water, sinks, even though not weighted with cargo. Some sailors have pondered over it, too, knowing that a small boat, built of wood, and fastened with nails, will float if water-logged.

"But the answer is simple. Most big craft are built of oak or hard pine, and fastened together with iron spikes and bolts—sixty tons at least to a three-hundred-ton schooner. After a year or two this hard, heavy wood becomes water-soaked, and, with the iron bolts and spikes, is heavier than water, and will sink when the hold is flooded.

"This craft of ours was like a small boat—built of soft light wood, with trunnels instead of bolts, and no iron on board except the anchors and one capstan. As a result, though ripped, twisted, broken, and disintegrated, she still floated even on her beam ends.

"But the soaked hemp rigging and canvas might be enough to drag the craft down, and with this fear in my mind I acted quickly. Singing out to the men to hang on, I made my way aft to where we had an axe, lodged in its beckets on the after house. With this I attacked the mizzen lanyards, cutting everything clear, then climbed forward to the main.

"Hard as I worked I had barely cut the last lanyard when that second wave loomed up and crashed down on us. I just had time to slip into the bight of a rope, and save myself; but I had to give up the axe; it slipped from my hands and slid down to the port scuppers.

"That second wave, in its effect, was about the same as the first, except that it righted the craft. We were buried, choked, and half drowned; but when the wave had passed on, the main and mizzenmasts, unsupported by the rigging that I had cut away, snapped cleanly about three feet above the deck, and the broad, flat-bottomed craft straightened up, lifting the weight of the foremast and its gear, and lay on an even keel, with foresail, staysail, and jib set, the fore gaff-topsail, flying jib, and jib-topsail clewed down and the wreck of the masts bumping against the port side.

"We floated, but with the hold full of water, and four feet of it on deck amidships that surged from one rail to the other as the craft rolled, pouring over and coming back. All hatches were ripped off, and our three boats were carried away from their chocks on the house.

"Six men were clearing themselves from their lashings at the fore rigging, and three more, who had gone overboard with the first sea, and had caught the upper gear to be lifted as the craft righted, were coming down, while the professor still declaimed from the alley.

"'Hang on all,' I yelled; 'there's another sea coming.'

"It came, but passed over us without doing any more damage, and though a fourth, fifth, and sixth followed, each was of lesser force than the last, and finally it was safe to leave the rail and wade about, though we still rolled rails under in what was left of the turmoil.

"Luckily, there was no wind, though I never understood why, for earthquakes are usually accompanied by squalls. However, even with wind, our canvas would have been no use to us; for, waterlogged as we were, we couldn't have made a knot an hour, nor could we have steered, even with all sail set. All we could hope for was the appearance of some craft that would tow the ripped and shivered hull to port, or at least take us off.

"So, while I searched for the axe, and the professor searched into the depths under the main hatch for signs of his menagerie—all drowned, surely—the remnant of the crew lowered the foresail and jibs, stowing them as best they could.

"I found the axe, and found it just in time; for I was attacked by what could have been nothing but a small-sized sea serpent, that had been hove up to the surface and washed aboard us. It was only about six feet long, but it had a mouth like a bulldog, and a row of spikes along its back that could have sawed a man's leg off.

"I managed to kill it before it harmed me, and chucked it overboard against the protests of the professor, who averred that I took no interest in science.

"'No, I don't,' I said to him. 'I've other things to think of. And you, too. You'd better go below and clean up your instruments, or you'll find them ruined by salt water.'

"He looked sorrowfully and reproachfully at me, and started to wade aft; but he halted at the forward companion, and turned, for a scream of agony rang out from the forecastle deck, where the men were coming in from the jibs, and I saw one of them writhing on his back, apparently in a fit, while the others stood wonderingly around.

"The forecastle deck was just out of water, and there was no wash; but in spite of this, the wriggling, screaming man slid head-first along the break and plunged into the water on the main deck.

"I scrambled forward, still carrying the axe, and the men tumbled down into the water after the man; but we could not get near him. We could see him under water, feebly moving, but not swimming; and yet he shot this way and that faster than a man ever swam; and once, as he passed near me, I noticed a gaping wound in his neck, from which the blood was flowing in a stream—a stream like a current, which did not mix with the water and discolour it.

"Soon his movements ceased, and I waded toward him; but he shot swiftly away from me, and I did not follow, for something cold, slimy, and firm touched my hand—something in the water, but which I could not see.

"I floundered back, still holding the axe, and sang out to the men to keep away from the dead man; for he was surely dead by now. He lay close to the break of the topgallant forecastle, on the starboard side; and as the men mustered around me I gave one my axe, told the rest to secure others, and to chop away the useless wreck pounding our port side—useless because it was past all seamanship to patch up that basketlike hull, pump it out, and raise jury rigging.

"While they were doing it, I secured a long pike pole from its beckets, and, joined by the professor, cautiously approached the body prodding ahead of me.

"As I neared the dead man, the pike pole was suddenly torn from my grasp, one end sank to the deck, while the other raised above the water; then it slid upward, fell, and floated close to me. I seized it again and turned to the professor.

"'What do you make of this, Herr Smidt?' I asked. 'There is something down there that we cannot see—something that killed that man. See the blood?'

"He peered closely at the dead man, who looked curiously distorted and shrunken, four feet under water. But the blood no longer was a thin stream issuing from his neck; it was gathered into a misshapen mass about two feet away from his neck.

"'Nonsense,' he answered. 'Something alive which we cannot see is contrary to all laws of physics. Der man must have fallen und hurt himself, which accounts for der bleeding. Den he drowned in der water. Do you see?—mine Gott! What iss?'

"He suddenly went under water himself, and dropping the pike pole, I grabbed him by the collar and braced myself. Something was pulling him away from me, but I managed to get his head out, and he spluttered:

"'Help! Holdt on to me. Something haf my right foot.'

"'Lend a hand here,' I yelled to the men, and a few joined me, grabbing him by his clothing. Together we pulled against the invisible force, and finally all of us went backward, professor and all, nearly to drown ourselves before regaining our feet. Then, as the agitated water smoothed, I distinctly saw the mass of red move slowly forward and disappear in the darkness under the forecastle deck.

"'You were right, mine friend,' said the professor, who, in spite of his experience, held his nerve. 'Dere is something invisible in der water—something dangerous, something which violates all laws of physics und optics. Oh, mine foot, how it hurts!'

"'Get aft,' I answered, 'and find out what ails it. And you fellows,' I added to the men, 'keep away from the forecastle deck. Whatever it is, it has gone under it.'

"Then I grabbed the pike pole again, cautiously hooked the barb

into the dead man's clothing, and, assisted by the men, pulled him
aft to the poop, where the professor had preceded, and was examining his ankle. There was a big, red wale around it, in the middle of
which was a huge blood blister. He pricked it with his knife, then
rearranged his stocking and joined us as we lifted the body.

"'Great God, sir!' exclaimed big Bill, the bosun. 'Is that Frank? I
wouldn't know him.'

"Frank, the dead man, had been strong, robust, and full-blooded.
But he bore no resemblance to his living self. He lay there, shrunken,
shortened, and changed, a look of agony on his emaciated face, and
his hands clenched—not extended like those of one drowned.

"'I thought drowned men swelled up,' ventured one of the men.

"'He was not drowned,' said Herr Smidt. 'He was sucked dry, like
a lemon. Perhaps in his whole body there is not an ounce of blood,
nor lymph, nor fluid of any kind.'

"I secured an iron belaying pin, tucked it inside his shirt, and we
hove him overboard at once; for, in the presence of this horror, we
were not in the mood for a burial service. There we were, eleven
men on a water-logged hulk, adrift on a heaving, greasy sea, with a
dark-red sun showing through a muddy sky above, and an invisible
thing forward that might seize any of us at any moment it chose,
in the water or out; for Frank had been caught and dragged down.

"Still, I ordered the men, cook, steward, and all, to remain on the
poop and—the galley being forward—to expect no hot meals, as we
could subsist for a time on the cold, canned food in the storeroom
and lazaret.

"Because of an early friction between the men and the second
mate, the mild-mannered and peace-loving skipper had forbidden
the crew to wear sheath knives; but in this exigency I overruled the
edict. While the professor went down into his flooded room to doctor

his ankle and attend to his instruments, I raided the slop chest, and armed every man of us with a sheath knife and belt; for while we could not see the creature, we could feel it—and a knife is better than a gun in a hand-to-hand fight.

"Then we sat around, waiting, while the sky grew muddier, the sun darker, and the northern horizon lighter with a reddish glow that was better than the sun. It was the Java earthquake, but we did not know it for a long time.

"Soon the professor appeared and announced that his instruments were in good condition, and stowed high on shelves above the water.

"'I must resensitize my plates, however,' he said. 'Der salt water has spoiled them; but mine camera merely needs to dry out; und mine telescope, und mine static machine und Leyden jars—why, der water did not touch them.'

"'Well,' I answered. 'That's all right. But what good are they in the face of this emergency? Are you thinking of photographing anything now?'

"'Perhaps. I haf been thinking some.'

"'Have you thought out what that creature is—forward, there?'

"'Partly. It is some creature thrown up from der bottom of der sea, und washed on board by der wave. Light, like wave motion, ends at a certain depth, you know; und we have over twelve thousand feet beneath us. At that depth dere is absolute darkness, but we know that creatures live down dere, und fight, und eat, und die.'

"'But what of it? Why can't we see that thing?'

"'Because, in der ages that haf passed in its evolution from der original moneron, it has never been exposed to light—I mean visible light, der light that contains der seven colours of der spectrum. Hence it may not respond to der three properties of visible light—reflection, which would give it a colour of some kind; absorption, which would make it appear black; or refraction, which, in der absence of der other two, would distort things seen through it. For it would be transparent, you know.'

"'But what can be done?' I asked helplessly, for I could not understand at the time what he meant.

"'Nothing, except that der next man attacked must use his knife. If he cannot see der creature, he can feel it. Und perhaps—I do not know yet—perhaps, in a way, we may see it—its photograph.'

"I looked blankly at him, thinking he might have gone crazy, but he continued.

"'You know,' he said, 'that objects too small to be seen by the microscope, because smaller than der amplitude of der shortest wave of visible light, can be seen when exposed to der ultraviolet light—der dark light beyond der spectrum? Und you know that this light is what acts der most in photography? That it exposes on a sensitized plate new stars in der heavens invisible to der eye through the strongest telescope?'

"'Don't know anything about it,' I answered. 'But if you can find a way out of this scrape we're in, go ahead.'

"'I must think,' he said dreamily. 'I haf a rock-crystal lens which is permeable to this light, und which I can place in mine camera. I must have a concave mirror, not of glass, which is opaque to this light, but of metal.'

"'What for?' I asked.

"'To throw der ultraviolet light on der beast. I can generate it with mine static machine.'

"'How will one of our lantern reflectors do? They are of polished tin, I think.'

"'Good! I can repolish one.'

"We had one deck lantern larger than usual, with a metallic reflector that concentrated the light into a beam, much as do the present day searchlights. This I procured from the lazaret, and he pronounced it available. Then he disappeared, to tinker up his apparatus.

"Night came down, and I lighted three masthead lights, to hoist at the fore to inform any passing craft that we were not under command; but, as I would not send a man forward on that job, I went myself, carefully feeling my way with the pike pole. Luckily, I escaped contact with the creature, and returned to the poop, where we had a cold supper of canned cabin stores.

"The top of the house was dry, but it was cold, especially so as we were all drenched to the skin. The steward brought up all the blankets there were in the cabin—for even a wet blanket is better than none at all—but there were not enough to go around, and one man volunteered, against my advice, to go forward and bring aft bedding from the forecastle.

"He did not come back; we heard his yell, that finished with a gurgle; but in that pitch black darkness, relieved only by the red glow from the north, not one of us dared to venture to his rescue. We knew that he would be dead, anyhow, before we could get to him; so we stood watch, sharing the blankets we had when our time came to sleep.

"It was a wretched night that we spent on the top of that after house. It began to rain before midnight, the heavy drops coming down almost in solid waves; then came wind, out of the south, cold and biting, with real waves, that rolled even over the house, forcing us to lash ourselves. The red glow to the north was hidden by the rain and spume, and, to add to our discomfort, we were showered with ashes, which, even though the surface wind was from the south, must have been brought from the north by an upper air current.

"We did not find the dead man when the faint daylight came; and so could not tell whether or not he had used his knife. His body must have washed over the rail with a sea, and we hoped the invisible killer had gone, too. But we hoped too much. With courage born of this hope a man went forward to lower the masthead lights, prodding his way with the pike pole.

"We watched him closely, the pole in one hand, his knife in the other. But he went under at the fore rigging without even a yell, and the pole went with him, while we could see, even at the distance and through the disturbed water, that his arms were close to his sides, and that he made no movement, except for the quick darting to and fro. After a few moments, however, the pike pole floated to the surface, but the man's body, drained, no doubt, of its buoyant fluids, remained on the deck.

"It was an hour later, with the pike pole for a feeler, before we dared approach the body, hook on to it, and tow it aft. It resembled that of the first victim, a skeleton clothed with skin, with the same look of horror on the face. We buried it like the other, and held to the poop, still drenched by the downpour of rain, hammered by the seas, and choked by ashes from the sky.

"As the shower of ashes increased it became dark as twilight, and though the three lights aloft burned out at about midday, I forbade a man to go forward to lower them, contenting myself with a turpentine flare lamp that I brought up from the lazaret, and filled, ready to show if the lights of a craft came in view. Before the afternoon was half gone it was dark as night, and down below, up to his waist in water, the German professor was working away.

"He came up at supper time, humming cheerfully to himself, and announced that he had replaced his camera lens with the rock crystal, that the lantern, with its reflector and a blue spark in the focus, made an admirable instrument for throwing the invisible rays on the beast, and that he was all ready, except that his plates, which he had resensitized—with some phosphorescent substance that I forget the name of, now—must have time to dry. And then, he needed some light to work by when the time came, he explained.

"'Also another victim,' I suggested bitterly; for he had not been on deck when the last two men had died.

"'I hope not,' he said. 'When we can see, it may be possible to stir him up by throwing things forward; then when he moves der water we can take shots.'

"'Better devise some means of killing him,' I answered. 'Shooting won't do, for water stops a bullet before it goes a foot into it.'

"'Der only way I can think of,' he responded, 'is for der next man—you hear me all, you men—to stick your knife at the end of the blood—where it collects in a lump. Dere is der creature's stomach, and a vital spot.'

"'Remember this, boys,' I laughed, thinking of the last poor devil, with his arms pinioned to his side. 'When you've lost enough blood to see it in a lump, stab for it.'

"But my laugh was answered by a shriek. A man lashed with a turn of rope around his waist to the stump of the mizzenmast, was writhing and heaving on his back, while he struck with his knife, apparently at his own body. With my own knife in my hand I sprang toward him, and felt for what had seized him. It was something cold, and hard, and leathery, close to his waist.

"Carefully gauging my stroke, I lunged with the knife, but I hardly think it entered the invisible fin, or tail, or paw of the monster; but it moved away from the screaming man, and the next moment I received a blow in the face that sent me aft six feet, flat on my back. Then came unconsciousness.

"When I recovered my senses the remnant of the crew were around me, but the man was gone—dragged out of the bight of the rope that had held him against the force of breaking seas, and down to the flooded main deck, to die like the others. It was too dark to see, or do anything; so, when I could speak I ordered all hands but one into the flooded cabin where, in the upper berths and on the top of the table, were a few dry spots.

"I filled and lighted a lantern, and gave it to the man on watch with instructions to hang it to the stump of the mizzen and to call his relief at the end of four hours. Then, with doors and windows closed, we went to sleep, or tried to go to sleep. I succeeded first, I think, for up to the last of consciousness I could hear the mutterings of the men; when I awakened, they were all asleep, and the cabin clock, high above the water, told me that, though it was still dark, it was six in the morning.

"I went on deck; the lantern still burned at the stump of mizzenmast but the lookout was gone. He had not lived long enough to be relieved, as I learned by going below and finding that no one had been called.

"We were but six, now—one sailor and the bos'n, the cook and steward, the professor and myself."

The old artist paused, while he refilled and lighted his pipe. I noticed that the hand that held the match shook perceptibly, as though the memories of that awful experience had affected his nerves. I know that the recital had affected mine; for I joined him in a smoke, my hands shaking also.

"Why," I asked, after a moment of silence, "if it was a deep-sea creature, did it not die from the lesser pressure at the surface?"

"Why do not men die on the mountaintops?" he answered. "Or up in balloons? The record is seven miles high, I think; but they lived. They suffered from cold, and from lack of oxygen—that is, no matter how fast, or deeply they breathed, they could not get enough. But the lack of pressure did not trouble them; the human body can adjust itself.

"Conversely, however, an increase of pressure may be fatal. A man dragged down more than one hundred and fifty feet may be crushed; and a surface fish sent to the bottom of the sea may die from the pressure. It is simple; it is like the difference between a weight lifted from us and a weight added."

"Did this thing kill any more men?" I asked.

"All but the professor and myself, and it almost killed me. Look here."

He removed his cravat and collar, pulled down his shirt, and exposed two livid scars about an inch in diameter, and two apart.

"I lost all the blood I could spare through those two holes," he said, as he readjusted his apparel; "but I saved enough to keep me alive."

"Go on with the yarn," I asked. "I promise you I will not sleep to-night."

"Perhaps I will not sleep myself," he answered, with a mournful smile. "Some things should be forgotten, but as I have told you this much I may as well finish, and be done with it.

"It was partly due to a sailor's love for tobacco, partly to our cold, drenched condition. A sailor will starve quietly, but go crazy if deprived of his smoke. This is so well known at sea that a skipper, who will not hesitate to sail from port with rotten or insufficient food for his men, will not dare take a chance without a full supply of tobacco in the slop chest.

"But our slop chest was under water, and the tobacco utterly useless. I did not use it at the time, but I fished some out for the others.

It did not do; it would not dry out to smoke, and the salt in it made it unfit to chew. But the bos'n had an upper bunk in the forward house, in which was a couple of pounds of navy plug, and he and the sailor talked this over until their craving for a smoke overcame their fear of death.

"Of course, by this time, all discipline was ended, and all my commands and entreaties went for nothing. They sharpened their knives, and, agreeing to go forward, one on the starboard rail, the other on the port, and each to come to the other's aid if called, they went up into the darkness of ashes and rain. I opened my room window, which overlooked the main deck, but could see nothing.

"Yet I could hear; I heard two screams for help, one after the other—one from the starboard side, the other from the port, and knew that they were caught. I closed the window, for nothing could be done. What manner of thing it was that could grab two men so far apart nearly at the same time was beyond all imagining.

"I talked to the steward and cook, but found small comfort. The first was a Jap, the other a Chinaman, and they were the old-fashioned kind—what they could not see with their eyes, they could not believe. Both thought that all those men who had met death had either drowned or died by falling. Neither understood—and, in fact, I did not myself—the theories of Herr Smidt. He had stopped his cheerful humming to himself now, and was very busy with his instruments.

"'This thing,' I said to him, 'must be able to see in the dark. It certainly could not have heard those two men, over the noise of the wind, sea, and rain.'

"'Why not?' he answered, as he puttered with his wires. 'Cats and owls can see in the dark, und the accepted explanation is that by their power of enlarging der pupils they admit more light to the retina. But that explanation never satisfied me. You haf noticed, haf you not, that a cat's eyes shine in der dark, but only when der cat is looking at you?—that is, when it looks elsewhere you do not see der shiny eyes.'

"'Yes,' I answered,' I have noticed that.'

"'A cat's eyes are searchlights, but they send forth a visible light, such as is generated by fireflies, und some fish. Und dere are fish in der upper tributaries of der Amazon which haf four eyes, der two upper of which are searchlights, der two lower of which are organs of percipience or vision. But visible light is not der only light. It is possible that the creature out on deck generates the invisible light, and can see by it.'

"'But what does it all amount to?' I asked impatiently.

"'I haf told you,' he answered calmly. 'Der creature may live in an atmosphere of ultraviolet light, which I can generate mineself. When mine plates dry, und it clears off so I can see what I am doing, I may get a picture of it. When we know what it is, we may find means of killing it.'

"'God grant that you succeed,' I answered fervently. 'It has killed enough of us.'

"But, as I said, the thing killed all but the professor and myself. And it came about through the other reason I mentioned—our cold, drenched condition. If there is anything an Oriental loves above his ancestors, it is his stomach; and the cold, canned food was palling upon us all. We had a little light through the downpour of ashes and rain about midday, and the steward and cook began talking about hot coffee.

"We had the turpentine torch for heating water, and some coffee, high and dry on a shelf in the steward's storeroom, but not a pot, pan, or cooking utensil of any kind in the cabin. So these two poor heathen, against my expostulations—somewhat faint, I admit, for the thought of hot coffee took away some of my common sense—went out on the deck and waded forward, waist-deep in the water, muddy now, from the downfall of ashes.

"I could see them as they entered the galley to get the coffeepot, but, though I stared from my window until the blackness closed down, I did not see them come out. Nor did I hear even a squeal. The thing must have been in the galley.

"Night came on, and, with its coming, the wind and rain ceased, though there was still a slight shower of ashes. But this ended toward midnight, and I could see stars overhead and a clear horizon. Sleep, in my nervous, overwrought condition, was impossible; but the professor, after the bright idea of using the turpentine torch to dry out his plates, had gone to his fairly dry berth, after announcing his readiness to take snapshots about the deck in the morning.

"But I roused him long before morning. I roused him when I saw through my window the masthead and two side lights of a steamer approaching from the starboard, still about a mile away. I had not dared to go up and rig that lantern at the mizzen stump; but now I nerved myself to go up with the torch, the professor following with his instruments.

"'You cold-blooded crank,' I said to him, as I waved the torch. 'I admire your devotion to science, but are you waiting for that thing to get me?'

"He did not answer, but rigged his apparatus on the top of the cabin. He had a Wimshurst machine—to generate a blue spark, you know—and this he had attached to the big deck light, from which he had removed the opaque glass. Then he had his camera, with its rock-crystal lens.

"He trained both forward, and waited, while I waved the torch, standing near the stump with a turn of rope around me for safety's sake in case the thing seized me; and to this idea I added the foolish hope, aroused by the professor's theories, that the blinding light of the torch would frighten the thing away from me as it does wild animals.

"But in this last I was mistaken. No sooner was there an answering blast of a steam whistle, indicating that the steamer had seen the torch, than something cold, wet, leathery, and slimy slipped around my neck. I dropped the torch, and drew my knife, while I heard the whir of the static machine as the professor turned it.

"'Use your knife, mine friend,' he called. 'Use your knife, und reach for any blood what you see.'

"I knew better than to call for help, and I had little chance to use the knife. Still, I managed to keep my right hand, in which I held it, free, while that cold, leathery thing slipped farther around my neck and waist. I struck as I could, but could make no impression; and soon I felt another stricture around my legs, which brought me on my back.

"Still another belt encircled me, and, though I had come up warmly clad in woollen shirts and monkey jacket, I felt these garments being torn away from me. Then I was dragged forward, but the turn of rope had slipped down toward my waist, and I was merely bent double.

"And all the time that German was whirling his machine, and shouting to strike for any blood I saw. But I saw none. I felt it going, however. Two spots on my chest began to smart, then burn as though hot irons were piercing me. Frantically I struck, right and left, sometimes at the coils encircling me, again in the air. Then all became dark.

"I awakened in a stateroom berth, too weak to lift my hands, with the taste of brandy in my mouth and the professor standing over me with a bottle in his hand.

"'Ach, it is well,' he said. 'You will recover. You haf merely lost blood, but you did the right thing. You struck with your knife at the blood, and you killed the creature. I was right. Heart, brain, und all vital parts were in der stomach.'

"'Where are we now?' I asked, for I did not recognize the room.

"'On board der steamer. When you got on your feet und staggered aft, I knew you had killed him, and gave you my assistance. But you fainted away. Then we were taken off. Und I haf two or three beautiful negatives, which I am printing. They will be a glorious contribution to der scientific world.'

"I was glad that I was alive, yet not alive enough to ask any more questions. But next day he showed me the photographs he had printed."

"In Heaven's name, what was it?" I asked excitedly, as the old artist paused to empty and refill his pipe.

"Nothing but a giant squid, or octopus. Except that it was bigger than any ever seen before, and invisible to the eye, of course. Did you ever read Hugo's terrible story of Gilliat's fight with a squid?"

I had, and nodded.

"Hugo's imagination could not give him a creature—no matter how formidable—larger than one of four feet stretch. This one had three tentacles around me, two others gripped the port and starboard pin-rails, and three were gripping the stump of the mainmast. It had a reach of forty feet, I should think, comparing it with the beam of the craft.

"But there was one part of each picture, ill defined and missing. My knife and right hand were not shown. They were buried in a dark lump, which could be nothing but the blood from my veins. Unconscious, but still struggling, I had struck into the soft body of the monster, and struck true."

SARGASSO

Ward Muir

Ward Muir (1878–1927) revelled in the full name of Wardrop Openshaw Muir. Born in Liverpool, he was the son of a Scottish Presbyterian minister and grew up with a strong sense of values and morals. It is ironic, therefore, that the one time one of his books was challenged was when some readers believed that Adventures in Marriage *(1920) was immoral and that Muir should be prosecuted. Dogged by ill-health, Muir found it difficult to hold down a full-time job, though he tried for a while to work in a publisher's office. Instead he turned to both writing and photography, and excelled at both. His book* A Camera for Company *(1923) was a bestseller in its day. Despite his health Muir volunteered for war work during the Great War as an orderly and wrote a much-appreciated book about his experiences* Observations of an Orderly *(1917). Muir is best remembered today for his spy story 'The Man with the Ebony Crutches' (1907) but otherwise his work has been forgotten.*

The following story was written during the period when the Sargasso Sea was a popular theme in fiction. The Sargasso was supposed to be a weed-clogged sea in the North Atlantic near Bermuda where ships became trapped. It was filled with derelicts, in some cases inhabited by descendants of the original sailors, in other cases by denizens of the sea.

A T THE END OF SEPTEMBER THE TRAMP STEAMER *WELLINGTON* was posted "Missing," and a number of placid persons in Cardiff and Liverpool and elsewhere, having speculated in insuring her when she became "overdue," became appreciably richer without any special effort, beyond that of enduring a temporary anxiety. The insurance company paid the *Wellington's* owners without the slightest fuss. The said owners made preparations to buy a new steamer. Two or three small milliners earned a trifling profit on selling black attire to the wives of various officers and sailors, and thus the matter ended. Cash changed hands, and here and there a heart was broken and a few families orphaned. That was all.

The *Wellington* had sailed from Cardiff for Trinidad—and vanished. The southern wastes of the North Atlantic had swallowed her up, and told no tale of her vanishing. No storms had been recorded; there were no rocks or shoals uncharted on her route; no derelicts, upon which she might have struck and done herself injury, had been reported. Obviously, she had sunk. There was no other explanation to offer. She could not have taken to herself wings and flown into the heavens; she could not have evaporated, she could not have blown herself to bits so small that none had floated and been recovered. Undoubtedly she had sunk. But what had caused her to sink? And why, when she sunk, had not the crew taken to the boats? Here was a mystery. The sea holds many similar mysteries—and holds them tight.

To this day the riddle of the *Wellington* might have remained unsolved (such unsolved riddles brood over innumerable homes in every seaport) had not the *Pennsylvania* happened to cruise across a certain patch of ocean on a certain day four years later. The *Pennsylvania*, belonging to the United States Navy, was on a scientific mission, looking for new kinds of fish, or new kinds of algae, or new kinds of something else—it does not concern us to inquire what it was looking for. Learned professors, with microscopes and dredging apparatus, were on board; and the learned professors were certainly not looking for the *Wellington*. Nevertheless, they found her; found her riding calmly on a silver sea, intact from her keel to the top of her masts, her engines apparently undamaged, her cargo untouched and perfect, but for some slight decay, her boats whole and sound, and her cabin—well, there were things (or the remains of things) in her cabin, which we need not dwell upon. To put the matter gently, the one passenger on board the *Wellington* was—Death.

"Extraordinary!" said the lieutenant commanding the exploring party which went aboard the derelict.

The *Pennsylvania's* doctor was set to work to examine the things in the cabin, and he pronounced a remarkable verdict. "Died of starvation," he said. "No disease otherwise, as far as I can see."

An engineer, who was sent below to look at the silent and rusted engines, said that with a little tinkering they could be put into good enough order to take the *Wellington* home. "Nothing wrong with the engines," he remarked, "except, maybe, a bit of strain. There's tons of coal in the bunkers."

Then came a professor, who had been employing the time paddling about the ship in the dinghy. "See this?" he said. He held up a string of weed. "I've been bathing, while you fellows made your examination. Dived and had a look at the screw. Found this."

"The screw's gone, I suppose?" asked the lieutenant. "The loss of the screw is the only thing that could have stopped them. Though why they didn't take to the boats or set sails, when they shed their screw, goodness only knows."

The Professor was grave. "The screw's all right; but there was some of this wrapped round it." Again he held up the dripping trail of weed.

"Naturally she's got weedy, drifting like this for goodness knows how long."

"Maybe." The Professor flung the weed on the deck, and took out a cigar. "Ever hear of Sargasso weed?" he asked, as he struck a match. Then he began to smoke, thoughtfully.

"It's only a guess," he went on. "Sargasso could have done it; and unless you people find a better explanation, mine is the best so far. Yes—Sargasso—that's my contribution to the problem. Sargasso's my guess."

The doctor returned from the cabin where the things were, carrying a little bundle of sheets of paper. "No need to argue," he said. "Here's the whole story. It seems there was a journalist on board, taking a voyage for his health. He's written it all down—at least, nearly all. The end wouldn't bear writing, I reckon."

This was what the journalist wrote in his diary:

SUNDAY MORNING

A curious thing has happened, and in order that I may keep the details clear in my mind, so as to be able to send an account to my paper when we reach Trinidad, I am writing a condensed description now. Last night, as we were steaming full speed ahead as usual, and I was below, lying on the cabin sofa reading a novel, I suddenly felt the ship give a most peculiar movement. The sensation of motion forwards is so permanently present in one's mind when one is travelling on board a vessel in mid-ocean that one forgets it. At this moment I suddenly, even violently, became aware not of this sensation, but of its stoppage.

The stoppage was not a sharp one; it did not feel as though we had, say, run on a rock, with a bump. There was no bump. Nevertheless, I was nearly rolled off the sofa, and only saved myself by a clutch at its back. The ship had, as it were, taken a dive backward instead of a dive forward. It had not done so with a jar. On the contrary, it had done so smoothly, and with a slur, much as a locomotive does when it glides, very gently, against a spring buffer. The only effect in the cabin beyond my own experience was that a bottle of sarsaparilla which stood on the table fell over, and rolled off it.

I sat up and listened. The screw was still going, and the ship was vibrating a good deal; but somehow I had lost the sensation of moving forward which one always feels when one listens to the screw. An instant later the captain, who had been in his berth, came running out in his trousers and shirt sleeves. "Stop the engines, Mr. Bunce!" I heard him yell to the mate as he ran on deck.

A second later the telegraph tinkled, and the engines slowed down and stopped. There was silence.

I followed the captain on deck. He was on the bridge now. I could see his face by the light of a lamp which hung there. He looked bewildered.

I joined him. "What's up?" I asked.

"Blowed if I know," he said, "If there were any sandbanks hereabouts—sandbanks in mid-Atlantic! Pshaw!" He stared into the darkness ahead.

The night was black. There should have been a moon, but it was hidden behind thick clouds. Now that the ship had stopped, one realized that the heat was considerable. Not a breath of wind stirred the air.

"Must have the arc," said the captain.

The masthead arc-light, which is used when the ship is loading in port, sputtered, and then blazed. Its pallid rays shot forth on every side, and illuminated the sea.

The sea? *Was* it the sea?

Ahead of us lay a vast and stolid tract of something, motionless and sinister. Mud? No, not mud. It was less motionless than I had thought. It moved slightly now and then with the swell. Its surface was not water, at any rate. It glistened, but it did not glitter as water does. And it was wrinkled here and there with solid yet sinuous markings. Certainly it was not water.

"Weed, by Jove!" muttered the captain. "Yards of it—hundreds of yards of it for aught I know. I've heard of gulf weed, but never seen anything like this. Too much trouble trying to plough through it. We'll back out, wait for the dawn, and then shape a course round the edge of it. Weed's no joke when there's such a lot of it. Full speed astern, Mr. Bunce, please!"

The mate signalled to the engine-room, and a hollow rumble rose from below. The ship trembled.

For a minute we stood. Then the captain sprang to the telegraph and swung round its handle to "Stop."

"Must have a look astern first," he said. "Weed's in the propeller, I fancy. May have to clean it out to be safe." He spoke jerkily.

I went with him to the poop, and we let down a lantern over the rudder.

There was weed there too; not much—a foot or two, maybe, crawling round our stern. The ship had swung, and instead of backing straight out of the weed, it was forcing its way into it in a path parallel with its margin. The margin was plainly visible; nice clean sea gleamed quite close to us.

"Awkward," said the captain gruffly. "Difficult to get steerage way on her. Must try, though." He went back to the bridge leaving the mate as lookout astern.

Again the engines rumbled, this time a shade more noisily than before, and one felt the ship straining to be free of its entanglement.

It heaved slightly and rocked; as it did so, a faint and not unpleasant odour rose from the weed overboard.

The captain wiped his brow. "No go," he said at last, and signalled afresh to the engineers to stop. "Must put out a boat astern to cut the weed. It's getting round our screw."

He thought for a while and then added, "Better wait till daylight, though."

We waited, and at last the dawn came, grey, from the east. The clouds furled like canopies, and when the sun rose the sky was clear and blue.

There was something cheerful about that blue sky, and I think it raised our spirits, although day showed us a grim prospect ahead. As far as the eye could reach the weed lay, thick matted, bubbling and blistering in the sun, and heaving oilily in the unseen swell. "It must be miles across," said the captain, after he had inspected it through a telescope from the masthead. "Miles, by Jove! Never heard of such a thing in my life. Chunks of weed a few yards square—yes, you meet them anywhere. Even in the blooming Mediterranean I've seen them. And there are islands of weed in the Pacific. But this isn't an island, it's a continent. Well, the sooner we're quit of the continent the better."

The space of weed which divided us off from the friendly ocean behind had grown a little wider, I thought, during the hours of the night; but a boat let down could clear a path through it without difficulty, and we could then back out and proceed on our way—and I should have a fine story for the newspapers.

The boat was lowered and sank squelching into the surface of the weed. Bubbles rose round it, and burst, giving off that peculiar smell which I had noticed before, and which I now began to dislike. Some of the crew—a queer set of ragamuffins of all nations from Cardiff—got down into the boat. It rode buoyantly on, or in, the weed. The crew got out the oars.

Then came the first hint of alarm. The boat would not budge.

The oars made no impression on the weed. They merely scooped it up in strings and skeins. The boat nosed the weed and moved elastically to and fro in it at each stroke of the oars. But not an inch forward did it travel. The men sweated at their oars and cursed. But their labours were utterly in vain.

The captain swore softly. "Vast there!" he called at length. The men stopped rowing. "Mr. Bunce, you must climb over the stern and find out whether we can do anything with knives. We'll swing you down on a rope."

Knives were useless. Mr. Bunce cut and slashed at the weed, lifted shovelfuls of it out of the water, and made no difference. Even if he had been able to clear a patch of water, fresh weed would have flowed in instantly and filled it up. But he had not even the momentary encouragement of making any clearance whatever. The weed was feet thick—fathoms thick, perhaps. A pole, pushed down into it, resisted the push to its full length. Somewhere beneath there must be open water, just as beneath the thickest ice there is open water. How deep beneath? It was impossible to tell.

The engines were set going again, furiously battling with this implacably enveloping monster. The ship trembled and swayed, pushed its stern perhaps a yard back, and then rebounded a yard forward again. Result: nil.

"We're stuck," said the captain.

And stuck we were.

Presently someone noticed that the boat, which had been put overside, was not so near as it had been. Exploring tendrils of weed had come between the *Wellington* and it. We were drifting apart, silently, hardly perceptibly.

A rope was thrown to the boat and it was hauled in, very, very slowly, and with an enormous effort. Our respect for the weed deepened as we saw how tenaciously it resisted the passage of the boat, and clung to its keel, as though with suckers.

The boat was hoisted aboard again, and the crew went to their midday meal.

MONDAY MORNING

We are still embedded in the weed, and the open sea is further astern. All yesterday, and all last night, the engines were kept going, intermittently, without the slightest appreciable effect. This is terrible. A lookout is kept at the masthead, in case some passing vessel could be hailed. If we could get a rope to a steamer in the open sea, she might tow us out. If no steamer comes—

The captain has declined to say what will happen if no steamer comes.

And every hour the strip of weed which divides us from the sea grows an inch or so wider. Either it is actually growing, and that at an amazing pace, or else the *Wellington* is being absorbed by some curious power into the centre of this slimy continent.

TUESDAY

The hands are beginning to murmur. They want to abandon the ship. The captain is loath to do so, as long as there is coal in the bunkers and the engines can continue to make efforts to free us.

(Later.)—As I wrote the above, the engines broke down. Cables of weeds have enveloped the propeller, and the engines, though not actually injured, have sustained a severe strain, and have had to be stopped for repair.

WEDNESDAY

The open sea is now a good hundred feet distant. On every side of us stretches this desert of oozy weed. It is horrible, and its stench is beginning to affect our health. Much of it appears to be dead matter, and undoubtedly is decaying. Possibly fish have got enmeshed in the weed and killed. Perhaps there are even embedded in it the carcases of whales.

THURSDAY

The crew are now openly revolting, and the captain has consented to make an attempt to abandon the *Wellington*. To leave her in boats is plainly impossible. No power on earth could drive the boats through the slough of the weed. The carpenter has suggested that boards could be laid down on the surface of the weed. They cannot sink. It may be feasible to make a sort of pathway or elongated raft of lashed boards, and walk along it, carrying a boat, till the edge of the weed-mass is reached. A party are to try the experiment this afternoon. Meanwhile, the boards are being prepared.

(Later.)—Horrible! Horrible!

The boards were let down overside, and sure enough they lay on the weed with reasonable firmness. Men got down on to them, and began cautiously to throw out other boards, which were lashed to the first lot, and so on. The pathway grew. It heaved up and down slightly, but otherwise gave a fair foothold. The men hardly got their boots wet walking on it.

It was an extraordinary sight. The men worked rapidly, even feverishly, and the odd path of wood grew longer and longer. At last the final planks were laid, their ends touching the verge of the weed. The men at the end of the path cheered wildly, and I don't wonder. The mere sniff of open water must have been exhilarating.

They came back to the ship, and a boat—the smallest we have—was let down. Under its weight the boards sank a little—really wonderfully little. Weed lapped up over the boards, but that was of no consequence.

The gang of men lifted the boat, and very slowly and with the utmost care carried it seaward.

It was now sundown, but already the moon had risen, and there was plenty of light. Those who were left on board watched the progress of the boat-carriers with intense excitement.

They were perhaps halfway towards the sea when an awful thing happened.

Words fail to describe it. It was an upheaval of the most terrible description. For a second or two I positively thought that some vast monster underneath the weed had lifted itself or rolled over. At any rate, what occurred was this.

A mighty billow, a giant undulation, suddenly arose in the weed, and swept across it. We on board the *Wellington* had to hold on for our lives. The ship literally stood on end. For one instant her stern was high in the air. The next her prow was high, and the stern fathoms beneath us.

We clung, I say, for we had seen the wave coming—if wave it could be called: a sprayless, solid, treacle-like mountain range.

The next instant the wave had reached the men who were on the plank pathway.

The pathway rose skyward and writhed...

There was a long cry of fear, and all was over. Men and boat and pathway had all vanished into the morass. They went down into its sticky depths, and their cries were drowned, smothered...

FRIDAY

The captain says that the upheaval was due to a submarine volcanic eruption. No one particularly cares what the explanation might be. All we know is that for an hour or so after the upheaval the weed in our neighbourhood was thinner. It had got broken and disintegrated, and, by a supreme effort, we might have forced our way out of it. But the engines were useless! The irony of it!

Such wind as there is seems to blow persistently towards the centre of the continent of weed, otherwise we should set sails and try what drifting can do to save us. We are, of course, preparing to make another wooden pathway—alas, now far lengthier than the first one. The end of the first pathway was roped to the ship, but we cannot draw it in. The weed hangs to it immovably, and is a dead drag on it.

SATURDAY

The second pathway was begun this morning, and when half made turned traitor. Its far end began to be crawled over by weed; then more weed, and then still more...

The pathways are useless.

SUNDAY

We have been a week in the weed, and now, except from the masthead, the open sea is no longer visible. Are we really doomed? It is difficult to believe that we are. There is plenty of food on board, plenty of coal in the bunkers—

But of what use are food and coal?

MONDAY

Still no hope. The engines are working again. They produce no effect whatsoever.

TUESDAY

Our position is getting on our nerves. An Italian, one of the crew, swears that in the night he saw an immense creature come out of the weed and try to crawl on deck. Pressed to describe the creature, he said it was like a stupendous lizard, with luminous eyes. Nonsense, of course; but I don't wonder at the fellow's alarm. This is an eerie place.

WEDNESDAY

We are on short rations. It is common-sense; but the crew are grumbling.

THURSDAY

The accumulators have given out, and we can only get our electric light at night by gearing straight on to the dynamos. The captain is looking queer. It seems that he was on deck last night, and he, too, confesses that he thought he saw something—some living thing—in the weed. He refuses to describe it, but says it had an audible voice.

Are there creatures? Last night I took a watch on deck. The moon is now waning, but there is still enough light to see the gloomy floor of motionlessness around us. Sometimes it bubbles a little, sometimes it seems to writhe and always it glistens—glistens iridescently.

In the middle of the night I heard a far-off sound. I gazed in the direction whence it came, and I seemed to see—to see something—a something which swept across the melancholy wastes towards the ship like a bird, and yet not a bird. It was too large to be a bird. And then, as it came nearer, I saw that it was not flying, as I had thought. It was really in the weed, but its head (if it was a head) towered above the weed at a height of several feet on top of a comparatively thin neck. The neck ploughed through the weed, hissing and gurgling, and the head came nearer and nearer…

It sank, and vanished. The weed closed over it with a swirl…

Had there really been anything there? Now that I think the thing over in the cold light of day I believe the whole vision was imaginary. But if this is the sort of vision we are to suffer from—well, we had better abandon our night watches on deck, or we shall have insanity to battle with as well as weed.

The crew have mutinied. They want to get at the stores, and particularly at the liquor. The captain, the mate, and the two engineers, and myself, have barricaded ourselves in the cabin.

SUNDAY

A fortnight gone!

MONDAY

We have parleyed with the men. No use.

TUESDAY

Yes, there certainly are creatures in this horrible weed-desert.

Last night, as we lay in the cabin, a something scraped against the side of the ship. A dark mass went across the porthole and momentarily blotted out the moonlight. Then there was silence. We saw no more, and we dared not go on deck, for fear of the crew, who have a revolver, and have threatened to shoot at sight.

WEDNESDAY

Are our brains becoming unhinged? Last night we all four woke at the sound of a bellowing, whistling noise, beside the ship. From the portholes nothing was visible. The origin of the sound was further forward.

Then came a scraping noise, like that we heard on Tuesday night, but lighter; more like the sound of gentle touching—the touching of a tentacle, whereas the previous sound was like the dragging of a heavy hawser.

The tentacle—if tentacle it was—withdrew after a while. Dawn came; and nothing was to be seen from the portholes but the old pavement of weed, empty and devoid of life.

THURSDAY

Last night the scraping came again, and this time the creature, whatever it was, dragged up on to the deck (at least, so it seemed) and swept to and fro for awhile, knocking things about. Before dawn it withdrew.

FRIDAY

It came again last night, and hardly had it reached the deck, when there was an awful cry from for'ard.

SATURDAY

The crew have joined us—in view of the fighting of a common foe. What the foe is none of us know. All we know is that the boatswain was on deck, and was carried off by the creature, shrieking.

SUNDAY

Three weeks gone now.

Thanks to the truce which has been called with the crew, we are now able to go on deck as much as we like. In the shelter of the chart-house we lay in wait for the coming of the creature last night; but it did not appear.

The captain thinks that we must now be more than a mile deep in the weed. It is plain that he has abandoned all hope of escape.

MONDAY

Tragedy to-day. The captain blew out his brains with his revolver.

Was he wise, I wonder? May it not be better to embrace death promptly than to wait, and wait, and wait—till some horrible slow torture kills one inch by inch, or till madness comes?

TUESDAY

Some of the crew have got at the liquor.

Reasoning logically, I begin to perceive that they are no more foolish than the captain.

WEDNESDAY

The junior engineer to-day fixed wide slabs of wood to his boots, and essayed to walk on the surface of the weed. What he expected to be able to do, even if he reached the open sea, I don't know. The experiment failed immediately. He capsized… and the weed swallowed him.

THURSDAY

The creature came again last night, and we all saw it… Heaven help us!

FRIDAY

The mate has gone mad.

(Later.)—The mate had to be shot, in self-defence.

SATURDAY

The ship's carpenter came to me to-day, and begged me to shoot him. "I haven't the pluck, sir, myself…"

Horrible! Of course, I could not do it.

SUNDAY

Four weeks!

The ship's carpenter had more pluck than he gave himself credit for…

I am now alone in the cabin, with the remaining members of the crew, all raving drunk.

To-night, if the creature comes again, I shall go out to meet it…

*   *   *

The diary ended here.

"Then it was Sargasso weed after all," said the lieutenant slowly. "You were right, Professor; but how the deuce did the ship get out of it in the end?"

"Another volcanic upheaval, only this time a real big one," said the Professor. "The weed is known to gather like that. It grows amazingly fast—a foot or more in an hour, I've heard say—and it dies quickly, too, and sinks like lead; but once it had got as thick as this poor chap describes—well, nothing but a volcanic upheaval would disperse it. I guess there was a grand bust up; the weed was shredded right and left; then there came, maybe, a stunning storm, and here we find the *Wellington* in clear ocean, practically none the worse."

The lieutenant chewed at his cigar. "And the—the creatures, to which the writer refers?" he queried tentatively.

The Professor shrugged his shoulders. "'There are more things in heaven or earth,'" he quoted.

"You think it really existed?"

The Professor held out his hand, the palm open. "Ever see a scale like that?" he asked.

The lieutenant gazed at the open hand. A large, scale—the scale apparently of an enormous fish-lay there, shining dully in the sun.

"Where did you find that? It's a darned big scale, by gosh! Two inches across, at least, and as firm as steel."

"That scale," said the Professor, carefully putting it into his pocket-book, "belongs to no fish, crustacean, or mammal, or reptile, or anything else that I've ever heard of. That's all I can tell you, except that I found it fixed—glued by its own slime—to the side of the wheel-house."

The lieutenant and the Professor looked at each other. Then the doctor, who had been listening, spoke.

"I thank my stars I wasn't on board the *Wellington*, anyway," he said.

HELD BY THE SARGASSO SEA

Frank H. Shaw

Frank H. Shaw (1878–1960), despite having been a serving sea captain for many of his early adult years, must qualify as one of Britain's most prolific writers of short stories. In his autobiography he reckoned he had written at least seven thousand stories, many of novella length. He recalls how one day he was in London, taking a break having written a complete novel the previous week, when a magazine editor contacted him because E. Phillips Oppenheim been unable to deliver a promised 20,000-word novella and he hoped Shaw could oblige—but it was needed the next day. Shaw asked for a typewriter to be delivered to his hotel room and, focusing the mind, he sat and produced the novella in time to get it into the evening post.

With so many stories written at breakneck pace it is difficult to single out too many because, inevitably, Shaw followed tried and tested formulas. But that number of stories also means that if even 10% was of any merit, that's still seven hundred stories, and Shaw's strike rate was better than that. Most of his stories have a nautical setting and deal with all and every drama of the sea, including the many legends. Using the same setting of the Sargasso as Ward Muir's story, Shaw comes up with a completely different result.

I

"I F I WERE YOU," SAID CAPTAIN CHISHOLM'S OLD FRIEND, Captain Welford, "I'd sell that old hulk and buy a ship."

Every hair of the old skipper's white beard stood on end with indignation. In all his fifty odd years of life, forty-five of which had been spent at sea, he had never heard such an insult passed on the ship that was his joy and pride. She lay alongside the wharf, and her age was written on every part of her, from the green-coated copper of her bottom to the warped wood of her lower masts. She was of a pattern that grew extinct almost thirty years ago: wood-built, copper-fastened, with heavy timber in place of the neat ironwork of a modern day, and her rigging was of hemp, not wire.

"To think that I should ever hear that!" exclaimed Chisholm, and his fiery old eye filmed over for a moment with sorrow, only to lighten again as it scanned the familiar outlines of the old craft. "Nay, James, but I thought you'd understand enough about a man's feelings to know that if you touch his ship you touch something else besides his pride—you touch his heart. I grant the *Swordfish* isn't much to look at, but she's a good 'un to sail, and she'll be a good 'un when I'm sewn up in a spare staysail and hove overside. Fifty-five years she has used the sea, and the men who built her knew their work as they don't now. I could go on talking for a twelvemonth and then only touch the fringe of what that ship and I have been through together. Storm and calm, fire and terror—ay, she's always stood by, has the old beauty, and, please God, I'll stick by her to the end. I'll never desert her. You might say she's not fit to hold a candle to some that are afloat now, but I know the ship's moods and humours, and I believe she knows mine. Talk about your dogs and horses! What can they know about a man when compared to a ship? There's something almost human about her. No, no, I'll never part with her, and she knows that. I fancy sometimes there's something like a soul in that old craft. When I've been at my wits' end, in a fog or a blizzard, with a lee shore not so very far off, I've just spoken to her confidentially, and she always seemed to understand. We weathered whatever came, and—we'll try to weather a bit more before we're both posted as 'missing.'"

As Captain Welford was not a sentimentalist, he looked shrewdly at his friend, and remarked in a gruff tone "that the sun seemed a trifle overpowering."

Chisholm snorted loudly.

"What can you expect nowadays, anyway?" he said vehemently. "What with your trades unions and such-like! Men don't take the pride in their work they used to do, and the result is a ship's nothing but a box of jumping machinery, that hasn't got the feelings of a ship. But with that vessel there"—he pointed to the *Swordfish* with the air of Cæsar pointing Albion out to his cohorts—"there's something like workmanship. Her designer put his soul into her, the men who worked on her were artists in their line. Each man put a bit of himself into the building, and the *Swordfish*, sir, is a sentient thing. Yes, sir, that describes her—a sentient thing."

"Well, I only hope she'll act up to her reputation, Captain Chisholm. When does she sail next? On the twentieth? Why, man, the strike isn't settled yet. You'll never get a crew together before that time. You might say ships aren't what they used to be, but I'll not deny sailors are very different from what I remember. They must have this, and they must have that: a pound of so-and-so here, and an ounce of the other thing there—I don't know what the sea's coming to. I was up at the Sailors' Home yesterday, and the crowd of sailors there—pah! Gaol-birds, they were, and road-sweepings. Landscape gardeners and matchbox makers, but not sailors. I don't know what the sea's coming to."

The two old cronies were embarked on a theme that promised endless possibilities of discussion. It was recognized by both that a bar-parlour and a friendly glass would do much to relieve the tedium of argument, and they adjourned by tacit understanding to The Captain's Arms. The *Swordfish*, left alone, lifted herself gently to the ripple of the tide, and poised her sharp prow over the wharf. At a distance, because of the two staring hawseholes, which had a ludicrous resemblance to eyes, she seemed to be watching her captain, as a dog, bidden to remain on guard, might watch its master recede into the distance. Her timbers groaned as she rolled lazily, and the summer wind sighed plaintively through her cordage.

Chisholm had a good deal of difficulty in securing a crew. Being something of a disciplinarian at sea, he liked to know the material he was working with, and in consequence spent many a bad hour in looking over the few non-strikers who presented themselves for engagement. These were either men who were at such a low ebb that they refused to starve for an imaginary principle any longer, or else hard-bitten, hard-hitting bravoes, who cared nothing for threats or expostulations. Men they were who would not be coerced, savages when in drink, and sullen idlers when sober. But it was a case of Hobson's choice, and the *Swordfish* was ready for sea.

"I don't want to pay demurrage," remarked Captain Chisholm when Welford joined him in solemn head-shakings over the prospective crew. "I reckon I've knocked worse crowds than that into shape, and I'll do it again. To be sure, I was younger then, but there's a lot in the power of a man's eye."

"There's more in the power of a man's fist," said Welford gloomily. "I was looking at that man you shipped as bo'sun to-day. He's a bad lot, if ever I saw one. Murderer was written all over his face. And you're carrying a lot of spirits in your cargo, aren't you?"

"Five thousand cases," said Chisholm triumphantly. "It's a lot at one go, but I'll get it stowed away down the after hatch, and I'll padlock the battens, so that'll be all right. But I'll let these fellows see they haven't got a kid-gloved extra master to deal with. I haven't forgotten my old tricks, I'd like you to know, Captain Welford. I used to be a terror at sea, and though I've quietened considerably of late, I'm not a chicken."

"Who's your mate?" asked Welford irrelevantly.

"Ah! now that's a drawback," returned his friend, with a wise wag of his grizzled head. "I haven't been very lucky in my choice. You see, young men won't go in sail if they can help it—they prefer the steamers—and so I had to take young Bilton, and he hasn't got much nerve, I'm afraid."

"Bilton!" The snort that followed the name told volumes. "I wouldn't carry him for ballast. He's in a blue funk every time he speaks to an ordinary seaman, and he always says 'please' to an A. B.! Bilton!"

But the *Swordfish* was loaded to her Plimsoll, and there was a favouring breeze. No master could stop too long to pick and choose amongst the material at his command, for Chisholm was a skipper first and last and in between. To him it was a sacred duty safely and speedily to deliver such cargoes as were entrusted to him and his beloved ship, come what might in the way of hazards and dangers and the manifold perils of the wave. The Blue Peter stood out gallantly at her fore; the clearance papers were in the cabin lockers, and the ship was ready for sea.

"I'll trust to the old barky to see me through, whatever might come," said Chisholm with a proud smile. "She knows I'm in a bit of trouble, and she'll do her best for me, I'm sure."

Welford watched the vessel depart, and, as he saw the aspect of her crew, he returned to the bar-parlour of The Captain's Arms shaking his head dolefully.

"That ship's just a floating convict settlement," he said to the innkeeper. "There's no telling what might come to her now. Poor old Chisholm!"

II

"That's no way to coil a brace down, Edwards. Please take it up and do it properly."

"Well, of all the dog-gasted cheek, I never saw! Here was I at sea afore you'd finished yelping for milk, an' you think you can teach me my work. Go and help the old man ter keep his whiskers on!"

The burly A.B. seemed to swell before the mate's frightened eyes, and there was distinct menace in his attitude. He coughed and flushed, then turned as white as a sheet, but attempted no remonstrance further. He was a coward to his very heart. But there was an old lion near at hand, and a voice like the cry of an angry god boomed through the breeze.

"What's that on deck there? Here, you—you loafer, you—come here!"

The sailor shuffled uneasily, and touched his forelock, for the sense of discipline was hidden somewhere within him. He advanced towards the carved and ornamented poop-break, and hung his head.

"Any more back-talk like that, my man," said Chisholm sternly, "and it's irons and the fore-peak for you—do you understand? I'm skipper here, and when I'm out of sight my mate must have my respect. Get forward, you swab, and move lively, or I'll help you along with my fist!" His eyes were blazing, but his fine old face was very calm. The man slunk away, muttering vague threats, and the mate breathed freely once more. He realized that his superior was a *man* in every accepted sense of the word.

"That's all right; I've sounded 'em," said the delinquent a little while later in the privacy of the forecastle. "The mate's just flabby, but the old man's a terror of terrors. He won't stand no jaw, not him. He looked belaying-pins an' capstan bars at me jist now. But I've got it in for Mr. Blooming Bilton, you mark my words."

With such a feeling in the forecastle, it may be granted that the opening of the *Swordfish's* voyage was not a monument of auspiciousness. Before the Bay of Biscay was crossed the crew were seething with incubating discontent. There was a feeling about the ship's atmosphere such as men have described as existing in a coal-mine before the deadly fire-damp exploded. It needed but the spark to set the whole combustible affair alight with disastrous results. But as yet the spark was not forthcoming.

The men realized that there was a man at the head of affairs with whom to trifle was no child's play. Let any seaman so much as allow a sullen expression to twist his face, and he was treated to such a volley of wholesome abuse as sent him sprinting forward at top speed with a regard for his captain's powers of persuasion difficult to express in ordinary English.

The boatswain did his best in that way.

"I ups an' tells the bloomin' mate as how I'd holystoned ther decks like mad, an' he ses as how I were a liar. So I just puts my fist under his nose, an arsks him ter take a smell o' that, an' he weakened right off—I knowed he would. But old Rough-and-Tough spots me, an' when he'd finished with his remarks I felt suthin' like a steamer fireman's sweat-rag after speed trials—all limp and flabby. There ain't no triflin' wiv him, I assure yer."

"But if he was out o' ther road," said one sailor darkly—a tall and lathy Yankee—"we could do what we blame well liked. Yew chaps don't know yew're born yit. This ship—blarsted old wreck an' all as she is—she's worth her weight in gold to us chaps. We could take what she's got in that forehold an' sell it tew one o' them potty republics in South America, an' never need tew work no more. Did yew see them cases down the forehold, any of yew? Rifles an' cartridges, or I don't know my hash from my wages. Just think what yew'd get for them from Botavia, say. An' ther ship air wuth somethin' herself."

It was the first breath, and the assembled men, grimy and tar-stained, with lowering faces and stealthy eyes, glanced from one to another. They were almost ripe for mischief now.

"We could do it, too, if we was drunk," said the man who was sowing seed of discontent.

"Garn!" sneered the boat-swain, "who's able ter git drunk on a bloomin' limejuicer? There ain't no sperrits nor nuthin' excep' a box o' medical comforts in the cabin."

"There's five thousand cases o' sperrits down the after-hatch," grunted the Yankee insinuatingly.

"Ay, bulkheaded off from ther main-hold, an' ther hatch-battens padlocked down," said the boatswain.

"What's that matter? Ain't this a wooden ship, and ain't her bulk-heads wood tew? What's to stop us cuttin' through from ther main intew ther after-hatch an' gettin' as much as we bloomin' well likes?"

The men pricked their ears at this information. Then the boat-swain rose from the green-painted sea-chest on which he was seated, and shut the door with some ostentation.

"Tell us that agin," he said as he reseated himself and crammed tobacco into his charred pipe-bowl. Then head was bent to head, and the foul air of the forecastle grew fouler because of the mutterings of treason there. And the old ship, booming along like a thing of life before the north-east trades, stirred herself uneasily and hung heavily on the helm. Captain Chisholm told the helmsman what his opinion of incompetent A.B.'s was in fluent language, but the man answered that "it weren't no fault of his if ther blamed ship were bewitched."

"Let's have hold of that wheel, my lad," said Chisholm grimly, "and if she steers all right I'll log you for cheek." But he failed to improve on the man's work. The *Swordfish* had the bit in her teeth, and she threw her head from side to side as a restless horse might before a thunderstorm. Though Chisholm humoured her with all his knowledge of many years, she refused to be comforted.

"I'm sorry I spoke," said the old man with no good grace. "The ship's restless." He left the wheel, and paced the poop in wonder-ing meditation. Never, in all the years that he had commanded the *Swordfish*, had she displayed such tantrums. It was inexplicable.

At four bells in the first dogwatch that night the boatswain was called aft. Chisholm's face was full of quiet anger.

"My mate says you have been talking back," he said, with a por-tentous frown. "Understand this, bo'sun, I'll disrate you without a chance if it occurs again."

"You go an' comb yer whiskers, skipper," said the boatswain insolently. "Yer'll need ther threads ter mend yer temper. "Ta-ta, old cock. Sorry I can't stop."

Chisholm thundered in his wrath, but only a derisive chuckle came to him from a fast-receding figure.

"What does it mean?" he asked himself anxiously. "There's something afoot. First the old ship's uneasy, and then that man was distinctly insubordinate. What is it, my beauty?" He asked the question of the ship, glancing at the towering pyramids of canvas that clothed her from truck to waterway, at the curved and booming canvas that was full of strenuous determination, at the cracking sheets that seemed straining with desire to get the voyage over at any hazard. But the ship herself was dumb. She could only speed erratically across the white-topped waves and betray her uneasiness in frightened plunges into shadows and in flurried poises over towering waves.

That night Chisholm sought out his old revolver, and loaded it carefully in every chamber. He slept with it beneath his pillow and did not undress.

III

The second mate had the first watch that night, and he thought the rats with which the old ship was infested were unconscionably busy in the holds. They gnawed loudly, and strange screeches now and then rose above the steady drumming of rope on canvas and the constant booming of the well-filled sails. Being a man who loved his ease, however, Mr. Thurston took but little notice of the happening, and had quite forgotten it by the time the first mate relieved him at twelve o'clock.

When the muster was called, the men answered in strange and unfamiliar voices, so that Bilton, peering through the almost opaque darkness of the sub-tropical night, felt an intangible shudder of fear stir his heart-strings. The wind veered a trifle towards two bells, and it became necessary to alter the trim of the yards slightly. In answer to the mate's whistle, only three of the watch appeared, and when he voiced his wishes they answered with a sneering laugh. As is the way with some cowards; the mate worked himself into a white heat of trembling anger—and the men laughed still louder. A belaying-pin grazed Bilton's head in the darkness, and before he could gather what was afoot there was a sudden hoarse cry from forward, a reeling rush of drink-maddened men, the scuttering run of many feet, and he was driven back, fighting like a suddenly-aroused lion.

Up the poop ladder he staggered, dealing blows to right and left at venomous faces that loomed wanly through the night. They followed him with a rush, and drove him still farther aft, until he turned at bay against the chart-room, and went down with a loose ring-bolt at his temple. But the tumult on deck had aroused other men, and the roar of the old viking's voice split the silence that followed on the mate's downfall.

"Back, you scum!" he bellowed, and his face was the face of a hero. "Get down to your kennels, dogs!" He sprang out of the companion-way like a youth, and the sheer menace of his voice held those men still for as long as one might count a score. The second mate was out on deck by this, and his young voice rang out clearly, "I'm with you, sir!"

"Get back! The first man who moves forward I'll shoot." A ray of moonlight escaped from a blanketing cloud, and shimmered on a bright barrel in the captain's hand. The men were cowed for the moment, but not for long. They saw the shadowy form of the murdered mate in the scuppers, and the sense of what they had done came upon them. They would hang for it in any case, they said; they might as well go the whole hog. But the revolver barrel never flickered from the boatswain's burly breast, and no man dared move.

The second mate was young, and wishful to show the kind of man he was. He bent his head, doubled his fists, and charged like a stone from a sling into the thick of the mutineers. Someone hit him under the ear, and he went down like a felled bullock. In the scrambling, yelling confusion, Captain Chisholm could not shoot for fear of hurting his own man, and he stood there powerless for a moment, until the men formed up again, and hissingly demanded his surrender.

"Never, you dogs! Get back!" It was gallantly done. Even then he might have carried his point, but the helmsman was not taken into consideration. The latter raced quickly—his bare feet made no sound—and gripped the skipper from behind, pinioning his arms.

There was a hasty conference there in the wonderful gloom of the night. Some were for murdering the skipper outright, on the "dead men tell no tales" plan; others, to whom the old man's gallantry had unconsciously appealed, were for milder methods. The latter section carried their point.

"Clear out that quarter-boat," commanded the boatswain. "Put ther old chap in it, an' give him some biscuit an' water. See how he fares on sailors' grub." They did it. The bemused, bewildered old captain was flung without gentleness into the boat, a jar of water and a bag of biscuit were thrown in after him, and the boat was lowered. Just as the tackles were being cast off, the boatswain staggered along under a heavy weight. He carried the almost dead second officer.

"Let him have comp'ny," he growled, and the body hit the thwarts below with a dull thud. Then the tackles were cast off, and the

Swordfish vanished into the unknown, leaving the boat alone on the black and mysterious sea.

Captain Chisholm raised his head and groaned as the truth was forced in on his dazed brain. The *Swordfish*, the ship that he had loved as few men can ever love the woman of their hearts, had deserted him in his dire extremity. She had gone without a sound, leaving him alone upon the ocean that he had conquered for fifty years almost. But his own position was nothing to him. He had taken the chances of the sea as they occurred, and knew that he might still find safety; but the thing that caused the dull gnawing ache at his heart was the knowledge that his ship, his pride, his beauty, was in the hands of a gang of unprincipled ruffians. He groaned again as he pictured them abusing the old craft that he had so carefully nurtured for so many years. It was misery of miseries to him, and he felt that the bitterness of more than death was on him in that hour of the old ship's desertion.

A groan from the near-by thwart aroused him from his bitter despair, and for the next hour he found occupation enough in bringing the second mate round. Then the two men sat down to await the chances the great deep might bring. The day dawned, and showed them no hope. A sea that was a vast expanse of cream-topped blue, a sky that was cloudless, and in the middle of the waste was nothing but a tiny cockle-shell of a craft, thrown hither and thither.

But they were saved. A homeward-bound steamer picked them up, and listened to their tale in wonder. The cables of the world were set to flashing messages of menace to those who had taken the *Swordfish* for their own ends. Every port was scrutinized carefully; every steamer kept a sharp lookout for the missing craft, but she had disappeared as completely as if the sea had swallowed her up.

Gradually men said that the *Swordfish* was lost, that her inexperienced navigators had run her under owing to their carrying too great a press of sail. She was posted as missing at Lloyd's, and Captain Chisholm sat himself down in the port that was his home, to wait for his death. The sea had no charm for him now—he refused to sail it in an alien craft. There were those who knew the cunning sea-lore of the man, and these offered him commands that would have caused the heart of a younger man to swell with gratified pride. He refused them all: what were other ships to him, who had owned and sailed a living thing for forty years or so? He said he had lived his life, and that he would wait for death. Life held no charms for him now—his ship was gone for ever.

IV

There lies in the Atlantic Ocean, far removed from all the ship routes, and shunned as the plague by sailing vessels which, by reason of adverse currents and baffling winds, have unwillingly sighted it, a mysterious and melancholy thing. It is called the Sargasso Sea. Columbus sighted it on his momentous voyage to the West, and brought back startlingly lurid tales of its wonderful powers. He said that it attracted everything that floated within a radius of many a mile; that it reached out horrible and slimy arms to drag the unwitting seafarers into its clutches like some octopus of fabulous size—which stories were certainly untrue, for no man has ever penetrated the Sargasso Sea and lived to tell the tale.

The sea is shut out here by illimitable tracts of loathsome weed. Thousands of years have passed since the Gulf Stream split up into two separate currents and caused a sort of backwater into which was swept all the raffle of the sea. The bottles that are thrown over from sinking ships are swept towards this common refuse heap of the deep; derelicts gradually sway into this vortex; the thick weed of the mighty rivers that feed the Gulf of Mexico all add their quota. There is a solid bed of vegetable matter, reaching down into the unknown depths of the sea, and spreading far to east and west, to north and south. And there are narrow lanes cut into and through this great bed of sea-raffle. Little currents drag the solid weed away, and so there are illusive roads that divide the solid thing into many parts. Not until the sea gives up its dead will the whole miserable history of the Sargasso Sea be known.

The mutinous crew of the *Swordfish* were in their element now. Given an unlimited supply of crude spirits, with the best of the cabin stores to satisfy a seldom-occurring hunger, no work to do and no one to exercise even the briefest authority, and you have a veritable sailors' paradise. But the *Swordfish* was fast becoming a floating place of horror. Men quarrelled with each other, and knives were drawn. The Yankee stabbed the boatswain in a drunken frenzy, and then dared the others to come on.

No man aboard knew the first elements of navigation. The wind held fair astern, and the easiest way to avoid work on the sails was to let the ship run straight away from the volleying wind that thundered ominously in her wake. The ship seemed to know that her guardian was gone for ever. She lifted her head and plunged madly forward into unknown seas, where she looked about her with a bewildered air, for here were strange curling tangles of floating weed—something through which she was hard pressed to bore a way. She seemed to know that a sweet rest from her ignominy lay behind the western horizon, for she headed for the silent places.

It was night, and the decks were shrouded in gloom. From overside came the steady rush and ripple of the ship's advance; but there was a curious dragging feel about the rudder, and the man who steered was bewildered. In the forecastle or the cabin, men drank deeply and swore foul oaths regarding their future. The Yankee talked fluently about the making of money without labour. The drink ran like a river. Greasy cards were shuffled and dealt, hot words followed hot words, and the ship still plunged on resistlessly through the silent night. Gradually the men slept where they had fallen, and lost all care. The ship glided on as though a shadow peopled by shadows. The drag on the rudder grew greater, but the ship's instinct bade her keep on and bring justice to the murderers.

It was a bright morning when the Yankee aroused himself and staggered to the deck for water to cool his aching head. The ship's sails were flapping idly against the quivering masts, but there was no refreshing lap-lap of parted water to greet his ears. Instead, was nothing but a ghastly silence. Unheeding, unafraid, the Yankee looked over the side to see the meaning of this strange happening, and then started back with a yell of utter dread. The ship lay in a sea of weed. Everywhere it stretched, astern and ahead, and far on either beam. No wind that ever blew could move her from that sinister grip that had tightened around her keel while men slept unheeding. The lane up which she had passed was filled in with a tangle of clogging weed: the drift of the sea left greasy streaks on her sides. Her rudder was tight jammed with a mass of vegetable growth, and her bow rested on a similar tangle.

Far away, yet painfully distinct in the clear air, the stumps of a derelict's masts protruded upward from the weed banks. It was an omen: no man might leave the place until his flesh had shrivelled on his bones and the light had left his eyes for ever. Still farther away was another derelict—a high-sterned, cumbersome thing this last, for the Sargasso's motto coincides with the Yorkshireman's: "What we have we hold." Centuries of mystery lay about the *Swordfish*, but she rested there motionless, quivering slightly from time to time, as though convulsed with mirth.

The Yankee's loud yells of fear brought the whole blear-eyed rabble on deck. They, in turn, surveyed the outlook, and then, with a unanimity that was amazing, turned-to and cursed the Yankee with all the tongues of the sea, as the author of their troubles. The Yank lost his quick temper, and one man went down with a heavy blow; but the others drew back afraid from the grinning gums and the glaring eyes of their self-elected leader.

They vanished below and found more drink. They fell into sodden stupor after sodden stupor, and so the slow days dragged past. Once, in a moment of sobriety, the Yankee kicked some of them into a boat, which he stored with food and drink, and then, launching the craft, they strove to make their escape from the horrible place; but escape there was none. The weed clogged the oars, and the bluff bow could not cut through the cumbering mass. It took them all of a day and a night to win back to the ship, and when they returned they bore on their faces the look of men who have been down into the depths of the pit.

So the weeks passed by, and the year drew to its close. They had ample food and drink, but their position unhinged their minds, and soon the ship was peopled by nothing but a few mowing madmen Time did its work with these—they killed one another in mad frenzies or died of thirst and their madness.

The sails rotted away in their ropes, the deck-seams opened wide. Some dry-rot began to work in the masts, and one by one they fell to the deck. But the old hull remained staunch and true.

The year passed, and a new year dawned. It found a silent ship in a desert of silence, a ship that was peopled only by sinister shapes that moved merely to the slow heave of the dismantled hull; and the years passed by, but the Sargasso held its grim secret staunchly.

V

They knew the old captain was dying. He had said it himself, and who should know better? He had no wish to live on in loneliness, and only his own heart knew how lonely he was since the *Swordfish* had deserted him. He had taken a little cottage that faced a wide and quiet bay, where the placid days passed peacefully, and here he nursed his bitter sorrow in silence. His old-time crony, Captain Welford, took a cottage near by, and strove to comfort his friend, but in vain.

"We'll get the doctor," said Welford one morning, when he came to persuade the old man to take a stroll along the beach and inhale the rich freshness of the sea-breeze, and found him in bed.

"Doctors 'll do me no good," returned Chisholm. "There's only one thing in the world would give me a fresh lease of life, Welford, and that's a sight of the *Swordfish*. But Welford urged and entreated, and finally young Doctor Smith was called in.

"No; there's nothing organically wrong," was the verdict. "Just a general decay of the tissues—senile decay, in short. Nothing to be done except to keep him cheerful."

"Senile decay, indeed!" snorted Chisholm, when the medico had gone. "My father died at ninety-nine, and his father topped the century. If things had turned out properly, I'd have been hale and hearty for another twenty years. No, lad; it's the loss of my old ship, and I can't get over it, try as I will. I've tried hard, but it's no use. My heart aches when I think of the old barky sinking alone, and weighted down with her shame."

The weeks floated easily by for the old man, and it seemed as if his grief were becoming assuaged with his growing weakness. He even took an interest in the doings of the outside world, and when Welford regaled him with long and tedious accounts of the earth-quakes that had recently devastated the New World, he ventured opinions in his old clear way.

"Mark my words," he said one day, "there'll be some changes and chances at sea with all these earthquakes and things. It isn't in reason that the earth should suffer and not the sea. There'll be need for a new Admiralty survey of the oceans before very long, for I tell you there'll be more than a few uncharted rocks springing up soon. Earthquakes and volcanoes work under the sea the same as above."

Seeing the old man's interest, Captain Welford said that he was regaining his lost strength; but it was merely a flash in the pan. He seldom rose now, but lay in bed, with his grave eyes fronting the sea he had fought and loved for the best of his life. From where he lay he could see over the quiet bay and out to the open sea. It was a vil-lage that lay out of the beaten track, where he lived. It was seldom that anything appeared to mar the perfect loneliness of the sea that he gazed upon, save that occasionally a far-distant curl of smoke appeared on the horizon.

"It was time, the old ship went, perhaps," he said one day, as his eyes watched such a curl fade away into the infinite. "She was out of date, and steam's the thing nowadays; but if I had her again I feel I could do some good with her."

It was a November morning when Captain Welford tiptoed into the silent cottage and made his cautious way upstairs. A dull, brooding atmosphere seemed to fill every room, there was a feeling as though the Death Angel were poised outside on dark wings, waiting for the end. Chisholm was very weak, and his breath came fitfully, but he strove to give the old cheery greeting, and Welford felt a strange lump in his throat as he marked the change that had come over his friend during the past night. It was a clammy, foggy day without. The bay was shut out in mist, and only the far-off bleatings of bewildered ships broke the stillness. The lighthouse at the bay's mouth brayed its futile warning, for all the ships of the port were safe at their moorings, and no stranger would come that way.

"It's fitting," gasped Chisholm weakly, "I shall go out in the fog—my life's been befogged for many a weary day. It's very close now, old friend; but—I feel as though I couldn't go without one last look at the grey old sea."

Welford understood him with a sailor's understanding. He dragged the bed to the window and threw the sash wide. There was nothing to be seen outside save the whirling and billowing fog-clouds, but over head the sun strove hard to penetrate the mist. So they sat for many an hour, and the old man's breath grew fainter and fainter.

Suddenly he lifted himself in the bed and peered through the open window with staring eyes. A long arm was lifted, and a wavering finger pointed out to the entrance of the bay.

"The *Swordfish!*" cried Chisholm, with an unearthly light in his eyes. His white hair was almost standing upright on his head, his eyes were narrowed to a mere crack, but his body was pulsating with eager expectation.

"She's coming!" he cried. "Ah! I knew she wouldn't desert me!"

And then the mystery happened. The sun tore down the fog-walls, and the bay lay aglow beneath the afternoon light. Coming up the bay steadily and surely, as though guided by spirit hands, was a ship. She was mastless and woebegone, her rigging hung in rotting tangles over her sides, and a long trail of weed floated astern. Her once black sides were bleached to a dirty white by many a tropical sun; her anchors hung rusting at the bow; her spars were broken and decayed. At her wheel, grasping the spokes, stood a grinning skeleton.

"Get the glasses," gasped Chisholm; and a flush of crimson was on his white cheek. "She's the old ship—I know it. She heard me call her, and she came." Wondering exceedingly, Welford found the glasses and scanned the vessel's bow. There, in rust-stained letters, yet plainly visible in spite of the lapse of years, he read the name, *Swordfish!*

Still she came on. Propelled by some submarine current, steered by a dead man's hand, the *Swordfish* made her slow way up the harbour, and a wondering crowd on the beach surveyed her with staring eyes. They were a superstitious race, the fishermen of that village, and they hesitated to touch the thing that was coming towards them from the sea. So the *Swordfish* crawled slowly up the bay. The old skipper was leaning out of the window now, and his face was ashine with joy. When the ship grounded easily under his very window he scanned her with a lover's glance, and lay for a moment exhausted, half afraid, and very wonderstruck.

He had been right about the effects of the earthquakes on the ocean. Some violent shock must have stirred the grim Sargasso Sea to its very core. The grasping, clutching weeds had parted, and the ill-fated *Swordfish* must have made her lonely, unpiloted way towards the open sea; then the Gulf Stream took her to its bosom, and floated her gently northwards, ever northwards.

With her crew of the dead, ghastly and unaided, she had come up out of the vasty deep to lay her poor old bones alongside those of the man who had loved her well.

Some may say that such a thing is impossible, that nothing could occasion such a coincidence as that the *Swordfish* should make her steadfast course towards Chisholm's home; but who shall solve the inexplicable mystery of the sea? Certainly, Chisholm made no attempt to solve the problem. He rose out of his bed, and stood alone with a new strength.

"Let's go down to her, Welford," he said calmly, yet with a sunny face. "The old ship wouldn't leave me, and I'll not leave her. She's got years of life in that old hull, and there are years of life in this body of mine. We'll patch her up and sail the seas for many a year. Senile decay, indeed! I've got the tonic I needed, and we'll never part again." And they did not.

THE FLOATING FOREST

Herman Scheffauer

Herman Scheffauer (1876–1927) was an American-born writer of German parentage who spent many years in England. Although influenced by German literature he also became a devotee of the works of Edgar Allan Poe. Though he trained as an architect his passion for literature became dominant and he earned an early reputation as a poet, encouraged by Ambrose Bierce who passed off one of Scheffauer's poems as being by Poe. From 1904 he toured Europe and North Africa, settling in London in 1905 where he mixed with the literary set, including G. K. Chesterton and Hilaire Belloc. Though he returned to San Francisco in 1907, where he began a new career as a novelist and dramatist, he returned to London in 1911, around the time the following story was written, married, and had considerable success with his play The New Shylock *(1913). Concerned with the anti-German feelings in Britain at the start of the War, Scheffauer went to Germany to better understand the situations. His allegiances were torn but in British and American eyes he had become a traitor and he was indicted for treason. Although there was some post-war reconciliation, Scheffauer remained in Germany working as a writer and journalist, but he sank into a deep depression and killed himself in 1927, when he was only fifty-one.*

Scheffauer's literary influences were diverse, but there seems to be more than an element of Edgar Allan Poe in the following story.

T HE TERRIBLE DISCOVERY, NOW THREE DAYS OLD, RANKLED
like a barb of rusted iron in the gentle bosom of Mary Vance.
It blotted the brightness of the day for her, and when sleep came it
brought dreadful visions and dreams. She saw doomed souls writhing in fiery torment, she saw the smoke-blackened hand of her
husband reach forth imploringly from the pit. And this had been so
only since three days.

What had seized upon the soul of the ship-captain James Vance,
he who had been so full of strange, rude tendernesses, with whom
she had sailed the sea since the day they were wed? Had she never
really known him, never sounded these abysses of terror so suddenly disclosed? For now he was as if changed by the wand of
some sorcerer, his blithe nature dashed with savage rancour, his
face disfigured with diabolical darkness. All day he brooded; sometimes he burst out suddenly in frightful curses upon the crew.
Ever since they had left Boston he had been sad and preoccupied.
She had marked him, tall and splendid, bearded like a sea-king,
standing with folded arms in the heaving bows, his rugged head
bent upon his breast, his eyes fixed on the blazing foam that flew
from the prow of the *Serapis*. But only since the last three days
had she known the truth.

In the presence of his wife the captain's stern features relaxed
a little, and his harsh voice grew somewhat softer. But reciprocal
anger stirred in the hearts of the crew against the monster passion
they could not understand. Mary Vance, isolated by soul and sex,
estranged from her husband by this new and remorseless secret,

stood alone and forlorn in the shadows cast upon the *Serapis* by the dread temper of all on board. The sunlight seemed merely to heat the gloom as the *Serapis*, with her big burden of cement and lime, tore on her way toward Callao. It was as if murder, unseen but sensed, moved among them.

Mary Vance was a Scotchwoman whom Vance had met and married five years before in Dundee. She was intensely pious with a piety such as was fixed, uncompromising, and of a day long past. Instinctively now she took to fervent prayers, pouring them upon the waters, uttering them to all the winds.

Three days before a storm had burst upon them. Why had Captain Vance deemed it necessary to provision the boats, to place charts and instruments in them? The *Serapis* had easily mastered fiercer gales.

It was on that very night that Mary Vance had seen her husband rise during one of the early morning watches and stealthily make his way toward the hold. In his eyes, revealed by a lantern's light, was a look she had never seen before. What was he doing in the hold at that hour? Why was he so secret, so silent, so crafty in look and movement? Why, after a wearisome time, did he not return?

The sad-eyed woman, with some strange, foreboding sense of doom weighing upon her, arose, and like a ghost crept on her slippered feet down the steep steps and along the narrow passage that led into the hold. Far ahead in the bows, where the ruddy lantern light bathed the enormous groaning knees and ribs of the bark and revealed the countless heads of the dusty barrels of Portland cement and unslaked lime, the woman saw her husband's head black against the glow. Fantastic shadows were flung toward her as he moved. The vessel pitched and plunged on the mighty swells that followed the gale, and the oaken timbers and beams groaned dolorously as the ship staggered and lifted and shook. Stealthily she crept between the barrels, and watched her husband at his work. He was heaping broken boxes and old ropes, oakum and pieces of oily sail cloth against the foot of the foremast.

"Jamie, Jamie, for the love of Heaven, what be you doing?"

Pale and spirit-like she stood there, her eyes dilated with alarm, her voice full of sorrow and accusation. James Vance wheeled about as though steel had stabbed him; he leaped forward with a roar like a lion and a blasphemous oath, his eyes afire, his clenched fist quivering above his wife's bare head. Cowering, she shrank away. Her husband's arrested fist sank slowly, then opened and clutched her by the braids of her long hair. Like angel and fiend they seemed to stand there, his eyes darting flame into her own, which were filled with terror and tears.

"Mary!" he shouted, "Mary! In a second I'd have killed you! What are you doing here? Go back to the cabin!"

The wife, trembling, crept away from the sombre scene; her white-robed form vanished like a mist from the circle of the red lantern-light and that rolling eye. The next day the captain spoke no word to his wife. The boats, provisioned and prepared for the emergency of the storm, still hung heavy from the davits. Mr. Monroe, the first mate, suggested replacing the stores. Gruffly the captain refused his consent. He was going to run the Straits of Magellan instead of doubling the Cape; the saving of time was worth the risk. The course was plain to him—and yet the *Serapis* was a rotten old tub.

Never had good woman been more defamed by slander's tongue than the good ship of Captain Vance by her master's words. The *Serapis* was framed out of the toughest white oak: her timbers were heavy and staunch, her seams new-caulked, her masts of picked Norwegian pine. From a famous Belfast yard she came twelve years before, and no ill of sea or shore had ever befallen her.

Dark green and flecked with foam, between black and gloomy headlands, flanked by ragged hulks of sinister rocks and helmets of basalt that thrust up their ugly shapes from the furious waters, the Straits opened before the *Serapis*. The savage and desolate peaks on both sides looked down like giants upon this white-pennoned bird of the sea that flew straight and undaunted between their formidable feet and the jaws of the white-fanged bluffs where bleached the skeletons of shattered ships. Perpetual rain and gloom brooded upon this region of warring elements. Yet safely and swiftly the *Serapis* fought her way through the fierce currents of the Straits, past this stormy gateway, to burst into the peaceful ocean of the West. The billows of the Pacific now broke against her sides.

Several days had passed, and still the *Serapis* was wrapped from keel to maintop in the black mood of the skipper. Mary Vance stood for hours by the taffrail, her pale blue eyes yearning for sign or portent, wandering along the illimitable sea-flats, searching the bland and unchangeable horizons. The soul of the unhappy woman was in torment, and she knew the soul of her husband writhed within him. All human things housed in the belly of the ship felt this bitterness as the *Serapis*, spreading her woven wings, foamed steadily northward on her track. To the east, at times, the sharp, snow-covered spines of the Andes glimmered pallidly through the grey sea-distances.

"Where be we now, Mr. Monroe?" asked the captain's wife as the mate stood at noon with sextant to the sun.

"Fifty-four south, seventy-six, thirty-one minutes west," replied the officer.

"And the course?"

"Due north."

"And when do we reach the Tiger's Tooth?"

"I think, ma'am, with this wind we'll be there at four bells."

When the slow, sweet strokes upon the bell pealed across the waters, Mary Vance was kneeling by the stern rail of the *Serapis*, the fallow glow of the sinking sun investing her as with the light of another world. In her hands she held a mass of white flowers and blue, poor crumpled flowers of cloth, torn from an old bonnet. These, with loving looks and trembling hands, she cast upon the white, boiling wake of the ship. Half a mile to the east a sharp, fang-like rock protruded above a ring of foam. It was the Tiger's Tooth.

The woman clasped her thin hands in prayer and inclined her waxen forehead upon them. So she knelt and prayed for a long time. The sailors moved by her, tip-toed, in silence.

As Captain Vance lay in his berth that night, staring with hot and sleepless eyes upon the darkness, which was filled with an oppressive heat, he saw the spectral form of his wife approach in the weak, weird light the stars cast upon the sea. She knelt beside him, her warm arms embraced his neck, and when she laid her lips to his ear he felt a tear pass from her cheek to his own.

"Jamie," said she, "did you see the log to-day?"

"No," he replied.

"Just a few hours ago, Jamie, we were in seventy-six, thirty-one west, fifty-four, twenty-three south."

"Well?"

"Do ye no' remember it, just three year ago, half a mile off the Tiger's Tooth? Do ye no' remember our darling bairn, our Robin, and the dark day we put his poor wee body over the side in this bitter spot? Oh, I've not forgotten it, Jamie, and to-day when we passed over the same place, I threw some blooms upon his grave and said prayers. It's over his head we sailed to-day, Jamie, and it seemed to me I could see our dear dead wean lying down there in the deep sea-bottom, in the thick kelp and the coral; the sweet fruit of our flesh sleeping thousands of fathoms deep with God's awful monsters swimming about his blessed curly head and his bonnie blue eyes looking up at me through the sea. And for the sake of our dear dead bairn, Jamie, and for the sake of them that never came to us, and for the sake of your own immortal soul, Jamie, ye will no' burn the ship?—tell me, Jamie, ye will no' burn the ship?"

Captain Vance loosed himself from the hold of the white and pleading arms, and dolefully the stricken voice broke from his lips:

"Leave me, wife—leave me alone with my thoughts, Mary—I promise."

Mary Vance pressed a kiss upon his bearded mouth and left him, a happy light in her eyes. But to the eyes of James Vance no sleep would come. The air seemed to grow more stifling, his brain was burning as with fever-flames. The vision that had been his insufferable torment through all the voyage, rose again, vivid, grim and ineffaceable.

It was the dingy office of Marcus Hood in Boston, where this crafty man lurked like a spider amidst dusty books, dirty maps, broken samples, and freakish things from the four quarters of the world, and peered from his littered desk through the grimy windows upon the bright, brave ships in the Bay. Marcus Hood was the owner of the *Serapis*, and Vance in his agony lived over again his temptation and his fall. Hood's gesture had been deliberate and the tones of his voice by turns hard and caressing as he pointed to his beautiful ship through the dusty panes.

"Burn her, sink her, wreck her before she reaches Callao, Vance," said he, "and a big share of the insurance goes to you. She is underwritten in Liverpool for twice her worth, cargo and bottom. I can afford to be liberal. You can afford to do it—and so be master of your own vessel;—you see, with what you'll save you can easily buy the *Isandula*."

Vance's ambition was like a demon planted in his breast. He longed for the splendid *Isandula* and his own freedom as a man longs for the woman of his heart. So in that fell hour, three months ago, the hands of owner and master had met to seal the infamous bargain and the doom of the faithful vessel then loading at the dock.

Last week he had sought to do the deed to which the tempter had bound him. Then his wife had come upon him like a seraph with a flaming sword. To night she had come again and held up to his guilty eyes the pure and radiant face of their dead babe, so mother and babe might plead as with the tongues of clarions for the life of the ship.

A heavy step sounded without, then a knock. Monroe, the first mate, entered the cabin with a lantern. The bloodshot eyes of the skipper looked up at him from the berth.

"Will you please come forward, sir? "asked the mate, "I fear there's trouble of some sort,"

The decks were warm to their feet. The captain ordered the forward hatch removed. A column of foul smoke, interwoven with a dull, struggling flame, leaped into the air.

"Shut the hatch!" he shouted. It was shut, all but a narrow orifice through which they thrust a hose. The water shot upon the barrels in the hold.

"Spontaneous combustion, sir," said Mr. Monroe.

They could not see that none of the water reached the smoulder-ing woodwork. The oil-soaked, close-packed sails had engendered heat and then fire as easily as a smothered coal-heap or a pile of mouldering straw. Within the ribbed body of the *Serapis* terrible convulsions were bred. The barrels of unslaked lime burst, and their contents, hissing hot, boiled forth like geysers and frothing volcanoes, turning the hold to an infernal cauldron. The cement set in the bar-rels and slowly turned to stone. Then the hatches blew up, and the dense white fumes enveloped the ship as with the snowy shrouds of doom. Like gigantic serpents the fires, freed once more, burst forth from the hatchways and darted their fierce tongues towards the stars. To and fro flitted the forms of the crew, in and out of the depths of the mountainous billows of blinding steam, half hidden or blackly stamped against the crimson background of the flames soaring into the night. Already the decks were intolerable with heat; the pitch bubbled from the seams. The *Serapis* was a hollow shell of seething lime and raging fire; she held her own destruction within her, red and unconquerable.

"Heave to!" shouted Captain Vance out of the impenetrable limbo of white steam. "Man the boats!"

He picked his way towards the cabin. There in the doorway, face to face, he met his wife. She was ashen pale, even in the glow of the flames; an iron and invincible conviction of the unforgivable crime was stamped on her every lineament. The captain seized her hand and dragged her forward. She followed, passively, deaf to the things he spoke, blind to the terror about her.

"Put Mrs. Vance in one of the boats," he commanded the second mate.

He went to the cabin again through the flame-and the smoke. When he returned with a roll of papers in his hand the last boat was ready to leave the side of the burning ship. He leaped into it, and the doomed *Serapis* stood masterless upon the sea, a floating shuttle of fire.

"Sheer off!" cried the captain, and the boat shot beyond the circle of glaring light cast from the *Serapis*. Like a wounded animal the vessel began to turn, warping from the wind and setting her head again toward the north. The sails flapped and filled.

"Where is my wife?" asked the captain.

"In the second mate's boat, sir, I think," replied the sailor.

"Mary!" cried Vance in the direction of the other boats, "are you there?"

There was no answer. The *Serapis* with swelling canvas was moving swiftly away.

"Mary!" cried the skipper again.

"She isn't here, sir," came over the water.

At that instant, as if in answer to her name, the white figure of Mary Vance appeared on the stern of the burning bark. Up from the boats arose impotent curses and groans.

"Pull! pull!" rang out the frenzied voice of the captain, and the sailors bent like racers to their oars. But the *Serapis*, steadily gathering headway, drew her burning robes about her, and slowly the gap of fire-dazzled water widened between blazing ship and straining boat.

"Jump, Mary, jump!" shrieked her husband. "For God's sake, jump!"

Mary Vance turned toward him her wide-open, sorrow-stricken eyes, and once more upon her face he saw that look of unutterable reproach. Like a martyr upon her death-pyre she stood there, the mast like a gigantic stake behind her, centred in the core of the brilliant rose of fire that spread over the ship, her form made radiant and holy by the solemn splendours of the sea and the threshing flames. She held her hands clasped, as in prayer, before her. So, like a saint in a fiery furnace, she drew away from their aching eyes and horror-writhen hearts. The great topsails, safe from the fire, shone like sheets of ruddy gold against the stars. The smoke and snowy volumes of lime-vapours billowed into the air like clouds in a summer sky, encrimsoned and gilded with the red elements in their hearts. And all about the ship as she sped northward, the sea turned to blood with the reflected glory of her death, and the stars paled, and her wake to the men in the helpless boats was a wake of fire. Through tears and smoke-smarting eyes they beheld the shining, solitary figure of the captain's wife, never moving from the stern. Eruptions of fire and smoke encompassed her, and golden showers of sparks,—a great yardarm fell hissing into the sea. So they looked their last upon her until the *Serapis* was but a blot of red against the cold, eternal skies, a vanishing mass of floating fire, which finally dimmed to a glowing coal upon the horizon and then to a spark that was lost amidst the host of sinking stars. Soon after immense clouds gathered in the heavens and poured their torrential rains upon the sea.

In two days the boats made the broken coast of Chile. And the *Serapis?*—ah! the *Serapis!*

Early in the world's infant years, when the American continents rose heaving from the sea and shook themselves dry in the beams of a younger sun than shines to-day, a resting-place had been wrought for the *Serapis*. A high, rocky wall was thrust up on part of the coast south of the Isthmus of Darien, fronting the sea. There came an earth convulsion and rent it asunder from its roots in the sea to its crest in the sunlight. Thither, after unthinkable ages, the *Serapis*, a blackened hulk steered by Death or Destiny, came at last in our day to lay her poor weary body on this rocky bed. The gap in the cliff had become a canyon, the outlet of a small river. Jungles formed on either bank, and the narrow estuary was soon filled with a smothered tangle of tropical trees and rank, riotous vegetation.

The *Serapis*, a masked vagrant of the desert seas, a blasted derelict, but with her bulwarks mostly intact and her mainmast still standing proudly, erring and drifting, crept northward to the equator. Then, caught in the tumult of a violent squall, she was cast shoreward and flung into the entrance of the estuary, high and dry in the river's bed. Here the *Serapis* reposed, washed by the river and the low tides from the sea that foamed up the narrow bight. Her single mast, charred but still solid, stood upright under the festooning arches of the trees that flourished high up on the banks. The soft luxuriance of the teeming forest surrounded her. Once a heavy earthquake shook up the heated and unstable land and loosened a mass of earth and rubble from the cliffs above. It thundered down upon the deck of the *Serapis* and against her sides, though these the river freed again. The trees and flowers cast their seed upon the earthen covering of the ship, and soon a tropical garden began to bloom with interwoven leaves and ferns and jungle creepers. Emblazoned blooms and tufted and clustered growths of a hundred shapes and colours began to flourish there. About the upright mainmast a dense host of sturdy vines entwined themselves like green serpents and made a mighty column of foliage. Several trees shot up where the soil lay thickest. Birds mated and nested in her trees: strange furtive animals made their haunts and burrows in the earth on her breast. So the *Serapis* lay for seven years buried in her fair cerements of earth, leaves and flowers, and her name was spoken no more upon the seas.

In the seventh year of her slumbers, in the season of the rains, a great flood devastated the mountains and inland valleys until the narrow sea-gulch roared and raved with the rushing waters. The *Serapis* was lifted from her nest in the river-bed, torn loose from her anchor-chains of flowering creepers and clinging vines, and vomited forth into the sea.

There, like some ancient barge of state, a fragment torn from the rich, primeval forest, trailing her long grasses and mats of tangled ferns through the waters, she roved idly, the sport of every wind and current. The salt spray soon blighted some of the jungle growths, and they hung down from her black bulwarks, rusted and yellow like rotting sails. Several brooding birds, brilliant parrots and flaming toucans, chained by instinct to their nests, remained in the floating forest with their mates. Sea-fowl came and lined the branches of the trees and flew screaming about the strange drifting islet.

The changing impulses of the ocean carried her west, then south. Once at night she lay in the path of a steamer from Sydney—a boat's length to port or starboard and the iron vessel and the wooden had run their heads together like two frantic bulls. The watch upon that steamer spoke in awed voices of a spectre island they had passed during the night, so close that the branches of trees had scraped the shrouds! Their captain, who swore by his charts, cursed them for drunken fools. But when he saw, caught in the ratlines, a small twig newly broken from the bough, fluttering its green leaves in the wind, his heart was confounded within him. Thus had the *Serapis* once more become the blind, dumb, and mindless terror of the deep, a floating menace hidden under beautiful floral robes.

Silent, swift and sure, out of the night came a magnificent clipper-ship southbound from Vancouver to Kingston in Jamaica. Every sail was set, the taut ropes sang in the breeze, her hull seemed lost beneath her towers of straining canvas. Her captain stood in the bow gazing toward the stern, his eyes rested on the vague form of the helmsman in the dull glow of the binnacle-lamp. To left and right of him the red and green stars of the ship's lights shone sharp and bright as living jewels. They were the eyes of the ship, eyes that saw not, yet could be seen.

A black mass, inert, blind and terrible, the dead ship heaved up her ponderous mass against the living. There was a monstrous shock, a rending crash—the thin, hollow, iron shell of the queenly clipper, striking the thick oak reinforced by the solid tons of cement that lay packed behind it, was crumpled up like pasteboard. She staggered and shook like a racehorse that has dashed its head against a stone wall. The seas poured into her hold. Even as the ships struck, down like a gigantic club rushed the tall mainmast of the *Serapis*, snapped off from its earth-rotted base and tearing with it all its entwining leafage. Like a bolt from the sky it fell across the foredeck of the clipper and upon the master of the ship as he lay prone on the deck where the shock had hurled him. The massive timber crushed him pitilessly beneath a cushion of leaves that exhaled strange fragrances.

Swiftly the stricken ship began to fill. Boats were lowered, the helpless form of the unconscious captain gently lifted over the side. Reeling and swaying, the noble, wounded ship went down to doom, making a maelstrom with sucking spirals and clashing waves that met above her decks and licked the sails ere they sank into the depths. Four boats rocked mournfully upon the sea. Close by drifted the sinister shape of the derelict; her fallen mast, freed from the sunken ship, hung slanting in the dark water; frightened birds, disturbed by the crash, circled screaming in the air.

Fear and ghastly wonder possessed the men. They rowed towards the floating monster. Beneath its ragged raiment of jungle foliage they discerned the familiar hull of a ship. They clambered aboard; their dark shapes and low voices broke the seals of the night and caused this sullen hull of destruction, this rank garden of death, to live once more. The soft, spongy soil felt for the first time the foot of man. The awestruck sailors bore their captain to an open space near the stern, where they laid him, crushed and helpless, with a ship's lantern beside him. The dying man opened his eyes.

"Where am I?" he asked, his eyes bent upon the branches of the tamarisk above his head.

"On the derelict we struck, sir," the first mate replied; "she's covered with earth and trees—most wonderful."

"And where's my ship?"

"Sunk, sir," murmured the mate mournfully, with lowered head. The captain feebly closed his eyes. The lantern-light beat upon his pain-blanched face, framed in a grey beard and long, iron-hued hair. One of the men, thrusting aside the light bracken, held a lantern over the stern, and spelled out the tarnished letters of gold.

"S-E-R-A-P-I-S—*Serapis*," he said.

The first mate started violently. The dying master caught the word through all the treachery of his failing senses.

"Mr. Monroe," he whispered to the officer, "did he say the *Serapis*?"

"Ay, sir, the *Serapis*—our old ship." Painfully the captain raised himself to a sitting position. His eyes were open with a mighty wonder. They were fixed upon the constellation of the Southern Cross, which seemed to rise and sink in a gap between the boughs of the trees.

"The *Isandula* sunk! The *Serapis* still afloat! and it's seven years since I saw her, burning like a torch, sail off through the night! Lord God!"

The soul of James Vance in its extremity was once more confronted by the vision that would not vanish, He covered his face with his hands; the men, hushed in the awful presence of the departing life, stood reverently about him. Then he sank back upon the earth, and it was seen that an inner serenity had settled upon his face.

"Mr. Monroe," he said faintly, and the mate bent down, "I'm done for. I'll be gone in an hour or so. I think—I feel she—Ma── still here. So it's fit I lie down beside her, she that was my good wife, here on the old ship that was our wedding couch, our cradle and her coffin. So let me lie here, old friend, you who stood by me through all the years—till the sea takes all."

His hand strayed forth and closed over the hand of the mate in a last pressure. When dawn came they dug a grave with the blades of their oars in the deep earth that lay upon the after-deck of the *Serapis*. At a depth of several feet they struck the deck of the vessel and came suddenly upon the fragments of mortality that once framed the body of Mary Vance. The trench was widened, and husband and wife at last reposed side by side, and the earth was piled upon them like a mantle. A sailor set a rude cross upon the grave, another decked it with ferns and grasses.

A day later a British steamer sighted the signals of the men on the derelict, and carried the officers and the crew of the *Isandula* to Valparaiso.

South and south the aimless *Serapis*, a floating tomb, wandered and strayed and crossed the path of many a ship. Master after master complained of this danger to navigation along the Chilean coast. So the Minister of the Navy of the Republic ordered forth a gunboat, which for days hunted for the derelict. At last, far to the south, the lookout saw the black, ominous hulk tossing upon the swells. Her trees and foliage were blasted by wave and wind, and she trailed her funeral veils like some mad widow through the bitter seas.

The swift white gunboat stood off—there was a flash of flame, then another, two puffs of smoke and a blended thunder across the waters. The steel shells burst in the hard unrotted oak of the valiant vessel, and the victorious floods, long denied, roared into her heart. She sank with a sound of rushing waters that was like a hymn of ... sank to sleep amid "the thick kelp and the coral." So the sea ... but never is broken, the sea that takes all, closed over her ... than half a mile west of the Tiger's Tooth.

TRACKED: A MYSTERY OF THE SEA

C. N. Barham

The Reverend Charles Nicolas Barham (1846–1923), served as a minister in several congregations throughout England until 1901 when he changed professions and qualified as a barrister. But he was also well known as an amateur hypnotist, fascinated with the potential of the human mind for clairvoyance. He once reported that he had hypnotized his maid-servant and placed her in a darkened room where he had hidden a silk covering and asked her to describe what was in the room. She rapidly identified the silk sheet despite having no prior knowledge that it was there. On another occasion he hypnotized a lady who had lost a ring and with his help she found it, even though it was many miles away. With this conviction, Barham wrote the following exploring how clairvoyance might be used to find ships lost at sea.

CLAIRVOYANCE IS TOO OFTEN LOOKED UPON AS BEING A peculiarly daring phase of imposture, with which the art of the begging-letter writer compares favourable. Authors of manuals on conjuring furnish their readers with elaborate instructions how they may best produce the various phenomena that are grouped under the head of Clairvoyance. As these details of information consist chiefly of how eyeholes may be arranged, and catch-words made to serve for stage cues, I am not concerned with them. Such manifestations of what is professedly an occult art are only deceitful displays of degraded powers.

Clairvoyance is a reality. Now and again the practical hypnotist, in the exercise of his avocation, will meet with it. It may be that a thousand hypnotic subjects will only furnish one lucid somnambulist. Consequently, while that one may be sufficient for the purposes of the operator, the sceptical world, which is condemned to kick its heels outside the scene of mysterious operations, refuses to believe in the reality of the phenomena which are produced. Not many persons have witnessed these.

It has been my privilege, or my misfortune, not only to see, but also to conduct certain clairvoyant experiments of an astonishing nature. Several of these I have described in the columns of the weekly and daily press.

The most extraordinary of them all I will now proceed to relate.

Let me premise that I had, at the time of which I write, a servant who was one of the most wonderful clairvoyantes I have ever met with. A single word would, at any time, suffice to throw her

into a state of hypnosis. From this she would pass, almost immediately, into the stage of somnambulism which nearly approaches
to ecstasy. When in this condition her mind seemed to be utterly
untrammelled by the limits of either time or space. The girl, when
she was in her normal condition, was not conscious of the fact that
she was clairvoyant.

It was the middle of February, 1885. The brig *Audacious*, of
Northwood, was lying at anchor in the French port of Havre. The
vessel had her ballast on board, and appeared all taut and trim. She
was waiting to run out, at midnight on the turn of the tide. The time
was Sunday evening.

The captain and mate, Fred and Harry Colwood (they were
brothers), were still on shore.

Havre, in common with many English and foreign seaports,
possesses a Sailors' Mission. In this work a Lady Beauchamp and
her daughters took deep interest. The two officers had been present at the service, which closed at nine o'clock. An hour later they
returned to the ship. Precisely at midnight the *Audacious* left Havre,
with a fair wind.

Two days later the brig showed her colours off Aldeburgh. From
that hour nothing was seen or heard of her. She vanished utterly
from human ken. It is certain she never entered Yarmouth Roads.

In due course the *Audacious* was written off the Northwood
Mutual Maritime List, and, except by the few who were most nearly
interested, was forgotten.

I had known Fred Colwood from his infancy. His aged father
and mother sat weekly under my teaching in the little old-fashioned
chapel at Northwood. I had been present when the good homely
old mother had wept over her son, and had placed the Bible in his
sea-chest, on the memorable occasion of his "going foreign" for the

first time. When Fred had successively taken his certificates as first mate and as captain, no one could have rejoiced more heartily and unaffectedly than I had done, unless it were his mother. Not the least of my simple ministerial pleasures had been to unite him in marriage to Bessie Ambrose, the rustic belle of our fishing village.

Nearly a month had elapsed before the anxiety respecting the *Audacious* approached the acute stage. We were a patient, slowly-moving people, who had been taught many lessons in long-suffering.

Grey-haired men loved to tell the story of how, in their young days, the *Hawk* had been blown away right up into the Gulf of Finland. When she came back in the following spring, with all her crew safe and well, the women, who feared lest they had been bereft of their husbands, were wearing black: all of them, that was, but one, and she, the heartless jade, was on the point of marrying again.

Younger seamen, congregating in the parlour of the "Bear and Beacon," loved over their pipes to tell admiring visitors how the schooner *Alexander Adam* had lain wind-bound for nine weeks in Boston Deeps, and everybody had thought her lost. These events, it must be admitted, lay back in pre-telegraph days. At the present time such would be next to impossible.

At the end of a month an event happened.

It was nothing less than the receipt, by Mrs. Colwood, of a letter from Lady Beauchamp. What a letter that was! It came like a sunbeam falling across the rugged field of the mother's sorrow, and conveying sweetest comfort. It was from a woman who knew how to write with unobtrusive sympathy, to a distressed sister. It told the broken-hearted one of the presence on that last Sabbath evening of the two young sailors at the Havre Mission, and of the evident interest which they had taken in the simple service.

That communication has ever since lain hidden in the village woman's breast. If Lady Beauchamp had never done anything for others except to write that letter, she would not have lived in vain.

The uncertainty as to the fate of the *Audacious* troubled me. I lost appetite—an unusual thing with me—and was unable to settle down to work. When ever I endeavoured to comfort mourners—and such were plenty in Northwood—the words which I would have spoken stuck in my throat.

What had become of the brig and its crew?

I was sitting, reading, in my study on an evening in early April. My wife was present sewing. The boys had gone to bed.

The servant entered. What prompted me I am unable to say, but it was an irresistible impulse. I waved my hand gently towards Abigail, who immediately sank back into a chair. She had fallen asleep. A few passes, made in the usual manner, sufficed to throw the girl into a somnambulic condition.

How shall what followed be best described?

The narrative will be unquestionably denounced as an utterly unreliable romance. It will be accepted as a positive proof that the writer is wholly destitute of the critical faculty. Nay, more: not a few will from henceforth conclude that I am *facile princeps* in the reprehensible art of lying. These things cannot be helped. Facts are given exactly as they occurred. The causes which underlie the phenomena disturb my philosophy and elude my search. My brethren, many-of whom ungenerously hint that I am a willing ally of the Prince of Darkness, may assist me somewhat. I am, I trust, not past praying for.

Turning to the girl, I asked if she were asleep. She replied, "I am."

The next step was a command, backed by all possible force of my will, that she should so annihilate the restraining influences of

Time as to cause it to be to her, at that moment, the third Tuesday in February.

This occasioned many convulsive spasms, coupled with considerable twitching of the facial muscles. In the end Science triumphed, and in a minute the sleeper announced that it was so.

"What is the day of the month?" I inquired.

Quick as thought the reply came. "It is Tuesday, February 17th."

A glance at any almanack for that year will show that the answer was correct.

Somnambulists do nothing, whether important or trivial, instantaneously. Time, however brief, is needed for the performance of every act, as well as for the conception of each thought. All things are effected by direct action of the mind. As the subject yields to the will of the operator, certain spasmodic movements indicate a condition nearly approaching to trance, while the compressed lips and puckered brow bespeak intense concentration of thought.

Time had been conquered. It was as though it had not been.

There remained Space.

In order to accomplish my purpose it was essential that I should transport the maid servant from North-wood to Aldeburgh, a distance of fully one hundred and fifty miles. This was not to be a bodily transportation, but a mental one. The corporeality was to remain sitting in my easy-chair, while the girl herself wandered freely through space. I was planning to stand face to face with a soulless body.

I succeeded in this purpose also.

Under the combined influences of will and of suggestion, the girl was conveyed by train to London. A cab bore her to Liverpool Street, whence another train hurried her away to the pleasant little Suffolk watering-place.

All this occupied about five minutes—not more.

Further questions elicited such a graphic description of the red-tiled houses, standing back from the sea, of the pebbly beach, and of Orfordness, that I am persuaded the clairvoyante must have seen all, as if in some panorama. Yet she had never visited the Eastern counties.

· The true difficulty began here. How should the *Audacious* be found?

Clearly only by the girl waiting upon the beach until the vessel hove in sight, and then joining it. This would scarcely be more difficult than the events which had preceded.

It was not long—in reality not quite half a minute—before she gave me the welcome intelligence that the brig was in sight. Here occurred a slight pause; then she continued, "I am on board."

Let me attempt to describe what followed in the person of the clairvoyante as nearly as may be in her own words.

"I am on board the *Audacious*. Captain Colwood is at the wheel; it is very cold, and both he and his brother Harry are wearing blue guernseys and sea-boots. I see three men, whom I do not know, and little Sammy Stephenson has just gone down the companion-way.

"The men are now bending on the flags, to signal the name of the vessel to the coastguards. The signal is seen, and Fred says, 'That is right. Now they will be satisfied at home. I will write from Yarmouth.'

"It is growing colder; the wind is going down with the sun; a thick mist creeps up; it is foggy and dreary. The waves lap against the bows; it will be a nasty night. We are nearing Southwold.

"The captain is anxious. He is talking to his brother; he says the brig drifts a little to leeward. What is that noise? It is too loud for the cry of the gulls, and it does not come from the shore. The men are talking; three of them are gazing anxiously astern. They say it is a steamer, and that we are lying directly in her track.

"Will she see us? Surely, yes.

"The captain hears her. He is porting the helm; but there is no wind, the sails refuse to draw, the brig continues to drift. That is all.

"Now the men are shouting, and the boy blows the horn. They are endeavouring to make themselves heard on board the steamer. Will they succeed?

"Evidently we are in danger; but of what? I cannot tell yet. We shall soon know.

"The steamer approaches. She looms up like a great mountain through the mist; the swish of the screw is distinctly audible.

"Help me! I am frightened. I am too young to die. Captain Colwood says she will run us down. All are alarmed; there is nothing but confusion on board. What shall we do? They do not hear us on board the steamer, for she has not altered her course by a hair's breadth. Is there no one on board her? Surely they do not intend to murder us in cold blood!"

The clairvoyante here almost sprang from her chair. Her cheek was blanched. Her whole attitude was expressive of alarm.

A slight pressure of the hand, and a kind firmly spoken word, tranquillized her. She resumed—

"The vessel is upon us. She strikes. The two ships grind together; the spars twist and twine. Oh, what a crash! The steamer is backing; she parts from us. Ah! what an awful collision! We are cut down from the quarter to below the water-line. A yawl might sail through the chasm. We are doomed to destruction.

"The captain speaks. He tells the crew that there is no time to launch the boats. They must jump for their lives. He is going to stand by the brig until the last.

"The men are in the water. They are unable to swim. Fear and cold have benumbed and paralysed them.

"The steamer is almost out of sight. Those on board of her have left us to die. They are guilty of murder.

"The men have disappeared from view. No, I see them: down, down below the black water. Harry Colwood has the boy Stephenson in his arms. I am looking upon the faces of the dead.

"The captain and I are left. The *Audacious* is settling down by the stern. Only her deck is above water. She reels. She is sinking stern-foremost. We are waist-deep in the water. Fred Colwood is muttering something—his prayers—No! He says, 'Bessie—'"

Here the sleeper once more sprang from her seat, crying piteously, "Help! I am drowning. Save me—do!"

The demands of Science are inexorable. Heart must not be permitted to triumph over brain. Quietly, but firmly, I compelled the maiden to be seated, and bade her continue. She went on—

"I am alone in the sea. I can see no one. The captain must be drowned."

This was sufficient. The fate of the *Audacious* and her crew had been strangely revealed by means of this occult art.

The vessel, like too many others, had been run down by a passing steamer, which, because merchants look on time as being of greater value than life, had inhumanely left its wretched victims to perish.

Who was the destroyer?

This was not difficult to discover.

Almost immediately the clairvoyante was placed upon the runaway's deck, and her detective commission was made clear to her.

With an air of mysterious excitement, the pythoness (was she not this?) re-commenced—

"I am on board a steamer. This is the first time I have been in such a place. How did I come here? What a wonderful ship it is! larger than the whole of our village.

"The crew are mustered on deck. There are forty of them—men and boys. The officers are present; all are talking together, it is quite a Babel, for not one-half of them are English. They are blaming the look-out, and say that he was asleep. What does he reply? I am unable to say. He is a foreigner, and his English is so bad that it is impossible to understand him. They are swearing horribly: the officers at the men, and the men at one another.

"The captain commands order.

"Now all is silent, except for the hollow thud of the engines.

"The captain is surely a bad man. Listen! He is offering each man and boy an additional week's pay if only they will swear to maintain absolute silence about the collision.

"They swear; and they will keep the secret of the sea locked in their own breasts.

"It is awful! I am among murderers!

"I shrink from addressing these men. Yet I must do so. A stronger power than my own will compels me to speak to them. I ask the name of the ship.

"The captain answers. He refers me to the mate. That person is rude and boorish. He swears at me, and bids me begone. No gentleman would swear at a woman.

"It is impossible to discover what the ship is or whence she has come. I question the men, but elicit no replies.

"I will search her.

"I am in the hold. The black yawning cavern is filled with barrels. These constitute the bulk of the cargo. They are filled with sugar. Having discovered this, I return to the light of day.

"What strange force impels me? I am dragged by invisible hands to the side of the vessel. They raise me. I am unable to resist; the water is beneath me. I stand upon the waves as upon the solid earth.

Above me towers the great square stern; upon it, engraven in golden letters, I plainly see her name. It is—*Alexandria*, New York.

"Once more I return on board. The captain is more calm. As he stands upon the quarter-deck, I approach him. What do I see? The bows of the vessel are stove in, the thick out-standing fore-mast is broken off close. Are the men intending to repair this?

"Now the captain replies to me; but he evidently does so under constraint. He must be compelled by the same mighty force which binds me to do its bidding. He no longer hides the name and destination of his vessel.

"Slowly and distinctly he utters the words. I do not miss one. It is the steamer '*Alexandria*, from Valparaiso to the port of Sunderland— last from Cardiff.'"

Then, with a sigh, the clairvoyante said—

"I am very tired."

Do any doubt the truth of this simple story? They need not do so.

I am aware that the evidence, thus strangely obtained, would be valueless in a court of law. The testimony of my eye-witness would be rejected as the cunning story of an impostor. But, notwithstanding all that may be advanced in opposition, I am persuaded that the *Audacious*, with the bodies of her ill-fated crew, rests off the Southwold coast, and that the steamship *Alexandria* was the guilty vessel which did those men to death. When He, whose hands hold the scales of justice even, shall bring the hidden things of darkness to light, it will be seen that the closed eyes of the young clairvoyante rightly and truly read the crime-laden story of this mystery of the sea.

The sequel remains to be told.

Inquiry elicited the startling information that the *Alexandria*, when she entered the port of Sunderland on the night of February

18th, had her bowsprit snapped off, while her bow-plates were also started. No satisfactory explanation of any accident had been vouchsafed by the captain.

What further corroboration of the truth of my story could be required or given than this?

THE MYSTERY OF THE
WATER-LOGGED SHIP

William Hope Hodgson

William Hope Hodgson (1877–1918) was, without a doubt, the master of the nautical mystery and horror story. He had run away to sea in his youth, in 1891, and served in the merchant navy until 1900. During this time he received a medal from the Royal Humane Society for rescuing a fellow sailor who had fallen into shark-infested waters off New Zealand. A health fanatic, who kept himself fit whilst at sea, Hodgson opened a physical culture school in Blackburn in 1901. It barely broke even, but Hodgson spent time writing about physical exercise for the leading magazines of the day and from 1904 onwards he turned to writing fiction as his primary source of income. The majority of his stories are set at sea and many involve the supernatural or inexplicable. The best of his weird tales were collected, in his lifetime, in Men of the Deep Waters *(1914) with a few other strange tales in* The Luck of the Strong *(1916). He completed four novels of which* The Boats of the 'Glen Carrig' *(1907) and* The Ghost Pirates *(1909) are classics of the genre.*

Hodgson was killed towards the end of the First World War at Mont Kemmel near Ypres in April 1918. His widow was determined to keep his name alive and managed to sell stories to various British and American magazines but his reputation faded until he was rediscovered by American devotees in the 1940s. Since then Hodgson's work has been regularly in print. I could have selected any one of scores of stories for this volume such as 'The Voice in the Night', 'The Derelict', 'From the

Tideless Sea'—another Sargasso story, 'The Stone Ship', 'The Haunted Jarvee', but these are all easily available in various collections of his work. Instead I have chosen a little-known story which nevertheless shows Hodgson's abilities at developing a puzzling problem with a derelict ship.

THE BIG STEAM-YACHT *WHITE HART* WAS DRIVING ALONG EASILY at half-speed through a dark, starless night in the North Atlantic. The Captain was pacing the bridge with Swanscott, the owner. At the little steam steering-wheel one of the four quartermasters stood drowsily, for the yacht almost steered herself, as the saying goes, and the man had little to do but listen for eight bells.

Abruptly the Captain stopped in his tracks, staring away over the bows; then, whipping round upon the helmsman, he roared at the top of his voice:

"Starboard your hellum! Smartly, now! Smartly, now!"

As the little wheel spun swiftly under the man's hands the Captain turned back quickly and stared over the bow into the darkness.

"What is it, Captain? What is it?" Swanscott was saying, glancing on every side through the darkness.

"What have you seen?"

"Light just under the starboard bow, sir," the Master answered. "It should be broad on the beam now."

He turned to the helmsman.

"Steady!" he called.

"Steady it is, sir," answered the man, and put the wheel over.

The Captain and the owner stood together and stared into the utter darkness to starboard; but the minutes passed, and never a sign of any light was there.

"Don't see anything, Captain," said Swanscott.

"Neither me!" replied the Master, and blew his whistle.

He gave word to the man who answered it to relieve the look-out for a few minutes and send him aft to the bridge. When the man arrived he asked him whether he had seen a light just off the star-board bow.

"Yes, sir," replied the man. "I thought I did; but it was gone before I could be sure. Then you starboarded, sir, and I knew you'd seed it, too. But I ain't seed it since."

The Captain dismissed the man forrard, with a word of warning to be smarter in future. Then he readjusted his night-glasses and took another long look out into the darkness to starboard; but nowhere could he see the light.

"Most mysterious!" said the owner. "What do you think it was?"

"Well, sir, it may be one of those fool timber-boys running dhowls across home and tryin' to save oil. I've known 'em do that, and just shove a lantern over the rail, if anything comes too near. They deserve hanging!"

"We ought to see her spars with the glasses," said Swanscott, "if she were as near as you think."

"Yes, sir," answered the Captain. "An' that's what's puzzling me. It might be someone got adrift in a boat; but they'd never hide the light till we'd got 'em safe. What do you say, sir? Shall we turn on the searchlight and just have a look round? You're in no hurry."

"By all means," said Swanscott. "This is interesting."

The Captain rang the engines to dead slow, and then whistled for a couple of the hands to come up and unhood the big searchlight, which was mounted on a platform at the after end of the bridge. Five minutes later the great jet of the light flashed out into the darkness to starboard, and swept round in a huge semicircle as the Captain revolved the big projector.

"Ah!" said Swanscott, who had come up beside him. "There she is. You were right."

For directly in the rays of the searchlight, apparently about a mile distant, there showed plain, with every detail of rope and broken spar standing out clear in the brilliant light, an iron, square-rigged ship.

"Derelict!" said the Captain. "Lord, we've had a shave! See how low she is in the water, and her fore and main topmasts gone. She's in the carrying trade; look at the deck cargo of her. It's shameful! Shall we take a closer look at her, sir?"

"Certainly, Captain."

The Master rang to half-speed and motioned to the helmsman, who muttered "Aye, aye, sir," and put the wheel over a few spokes. They steamed down for the strange vessel, and in a few minutes had passed under her stern and reversed about a hundred yards to leeward. Here they rode easy on the slow swells, with the searchlight playing full upon the derelict ship. Her condition was plain now to be seen. Her fore and main topmasts had gone, as I have said, with all their yards and gear; also the spike-boom had been carried away over the bows. Her mizzen t'gallant and royal masts also were gone; but the mizzen topmast was standing, so that she rolled there in the gloom, a derelict dripping hulk, with little more than her naked lower masts and yards above the deck to show what she had been.

"'That's a fine thing to have floating around in the dark!" said the Captain, examining her through his glasses. "That's the sort of thing that accounts for the missin' packets. Just fancy hittin' it under a full head of steam! I'll bet that's what's ended the *Lavinia*, if the truth could be known."

Here he referred to one of the North Atlantic boats which had been reported missing just before they left home.

"Yes," said Swanscott thoughtfully. "It might have been us, if you hadn't spotted the light. But where the deuce *is* the light?"

This neither of them could decide; for the whole length of the dripping rail was unbroken by any sign of light or life, and beyond it there rose in great mounds the timber masses of her deck cargo. After a further time of watching and keeping the searchlight going, Swanscott suggested that he would go aboard and have a look round, and whilst the boat was being lowered he hurried below to wake his friend Hay, who, he knew, would be keen to accompany him.

When they both came on deck the boat was in the water, with the First Officer in charge, and a few minutes later the two of them were standing on the water-soaked decks of the derelict, with below them the dull pounding of the imprisoned timbers as they rolled sluggishly, grinding against the deck-beams and hatch-coamings in the water-logged hold. The hatches were off, and odd whiles some heavier roll than usual would send some of the water slopping up out of the hold over the coamings of the hatches, and all the time there was the lone-some swish of water upon the dripping decks and the low groan of the great masses of timber as each roll threw new stresses upon them and the bulk of water in which they floated. So that just to look down through the open mouths of the holds was to have dank thoughts and dismalness, with the grim suggestiveness of desolation and the nearness of the ocean deeps, which came to the mind as they stared down into that gulf of gloom and water and soaked timbers.

Swanscott and Hay, with the Officer and two of the men, explored the whole of the vessel—that is, all that was still above water. Forrard they found the fo'c's'le empty and glimmering wet and dank in the light from the lamps. All the bunks had been washed out, and below them, under their feet, was the same suggestive pounding and grinding of timbers and the sullen roll of the great bulk of water imprisoned in the holds.

"Makes me feel creepy," said Hay. "Let's get out of here!" and he led the way out of the gloomy iron cavern, where the very decks seemed to have grown soft and mushy with the long and continual soaking. Then away aft, and here they looked down the poop sky-light into the darkness of submerged cabins, and, for all they knew, into places where dead men rolled to and fro hideously in the black waters.

"Ugh!" said Hay, again expressing the general feeling. "Beastly! Let's leave her!"

And they went aboard the yacht. Here, however, more practical things were discussed.

"Yes, sir," said the Captain. "You ain't in no hurry, an' if we go jog-trot for a couple or three days, we needn't strain ourselves or tow the blessed stern out of us. It'd be a blessing and a duty to all shipping if we was to remove her; for sink her you can't, not without you took her to pieces or blew her to pieces. I know. I've tried. She'll float as long as them timbers has any sort of framework to hold 'em together. An' then there's the salvage."

This was talked over in all its bearings, and Swanscott told his Captain that he could "take the job on", and he'd make him and the men a present of the yacht's "share". The only thing he stipulated was that a crew should not be put aboard of her unless it was a certainty that she would not sink under their feet.

"Sink!" said the Captain. "She'll not sink this side of the Judgment, not that way."

And so it was arranged. Volunteers were called for, and out of those who stepped forward four were chosen. These were put aboard the derelict, and some food and water. One of the boats, with which she was well supplied, was sent astern at the end of its painter as a precaution, lest, as the Captain said, "the im-bloomin'-possible" happened, and the wreck did sink. The sidelights were lit, and a very long spring was shackled on to the tow-line so as to ease the "pluck" of the deadweight of the "tow" as much as possible. The Bo'sun was sent aboard with the four men to take charge, and the Captain told him to put a man on the fo'c'sle head to watch the tow-line, and that the helmsman must steer by the yacht's stern-light. Then he went ahead with the line, and took a strain, and so began to jog forward through the night, slow and easy, with that dismal "tow" about a quarter of a mile astern.

For a while after they had "got going" again Swanscott and Hay walked the bridge with the Captain, discoursing on the danger of just such lonesome derelicts as the one they had come across that night. Presently the talk came upon the light which the Captain insisted he had seen. Both Swanscott and Hay were of the opinion that it must have been one of those strange "fancy lights" which sailors sometimes see suddenly at night through overstraining the eyes. On his part, the Captain was positively sure that he had seen a light; but more than that he would not say at first, until Hay perceived that if they ceased to "rag" him he might be got to explain what was at the back of his silence. He gave Swanscott the hint to cease "baiting", and by showing a sympathetic attitude they coaxed the Captain finally into admitting seriously that what he had seen must have been what he called a "sailors' light."

"A what?" said Swanscott, half amused, half impressed by the old man's earnestness.

"A sailors' light, sir," said the Captain. "It's always give as a warnin'. My father, as was fifty-five year at sea, an' died there, seen it three times, an' if he hadn't took notice he'd have smashed up his ship every time. He always said it was the spirits of them that's drowned warnin' the sailors. I half believes it, you know, and half don't. When I'm ashore it seems just sailors' talk; but on a night like this—Well, you know the feeling yourself. You saw she was *empty*, not a soul aboard. And I *know* I saw that light. You think I'm mistook; but if I hadn't seen something, where'd we be *now*? I tell you it's as queer one way as the other."

"I think I understand your attitude," said Hay. "Anyway I must admit that the sea's a place to breed fancies, especially at night, and with old wrecks and drowned men knocking around," and he peered away into the darkness, where the lights of the derelict showed astern in the gloom. "All the same, you know, Captain, we mustn't get superstitious. It may have been that you saw nothing really, but you had a premonition."

The old man snorted.

"What's the difference, mister?" he said. "What's the difference?"

Presently, leaving the Mate in charge, the Captain went below with the two friends, and they sat awhile in Swanscott's cabin having a whisky before turning in. Then, just before they said good-night, the old Captain raised his head and looked round the cabin as if he were listening.

"That's a pretty smart squall we're into," he remarked; "hark to it!" For outside in the night the wind was going over them with a scream, as one of those heavy squalls which wander the seas alone passed them. "That'll wet 'em!" he said, meaning the four men and the bo'sun who were in the derelict. "Guess she'll just be lumpin' it aboard. Well, they'll get dry on the salvage."

He drained his glass, and set it down in the fiddles; then once more raised his head, with that suggestion of listening and half-expecting. Abruptly he jumped from the locker.

"I knew it!" he said, reaching for the door-handle. "She's parted! I thought she was ridin' different."

He opened the door and hooked it back, then ran for his oilskin coat and sou'wester. The two friends did the same, and followed him on deck. Here, at first, they were half stunned by the storm of wind and rain which met them. They struggled to the bridge after the Captain, and heard him singing out to the Officer that the "tow" had parted from them. He did not attempt to blame the man; for he knew by experience that up there in the wind and rain the altered "scend" (motion) of the yacht would be less felt than down in the calm of the cabin, where the senses were not bewildered by the blinding force of the rain and wind. Also, the rain made a curtain between the two vessels, so that it was no use expecting to locate her by her lights until the squall had passed, as Swanscott and Hay discovered for themselves, and by then she might have soused them out, or be slewed off before the wind, and so hiding them.

The searchlight was unhooded and turned astern; but so heavy was the rain that the light simply made a glittering tunnel amid the raindrops, and was lost in strange rainbows in the night, without showing any sign of the missing vessel.

"You think they're all right, Captain?" asked Swanscott anxiously, for he began to fear that the wreck might have foundered, in spite of the Captain's sureness of her powers to float beyond the Judgment.

"Certain, sir," said the Captain. "Just wait till the squall's eased a bit, an' you'll see her."

"There she is!" he said a few minutes later, as the squall cleared away to leeward. "There she is! My goodness, she's drifted more than I'd have thought! A power more than I'd have thought."

She was plain now in the great jet of the light, about three miles astern, and running off before the wind.

"That's queer, Mr. Marsh," said the Captain to the First Officer, who was standing near, looking through his night-glasses. All that top-hamper aft ought to have brought her up into the wind, dead sure."

The Mate agreed, and the Captain told him to run the yacht down to leeward of the wreck, which was done. Here, with the glare of the searchlight full upon the derelict, they ranged up to within thirty or forty yards of her, and hauled. Yet the most inexplicable thing greeted them—*nothing*! There came no answering faces to the rail, nor any answering sound across the quietness left by the departed squall; nothing, save, as it seemed to Hay, who was the most impressionable, a strange little dank echo of their hail, that seemed to beat back at them vaguely from the dripping iron side of the ship.

"Good Lord!" said Swanscott, "what's up, Captain?"

"I don't know, sir," said the old man, seriously enough. "I don't understand it one bit. We must go aboard." He turned to the Mate, "Where did that hawser carry away, Mr. Marsh?" he asked.

"Didn't carry away at all, sir," replied the officer. "Must have come free off the bollard or the bitts, or wherever that fool Bo'sun made it fast!"

"Mighty queer," said the Captain, and went down to see whether the boat was all ready; for he was in trouble to discover what had happened, and intended personally to investigate this curious happening.

Presently he and the two friends, with three of the boat's crew, stood on the soaked decks and looked round. The Captain looked forrard and aft; then he put his hands to his mouth:

"Bosun!" he sang out. "Bo'sun!"

But there came back only the little hollow echoes from the high bulkhead of the t'gallant fo'c'sle, and the low break of the half-poop. He turned to one of the men.

"Back into the boat, my lad, and go across to the yacht. Ask Mr. Marsh to pass you down two or three lamps. Smart, now!"

When the lamps arrived they were distributed among the party, and a thorough search was made; but nothing was found. The four men and the Bo'sun had gone utterly and entirely; and the only supposition that could be made was that the wreck had shipped a heavy sea during the squall and washed some of the men overboard, and that the rest had been lost in trying to save them; for it was folly to suppose that one sea, or even a series, would remove five men from the *different* parts of the decks of the derelict; for except under the circumstances suggested by the Captain, if the wreck had been much swept by water, the crew would have taken refuge in the rigging until the squall was gone. And you must know that all the time under their reasoning everyone was vaguely uneasy. The explanation was possible, just barely possible, but certainly improbable. But then, again, so was any other explanation that anyone had to offer. Hay thought of the Captain's talk about "sailors' lights," and stopped himself; for it made him uncomfortable and miserable; so that in a less impressed mood he would have reproved himself for feeling superstitious.

"And you know," said the Captain in an undertone to Swanscott and Hay, "you know she ain't sloppin' any water aboard to speak of, an' I can't see how she done much in that squall. It was stiff, that's so; but there was no time for the sea to rise. It's a corker."

Presently they left the wreck and went aboard the yacht for a consultation. Here it was decided finally to wait for the morning, and then to see what could be done in the way of blowing the wreck to pieces, though the Captain was not sanguine, for, as he said: "You can't get at 'er to put the charges in."

It was at this point that the Second Mate arrived on the scene.

"I hope you'll forgive me, sir," he said, looking at the Captain and the owner. "I feel it's cheeky of me to push myself in like this; but the Mate tells me you're giving up the idea of our salving the derelict," and he nodded towards where she lay, with the searchlight still playing upon her.

"Yes," said Swanscott gravely. "We can't allow anyone else to risk it aboard of her, even if we could get them to go. I'm very grieved indeed about what has happened."

"Well, sir," said the Second Mate, "let *me* go. I'll go alone. I'm not afraid. I'll lash myself secure and rig a few life-lines. The salvage money means a lot to me, sir. I wish you'd let me."

At first both the owner and the Captain were firm that no one else should be allowed to risk their lives aboard the somewhat mysterious wreck; but in the end he showed himself so determined and without fear that they allowed him to have his way, and, more than this, to take three of the men with him, if he could induce them to volunteer; which, indeed, he managed by sheer force of personality, persuading them and holding up to them that their share of the salvage money would more than double their wages; for it had been agreed by the owner and the Captain that the bulk of the salvage should by rights belong to the plucky Second Mate and the three men who accompanied him.

"And a good sailorman he is, too," said the Captain, "an' plucky as they're made."

The tow-line was once more passed, and the Second Mate himself saw to the making fast of it; also to the re-lighting of the sidelights, which were found to be out. Then he rigged life-lines along the decks, and so prepared to meet whatever danger there was ahead.

Presently the yacht took up the tow, and the watches settled down somewhat; but no one went to sleep, for the loss of the four men and the bo'sun had upset everybody; the curious mystery that hung about their death had tinctured the general gloom with queer thrills and wonderings.

For a good hour the yacht went forward at a slow pace through the night, and her side-lights could be seen burning clearly about a hundred yards astern, for the Captain had given orders to shorten the tow-rope.

The Captain and the owner and his friend were all grouped together under the weathercloth on the weather side of the bridge, and the old man was spinning them a yarn about another curious happening which had come to him one night in mid-ocean some ten years before. Abruptly his tale was cut short by an astonished shout from the Mate:

"My God! She's parted again, and both lights are out!"

"What!" yelled the old Captain, and jumped into the after corner of the bridge, where he could see, unimpeded by the angle of the weathercloth. "Yes, she's gone again, mister. There's some devilment in this. Man that searchlight—smart, now! Starboard your hellum. Smartly now, my lad!"

This latter to the man at the wheel.

The yacht came round in a big curve, and half a minute later the great beam of the light drove out through the darkness to port. It swept across the empty miles, showed nothing, and abruptly drove back again in a wider circling. Then they saw the derelict, a good two miles away to port.

"Got her again!" sang out the Mate. "Lord! How's she got left all that way?"

The man's astonishment was plain; and the Captain was equally surprised.

"Full speed ahead!" he shouted. "Keep the light on her," and within six minutes they were reversing to leeward of her. The Captain leaned over the end of the bridge and hailed: "Mr. Jenkins!" he shouted (that being the Second Mate's name). "Mr. Jenkins!" But there came no answer, beyond the vague echoing of his voice from the iron side of the ship, and strange little mocking echoes which seemed to sound vaguely about her empty, lumber-stacked decks.

"Starboard lifeboat!" shouted the Captain. Then, to the Mate:

"Bring up half a dozen rifles and cutlasses, and arm the crew. Put a lamp for every man in the boat. Call the other watch. Pass them out rifles and ammunition, and have the port lifeboat ready to lower away. Keep the searchlight going."

"Aye, aye, sir," answered the Mate, and hurried away to obey, whilst the Captain turned to the owner and Mr. Hay.

"I don't know what it is, sir," he said. "But if you're coming, you'd best have some sort of weapon, and your friend too. There's something devilish aboard that craft, you mark my word; but whether carnal weapons is any use, the Lord He knows. I don't."

Five minutes later they were away in the boat and aboard of the derelict, gazing fearfully round, not knowing what they might see. Yet from end to end they searched her; from the dank and water-sodden fo'c'sle to the deserted wheel, where, but a few short minutes before—as you might say—one of their shipmates had stood. And now everywhere the silence, and the utter mystery that shrouded the end of the nine men who had gone utterly during the night, leaving no trace of any kind to tell what extraordinary thing had happened.

When the search had been completed the Captain gathered the men together, whilst he held a short consultation with his owner and Hay, in which it was decided to stand by the wreck during the rest of the night, and to make a more drastic search by daylight. As they talked they could hear under their feet the constant dull grind of the timbers, and the low, hollow boom and swirl of the great bulk of water in the holds rolling and rumbling to and fro; and this, combined with the peculiar and frightening mystery which now hung about the vessel, made everyone very thankful when the Captain gave the word to get down once more into the boat and return to the yacht.

During the remainder of that night the yacht steamed slowly round and round the derelict, keeping her searchlight playing full upon her; and so the dawn came in presently, and they prepared to make their great attempt to solve the mystery. As soon as the day had broken properly two boat-loads of men, fully armed, were sent aboard the wreck, the Captain, Swanscott, and Hay accompanying them. Then, the search began in earnest. Every piece of timber on the decks was shifted, lest they should prove to be shelters for anyone or anything; the fo'c'sle was visited, and the forepeak examined; but only to find that even here the water had entered, showing that she was full, fore and aft. The after-cabins were inspected; for it was found that a couple or three feet of air-space existed between the poop-deck and the surface of the water; though, indeed, the rolling of the vessel sent the great bulk of fluid from side to side in a manner that nearly drowned the searchers, whilst several were hurt more or less by the blows of the various objects afloat in the saloon and cabins. Yet nowhere—though not a cabin was left unexplored—did they find anything remarkable; only everywhere the dismalness of the water, and the smell of dampness and brine; and all the while, under the feet, the great bulk of water in the holds rolling to and fro, and the dull grinding and pounding of the water-logged timbers.

The search occupied the whole of the day, and all day the yacht had towed the derelict landwards, for Swanscott had sworn now to tow her into port, even though they towed only by day and removed the men to the yacht at night and stood by for each dawn.

In the late afternoon the Captain removed most of the men to the yacht, leaving half a dozen with their rifles to guard the man at the wheel, under the command of the Third Officer.

"What on earth can it be, Captain?" said Hay that evening at dinner for about the hundredth time. "Could it be an octopus?"

"No, sir," said the Captain. "You don't get octopuses in these seas. The devilment's something in that packet herself. She's a wrong 'un."

"How do you mean—a wrong 'un?" asked Swanscott seriously.

"Well, sir," said the Captain, "I don't quite know what I do mean, except just that. If I said she was haunted, you'd laugh; but she's a wrong 'un, you mark my word, sir. I'll have those men aboard here again as soon as ever it gets dark."

"Well, Captain," said Hay, "it's getting dusk now," and he pointed at the open ports. "I know I'll feel happier when they're aboard again."

Even as he spoke there was a loud shouting on deck, and the Mate's whistle was heard blowing shrilly.

"My God!" said the old Captain, "she's parted again. My God! We're too late; we're too late!"

They rushed on deck after him, and here they found that it was as the Captain had said. The "tow" had just parted, and showed dimly away astern in the dusk. Something extraordinary was happening aboard of her, for strange cries and sounds came over the sea, but never a shot to tell of any fight.

In two minutes the boats were manned, each man armed, and the yacht was running down at full speed on the derelict, her searchlight playing upon the wreck, yet showing nothing. She dropped the two boats within fifty yards, and they raced to the side of the wreck. There was a scramble aboard, with Swanscott and the old Captain leading; lanterns were passed up, and the rest of the men followed, whilst the searchlight played from end to end of the derelict craft. There was an absolute silence as the Captain put his hands to his mouth and sang out:

"Mr. Dunk! Mr. Dunk!" which was the Third Mate's name.

There came no answer; and the search began again, every man nervous, and glancing fearfully behind and on every side. Yet not a sign of any kind could they find of the men or of their arms, nor anything to show that there had been any struggle. The wreck looked as if no living thing had stood aboard of her for months.

"Into the boats!" said the Captain, and there was the beginning of a rush, which, however, he checked. "Easy now, lads! Easy! Easy!" he shouted. "Keep your heads!" And so in a few minutes they were all back on the yacht.

On the bridge Swanscott held a long talk with his Captain, with the result that all night they stood by the derelict; steaming slowly round and round her, and keeping the searchlight full upon her. The next morning the Captain and the two friends went aboard the wreck with the carpenter and two boat-loads of men, who were set to work building a big, roughly made, but powerful shelter on the poop, using for the purpose the timbers which comprised the deck-load. This was finished by the afternoon, and a strong sliding door was fitted. There were left also a number of openings round the sides and in the roof; but these were crossed closely with iron-bars which the engineers supplied.

Returning to the yacht, Swanscott called all hands together and told them that he intended to pass the night in that shelter aboard the wreck, and that he wanted volunteers to accompany him. At first no one offered; but suddenly one of the firemen said he had no wife, and he would risk it, and after that others followed, until a dozen had come forward. These Swanscott took aboard with him, all armed, both with rifles and revolvers and cutlasses; they were all naval reserve men, and knew how to use their weapons. He gave directions to the Captain to hide every light, and keep the masthead light and sidelights unlit, also the searchlight. The yacht was to lie about a hundred yards away, and the instant he fired a shot the searchlight was to be flashed upon the wreck, to and fro, to see whether anything could be seen. No sound was to be made in the yacht, and there was to be no smoking; whilst every man left aboard was to line the nearest rail, and be ready with his rifle, but no shot to be fired until the Captain passed the word. This was the general trend of the orders for the night.

As soon as Swanscott, his friend Hay, and the dozen seamen and firemen had entered the shelter he pulled across the sliding-door and secured it. Then, having passed the word for absolute silence, and stationed a man at every barred opening, he settled down to wait. Presently the dusk was upon them, and soon the night, and after that the darkness, slowly intense, almost unnaturally so it seemed to Hay, whose more sensitive spirit was open to a thousand vague influences. Far down under them, as the ship rolled, they could hear the gloomy motion of the water in the holds, and odd whiles the dull grind of the sodden baulks would change into lumpish poundings and bodgings as there came a heavier swell under the vessel. Of wind there was none, save occasionally a little breath that would come sighing out of the night, making slight eerie sounds through the barred openings, and passing on again into the distance, leaving a double silence, because of the contrast. And so the hours passed on. Every now and again Swanscott would tiptoe quietly from man to man to make sure that all were awake and watching; but, indeed, there was little fear of anyone sleeping in that dark silence, for there was an utter weirdness and suspense in the night all about them, as it might be said, and each man was tensely awake; so that Swanscott had to be careful when he made his rounds not to touch any man suddenly, lest he cry out or turn blindly upon him in the darkness.

Then, after a great time had passed; there came a sound foreign to all the natural sounds of the ship and the slight movements of the men. It seemed to Hay, who was the first to notice it, that a vague, strange noise passed up through their midst. It was quite distinct from the dull booming of the waters in the hold, and could not be mistaken for any sound of the sea conducted upward by the framework of the vessel. It was near, very near, among them, so it seemed; and Hay heard the breathing of the men stop, as they harked, fiercely tense, to this thing, which might betoken some unknown horror right among them.

Then Swanscott realized that it was necessary to *learn*, and he struck a match. As the light flared up the men moved nervously and restlessly, but they all saw that the shelter was empty of everything except themselves.

There came a further space of silence; then, abruptly, Hay knew that something was near the shelter; it was more as if his spirit knew than any coarser sense. He reached out and touched Swanscott, and Swanscott thrilled under his touch, so that Hay perceived that he too had learned. Then Swanscott slipped from his hand, and there was not a sound in the shelter; thus Hay perceived that the men also were aware of something, and held each his breath—listening.

Suddenly, like thunder in that confined space, a shot was fired, and the flash lit up Swanscott's face momentarily. The following instant a great glare of light blazed upon the structure, pouring in at the barred openings and showing each man tense and strained, holding his weapon ready, and looking blindly towards where Swanscott stood with his smoking revolver in the middle of the shelter. He was staring upward through one of the barred openings in the roof. The blinding glare of the searchlight swept away from the house, leaving all in darkness; but now Hay was at one of the openings, and saw the huge shining jet of the light sweep forrard along the decks of the wreck. Then with a jerk it lifted and poised itself in mid-air, motionless, showing every detail of the mizzen-mast right above their heads. Hay saw something incredible, and craned his head more, so that he could see higher. There were dozens of strange men coming down out of the night—coming down from aloft—down the mizzen rigging. There was a sound of confused shouting from over the sea from those in the yacht, and still the searchlight burned relentlessly, showing those strange men constantly descending out of the night.

"Stop!" shouted Swanscott abruptly. "Stop, or we fire!"

"Onto them; lads!" shouted a voice far up in the night. "Wipe them out!"

There was the report of a weapon up in the darkness, and a bullet struck the bars of the opening just above Swanscott's head. He replied with his revolver, and three of those black descending figures toppled headlong. Then there was a sound of distant firing, and Hay knew that the riflemen in the yacht had opened on the strange men who were coming to wipe them out. He saw a dozen black figures sag and fall away—some went into the sea, but more on to the decks. Then the shelter was ringing with the noise of rifle fire, and he found his own pistol spitting viciously in his hand, and saw more than one figure at which he had aimed come downward.

In five minutes all was over, and the Captain of the yacht was alongside with a fully armed boat's crew, whilst the men in the house came forth and joined them. Swanscott gave an order, and led the way aloft, followed helter-skelter by his men. He went up over the mizzen-top, and saw a man sagging forward out of the top of the hollow steel mizzen-mast. They removed the man and entered the mast, where they found rungs fitted down the inside. This led them downward right to the keelson, in the bottom of the ship, where one side of the mast had been cut away and hinged on to form a door. Through this strange doorway they stepped, and found themselves in a huge hall, which was plainly the hold of the vessel. It was lit with electric light, and there were electric fans spinning.

Swanscott was utterly amazed. The hold of the derelict was full of water. He had seen for himself. Then, suddenly, he understood. It was only the upper part of the vessel that was full of water. Whoever had arranged that strange and mysterious craft had put an iron deck across the 'tween-deck beams about midway down the broad part of the hold, and extending from end to end of the vessel. By this simple expedient they had made the whole lower part of the vessel a huge water-tight tank of iron, about two hundred feet long and about fifteen feet deep, by about thirty-seven wide at the widest part. Ventilation had been arranged up and down the hollow steel masts; as also the methods of ingress and egress; though, as Swanscott discovered afterwards, they had other methods which they used for passing in and out of bulky objects, and this was by means of a concealed hatch under the galley, which led an iron shaft right down through the water with which they had filled the 'tween-decks, even as the hollow steel masts went down.

The missing men were all found ironed "head and tail", but safe and well, save for the rough handling which they had experienced. They each told the same story—how they were seized before they had any idea that anyone was near them, and those who struggled were stunned or drugged and so removed from sight; the idea obviously being to frighten the yacht away from attempting to tow them.

The object of all this planning and mystery was revealed when they came to examine the contents of the underwater hold. Here they found an immense amount of bullion, which had evidently been removed from the missing steamship *Lavinia*, of which previous mention has been made. Questioning one of the wounded, it was made finally plain that the derelict had been planned for an elaborate piratical cruise on a gigantic scale. There was, as Swanscott knew from the papers, an immense amount of gold being shifted that week from east to west, contrary to the usual conception of the "gold-current", and this old iron ship had been fitted up like this with the sole idea of transferring the gold from the transatlantic liners to the secret hold of the apparent derelict. That she had succeeded with the *Lavinia* the bullion bore silent witness. But where was the *Lavinia*? No questioning could elicit this; so that it was plain there could be only one answer—at the bottom of the sea, where, but for the inter-position of the yacht, it is likely enough each of the succeeding gold ships would have followed her with all hands, minus only their gold. It was certainly a somewhat ghastly discovery.

The method of procedure was simple: the apparent derelict, on seeing its victim approach, would put up a distress signal; the liner would stop to pick them up; then the succoured would turn upon the saviours, and the rest can be easily imagined. Perhaps, also, there were a certain number of confederates aboard; but of this there can be no surety.

The strange sound which so disturbed the watchers in the shelter was the creeping of one of the pirates' spies up the hollow mizzen-mast, which passed through the centre of the shelter. The timber baulks were to explain why a ship apparently full of water did not sink. One final little mystery was also cleared up. The reason why the derelict appeared to drift so fast was that she was aided by an electrically-driven screw deep down under the counter, by means of which she was able to keep her position on the track of the liners, or to retire discreetly, as suited best the purposes of her masters—the gold thieves.

FROM THE DEPTHS

F. Britten Austin

Frederick Britten Austin (1885–1941) was a prolific contributor to the magazines in the years between the First and Second World Wars, particularly to The Strand. *His appearances started before the War whilst working as a clerk in the London Stock Exchange but on the day War was declared in 1914 he signed up for the London Rifle Brigade. He served with the British Expeditionary Force and Royal Army Service Corps throughout the First World War, rising to the rank of Captain. He used his military knowledge in many series. A* Saga of the Sword *(1928), traced the history of warfare in fictional form, A* Saga of the Sea *(1929), likewise retold early naval exploration and battles and* The Red Flag *(1932) looked at the power of the people through the centuries. Amongst Austin's other stories was his series featuring the detective Quentin Quayne which, unaccountably, was not collected into book-form. The following story was included in his 1922 collection* On the Borderland, *which contains several more of his strange tales.*

T HE S.S. *UPSAL*, TWO THOUSAND TONS, THE SWEDISH ENSIGN at her taffrail, her one black-spouting funnel still daubed with remains of wartime camouflage, lifted and plunged doggedly into the teeth of the September south-west gale. But her look-out no longer scrutinized every flitting patch of foam in apprehension of the dreaded periscope. The violences of sea and sky were dangers as of yore. From the depths came now no menace.

The group upon her bridge was more numerous than is customary on a cheaply-run little freighter of her class. In addition to the second officer, whose watch it was, and the look-out man on the opposite corner of the bridge, were three others. Two of them, young men oilskin-clad like their companions, stood close together in an attitude which indicated a personal acquaintanceship independent of the working of the vessel. The third man held himself aloof.

The buoyant twist and roll which accompanied the lift and plunge of the *Upsal*, the frequent racing of her propeller, indicated that she was running in ballast. Almost for the first time in her drab, maid-of-all-work career, indeed, the *Upsal* carried no cargo. She was on a special mission. A Scandinavian salvage syndicate, having come to an arrangement with the underwriters of a few out of the hundreds of vessels which strew the bottom of the entrances to the British seas, had chartered her to locate and survey a group of promising wrecks, preparatory to more extended operations. The two young men were their technical engineers: Jensen, the taller of the pair, and Lyngstrand, his assistant.

The third man, who stood aloof from them, was Captain Horst, the master of the ship. He was, of course, primarily responsible to his owners, and not to the syndicate who had chartered his vessel. Until they reached the location of the wrecks the submarine engineers were merely passengers. Reticent and sombre as he had been since the commencement of the voyage, he ignored them now, stood apparently lost in abstract contemplation of the grey waste of sea. But one who could have looked into his face would have been impressed and puzzled by his expression. His glance looked down, apparently fascinated, upon the seas which raced below him as the *Upsal* lifted on yet another crest, as though there were something strange in being so high above them—and then jerked up, automatically, to the horizon as in swift, instinctive doubt of impunity. A psychologist would have suspected that he allowed a fear of some kind, so long-abiding as to have become a subconscious mental habit, the relief of free play when he knew himself unwatched.

When at last there was no object to claim the eye on all the tumultuous stretch of ocean ahead, Jensen turned to his companion and pointed downwards. Lyngstrand nodded assent, and they both staggered across the wet, reeling bridge towards the ladder which led below.

The skipper, staring aft, his back to them, blocked their passage. Jensen touched him on the shoulder. He swung round abruptly with a startled curse. Then, recognizing them, he moved aside grudgingly. His face was turned from them as they passed.

The two young men descended to the deck below. They were berthed in the saloon under the poop, but they took their meals in the chart-house immediately beneath the bridge, in company with the skipper, who slept there. In addition to mealtimes, the chart-house was a convenient refuge from the weather common to all of them. It was their objective now.

"Filthy weather!" said Jensen, producing pipe and tobacco-pouch. "But we ought to get there to-night. We're changing course now to the north-west. Feel it?"

Jensen, having lit his pipe, produced a type-written sheet of paper from his pocket. It was a list of ships, followed by indications of latitude, longitude, and other particulars.

"No. I—*Gloucester City*, seven thousand five hundred tons, latitude fifty degrees fifty-five minutes north, longitude nine degrees fourteen minutes west, sixty fathoms, torpedoed September 20th, 1918," he read out. "Get the chart, Lyngstrand, and let us prick down its exact position."

His fair-haired junior obediently spread out a chart of the exit to the English Channel upon the table.

"September 20th!" he said, reflectively. "That's curious, Jensen! Exactly a year ago to-day!"

"Coincidences must happen sometimes," replied Jensen, with the superior indifference of three or four years' seniority. "I see nothing remarkable in it."

"It just struck me," said Lyngstrand, apologetically. "No—I suppose there's nothing remarkable in it—it might just as well have been any other day."

Jensen threw a cursory glance at the chart.

"You've brought the wrong one," he said, snappily. "This doesn't go far enough north. Look in the drawer there—there must be another one."

"It is up in the wheelhouse, I think, Jensen," demurred the young man, mildly.

"Yes—I know—but old Horst is certain to have a duplicate. Look in the drawer and see!" replied Jensen, with an impatience invited by the docility of his junior.

Lyngstrand obeyed, rummaging among a number of charts in the drawer of the locker under Captain Horst's bunk.

"Here we are!" he cried at last, unrolling one of them. "This is a special one, evidently! Someone has marked it all over with red ink."

Jensen snatched if from him, spread it out. In fact, as Lyngstrand said, it was marked in many places with little red-ink crosses, and under each was a date. Jensen ran his finger across it, stopped just off the south coast of Ireland.

"By all that's wonderful!" he cried, in a slow, long-drawn accent of amazement, raising his head and looking at his companion. "*He has marked our wreck!* Look!—Fifty-fifty-five north, nine-fourteen west—and there's the date under it—20–9–18!"

"Then all those other crosses—?" queried Lyngstrand, in a voice of puzzled interest.

"They must be— Wait a minute!" He compared some of them with the indications on his list. "Yes! They are wrecks, too—all torpedoed ships—look! this and this and this are marked on the chart! There are others not marked—but there are many more marks than there are ships on our list. They must be all torpedoed ships!"

"But why?" asked Lyngstrand. "Why has he got them all marked like this? Where did he get this chart, I wonder?"

Jensen glanced to the bottom of the sheet.

"*This is a German chart!*" he exclaimed.

Lyngstrand stared at him.

"German—!" he began, and stopped. They looked into each other's eyes in a long moment when suspicion defined itself as almost certitude. For that moment they forgot the sickly rolling of the ship thrashing and wallowing on her way to one of those tragic little red crosses. They forgot everything except the slowly-dawning possible corollaries of this discovery.

Before either could utter another word, the lee door of the chart-house opened and Captain Horst stood framed in the entrance. He glared across at them, his face livid with a sudden anger, his eyes blazing. Then, with a scarcely articulate but vehemently muttered oath, he sprang across the little room, snatched the chart from the table, thrust it into the drawer, locked it up, and put the key in his pocket. He uttered an exclamation of angry contempt and, without further speech, walked out of the chart-house.

The two young men looked at each other.

"That is the second time this morning!" said Jensen, at last, glancing towards the door, now once more closed on them.

"What is?" asked Lyngstrand, curiously.

"*That he has cursed in German!* Lyngstrand! I am beginning to see into this!"

"But it's impossible!" exclaimed Lyngstrand, his mind leaping to his friend's deduction and then rejecting it. "He is a Swede, like ourselves!"

"He is a German!" said Jensen, positively.

"But he speaks Swedish without a trace of accent!"

"And other languages also, I expect—French and English as well—better than you or I speak them, I have no doubt. Swedish would much facilitate service in the Baltic—and your German naval officer was linguistically well equipped for any possible campaign."

"German naval officer!" echoed Lyngstrand, incredulously.

"I will bet on it!" asserted his friend.

"But—a German naval officer commanding a rotten little tramp like the *Upsal*?" said Lyngstrand, emphasizing his incredulity. "I can't believe it!"

"Even German ex-naval officers have to live, my friend," responded Jensen, axiomatically. "And—I ask you—what is open to them but to take service in the mercantile marine of other nations? There is no more German fleet—there are not enough merchant vessels left under the German flag to employ all their trained officers. On the other hand, all the Scandinavian nations have multiplied their trading fleets—they cannot find officers enough for them. A first-class seaman like Horst, speaking Swedish like a native, would find plenty of owners only too willing to employ him."

"It sounds plausible," agreed Lyngstrand, but somewhat doubtfully.

"Plausible!" repeated Jensen, scornfully. "It is more than plausible—the more I think of it, the more certain I am. He is a German naval officer, I will swear to it! More than that, I am convinced that he commanded a submarine!"

"That chart, then?"

"Is the chart of his sinkings!"

"By God!" said Lyngstrand, solemnly, setting his teeth and staring sternly at the chart-house wall. "If I were sure of it—"

"What do you mean?" asked Jensen, struck by this sudden change from his friend's ordinarily meek demeanour. "What has it to do with you?"

Lyngstrand turned to him with a bitter little laugh. He seemed, indeed, a different man.

"More than you think, my friend," he said, briefly. "I am not good company for U-boat commanders!"

"But why? You lost no one?"

Lyngstrand's serious eyes held his.

"You remember I went to America in 1917, Jensen? I met a girl there—we were betrothed. She was coming to Europe to me last year. She never arrived. Her ship—a neutral—a small Norwegian ship, the *Trondhjem*, on which I had arranged for her passage—was torpedoed in the Atlantic last September—*spurlos versenkt!*" He finished in a tone of bitter mimicry, and then suddenly hid his face in his hands through a silence which Jensen felt incapable of breaking. At last he looked up again. "If ever I trace the scoundrel who murdered her—" The ugly menace in his voice supplied the final clause to his unfinished sentence.

"A difficult task!" murmured Jensen, sympathetically.

Lyngstrand glanced at the closed drawer of the locker.

"When I think that perhaps on that chart—one of those little red crosses—" He crashed his hand upon the table. "By God, Jensen, I would give something to have another look at it!"

Jensen laid a friendly hand on his shoulder.

"We will do our best, Lyngstrand, to see it again. But don't torture yourself about it now. Come out on deck. The barometer is rising, and if the sea goes down to-morrow we shall want to keep clear heads for our investigation of the *Gloucester City*. Come!"

He rose and held out his friend's oilskins, helped him on with them.

They went out and stood in the shelter of the lee-deck, watching the foam-froth sink down and melt in the depths of the malachite waves that rolled away from them, until soon after eight bells the white-jacketed steward clanged out his announcement of dinner.

"I think the weather is moderating, Captain Horst," Jensen said, pleasantly, as he sat down.

"*Ja*," responded Captain Horst, gruffly, throwing a perfunctory glance through the unshuttered forward windows of the chart-house.

"We ought to reach the neighbourhood of our wreck some time to-night?" pursued Jensen, in affable inquiry.

Lyngstrand had addressed himself in silence to the food the steward set before him, but he glanced up as though some undertone of significance in his friend's voice had caught his ear.

"Thereabouts," conceded Captain Horst, in a tone which sufficiently indicated that he was disinclined for conversation.

But Jensen was cheerfully loquacious.

"I wonder whether we shall hit on some other wreck instead?" he surmised. "These seas must be strewn with them."

Captain Horst shrugged his shoulders.

Lyngstrand looked up.

"If I were a German U-boat commander," he said, with a quiet deliberation, his eyes straight on Captain Horst's face, "I should not dare to sail over these seas again. I should see drowning faces sinking through every wave."

His last sentence seemed to ring through the silence which followed it. Captain Horst sat impassive, but his brutal jaw locked hard and his cruel mouth thinned during the moment in which he returned Lyngstrand's glance.

"Bah!" he said. "The dead don't come back!" There was something of defiance in his harshly contemptuous tone. "They are finished with—for ever!"

The blood went out of Lyngstrand's face as he bent down again to his plate.

There was no further conversation during the meal.

When, a little after four bells, they were summoned to tea, the sun was setting in a golden splendour that promised a peaceful dawn. The gale had obviously blown itself out.

Excited by the prospect of the next day's work, the two young men forgot their suspicions of Captain Horst, could talk of nothing but their plans for diving despite the after-swell of the gale which would surely still be running. The captain listened to their impatience with the ghost of a grim smile, but volunteered no part in the conversation.

"Do you propose to keep under way all night, Captain Horst?" inquired Jensen.

"No," he replied. "By my dead reckoning we ought to be in the vicinity of the wreck at about eight bells to-night. I shall anchor then if the glass is still rising. To-morrow we will take an observation and get as close as we can to the position of the *Gloucester City*—presuming that you have it correctly stated."

His tone was perfectly indifferent, but Lyngstrand thought suddenly of that chart with the little red crosses—and particularly that cross on their indicated spot, fifty degrees fifty-five minutes north, nine degrees fourteen minutes west, with the fatal date of exactly a year ago—20–9–18. Surely it could not be mere coincidence! He thrilled suddenly with a dramatic perception. If—if it were so—if the man so calmly smiling at him had really sent the *Gloucester City* to the bottom!—and now, on the anniversary of the crime, was coolly proposing to anchor himself as near as might be over her ocean grave, preparatory to disturbing it on the morrow! No! He ridiculed himself. No man could have the iron will—he glanced straight into the blue eyes of the impassive Horst, read nothing—no man could stand the strain without betraying himself. The thing was impossible! Another glance at the hard but emotionless face opposite him reassured him. He banished his hyper-dramatic idea in a spurn of self-contempt for his too excitable imagination.

The skipper and his passengers came together again some three hours later, when a glance at the clock reminded them that it was the hour when the steward brought biscuits and cocoa to the chart-house. The unwonted stillness of the ship's engines was suddenly vivid to their consciousness as she eased and tugged at her anchorage.

"Come along," said Jensen. "Our cocoa will be cold."

At the chart-house door they hesitated for a moment on an indefinable impulse, peeped through the unshuttered window which allowed a broad ray of light to fall across the deck.

Captain Horst was seated at the table, his head in his hands, his back to them. Spread out before him was the chart with the little red crosses. He sat motionless, staring at it, as though absorbed in reverie. The three cups of cocoa were steaming on the table. His was untouched.

For one wild moment Lyngstrand thought he might be able to surprise a glance at the chart. He turned the handle of the door as stealthily as he could. Slight as the sound had been, however, Captain Horst had heard it. When they entered he was stuffing something into his breast pocket, and the chart was no longer on the table.

They drank their cocoa in silence, Horst staring moodily at the floor, Jensen and Lyngstrand risking a glance of mutual comprehension. Suddenly two loud, sharp knocks broke the stillness—knocks that seemed to be on the chart house wall.

Captain Horst raised his head.

"*Herein!*" he cried, automatically, obviously without thinking.

Jensen shot a swift look at his friend, eyebrows raised at this German permission of entry. Horst bit his lip, suddenly self-conscious. He repeated the authorization in Swedish.

No one entered.

Expectation was just passing into a vague surprise, when the knocks were repeated—three heavy blows, obviously deliberate, upon the after-wall of the chart-house.

Horst sprang up, with a savage curse of exasperation. He was self-controlled enough, however, to utter his thought in Swedish. "I'll teach them!" he exclaimed, as he flung open the chart-house door. "Fooling around here!"

He disappeared into the night, and they heard the tramp of his heavy sea-boots as he ran round the chart-house. But no other sound woke upon his passage. The circuit completed, they heard his angry yell to the look-out man on the bridge above, heard the quietly normal response, the surprised denial. The interior of the chart-house was a hushed stillness where Jensen and Lyngstrand sat exchanging a smile of malicious enjoyment. Horst vituperated the stammering look-out man in a flood of ugly oaths that were plainly a break-down of nervous control.

The door opened again for his entry.

"Extraordinary thing!" he scowled across at them. "No one there! You heard them, didn't you?" He seated himself with an angry grunt.

Before they could answer, the knocks recommenced in a sudden vehemence—not slow and deliberate this time, but in a rapid succession which quickened to a fast and furious fusillade from origins that seemed to play, flitting arbitrarily, all over the walls and roof. The chart-house reverberated with them. Their intensity varied at every moment from sharp, hammer-like blows to rapid, nervous taps from what might have been a feverishly agitated pencil. The wild and uncanny tattoo culminated in three crashing blows that seemed to be on the underside of the table itself. There was silence.

"What are you playing at?" cried Horst, glaring at them in fierce suspicion of a hoax.

For answer, they both lifted up their hands, obviously unoccupied, into the air. Even as they did so, the knocks started again, still rapid, but with a certain deliberate rhythm, and much less violent. Again they seemed to be on the underside of the table. Horst looked, with a scowl of distrust, under it to their immobile feet. The two young men glanced at each other, as puzzled and alarmed as Horst himself.

"What in the name of Heaven is it?" cried Jensen.

The knocks swelled suddenly louder as though in answer to his voice.

"Listen!" said Horst, holding up his hand. The colour had gone suddenly out of his face, his eyes fixed themselves in a recognition charged with vague fear. "It's—!"

"Yes!" cried Jensen, "by all that's wonderful—!"

"The Morse code!" Lyngstrand completed the sentence.

Once perceived, there was no doubt of it.

"But," cried Lyngstrand, "where does it come from? We have no wireless and even wireless could not produce that!"

"Listen!" Jensen reproved him. "It's a message of some kind!" He glanced across to Horst, who sat speechless, his face grey, his eyes terrified. "Not Swedish! Take it down, Lyngstrand, while I spell it out!"

The young man feverishly produced pencil and paper from his pocket. "Listen!" he cried. "Good God! Do you catch it?"

Three sharp taps—three more widely spaced—three sharp taps again—the series was reiterated insistently—S-O-S!—S-O-S!—S-O-S!

"Ready, Lyngstrand?" queried Jensen, in the sharp tone of a man concentrating himself for action. His comrade nodded.

Jensen rapped sharply upon the table the wireless operator's signal of reception. In immediate answer the raps from the invisible source renewed themselves, continued evidently in a message. Lyngstrand jotted down the letters as Jensen spelled them out.

"'s-t-e-a-m-s-h-i-p'—it's English!" he interjected. "Got it?—" The raps had continued, noted by his brain and coalesced by it into definite words. "'*gloucester city*'—"

"*What*—?" ejaculated Lyngstrand, in incredulous amazement, as he rapidly wrote the words.

Jensen continued, his attention fixed upon the unceasing raps.

"—*torpedoed, fifty-fifty-five north nine-fourteen west—sinking fast—come quickly—done in—*"

He glanced up to see Horst springing at them like a maddened animal.

"Stop that!" cried the captain. "It's a trick!—it's a trick!" In another second he had snatched paper and pencil from Lyngstrand's hand.

A formidable series of violent crashes, emanating from walls, roof, and table, was the instant response to his action. He shrank back, appalled, crouching with eyes that searched the surrounding walls in agonized apprehension. "It's a trick!—it's a diabolical trick!" he muttered. "*It must be!*"

"Captain Horst!" said Jensen, with sternly level authority. "Be good enough to sit down and remain quiet. All matters relating to the *Gloucester City* come within my province."

Horst, his arms up as though to guard himself, went slowly backwards to his seat, but did not sit. There was madness in his eyes. "How could they know?"—he said to himself, in a sharp-breathed whisper; "*the exact words!—*"

"What do you mean?" queried Lyngstrand, curiously.

Horst replied without thinking, more to himself than to his questioner.

"The exact words of her call for help—a year ago! My wireless picked it up after we had left her—" He stopped suddenly, realized that he had betrayed himself.

"Then—!" cried Lyngstrand, jumping up from his seat and taking a step forward. His eyes, full of menace, searched the ex-U-boat commander's face.

"Be quiet—both of you!" commanded Jensen, holding up his hand. The regular succession of raps had commenced again. Jensen listened to them, nodded. Then he himself rapped a message in English on the table: *"who are you?"*

Horst and Lyngstrand listened in dead silence as the answer spelled itself out upon the table:—

"h-e-n-r-y s-m-i-t-h w-i-r-e-l-e-s-s o-p-e-r-a-t-o-r g-l-o-u-c-e-s-t-e-r c-i-t-y."

Jensen turned a glance of wonderment to his comrade. Horst, reading the message as currently as the others, looked as though about to faint.

"Stop it!" he said, hoarsely. "Stop it!"

Jensen ignored him, rapped again upon the table: *"where are you now?"*

The answer came immediately:—

"a-t y-o-u-r s-i-d-e."

The three of them sprang back simultaneously, as from the presence of a ghost. Their eyes probed empty air.

Jensen spoke aloud, still in English.

"Can you see us—hear us?"

The raps of the invisible hand upon the table replied at once: *"y-e-s."*

"Mein Gott!" muttered Horst. "I shall go mad!"

Jensen continued his colloquy.

"Where is the *Gloucester City?"* He smiled to himself as though setting a trap for this unseen intelligence. "Is she still afloat?"

The raps recommenced without hesitation.

"y-o-u-r a-n-c-h-o-r f-i-x-e-d i-n u-p-p-e-r w-o-r-k-s."

Lyngstrand uttered an ejaculation of awed astonishment. He looked to see the sweat pearling on Captain Horst's forehead.

The raps spelled out, spontaneously, an explanatory afterword:—

"w-e l-e-d y-o-u t-o i-t."

"We?" queried Jensen. "Who are *'we'*?"

"*t-h-e d-r-o-w-n-e-d.*" The raps were decisive.

"Why?" Lyngstrand admired his comrade's steely self-control. "Why did you lead us to it?"

"*h-e c-a-n g-u-e-s-s.*"

"Who?"

"*t-h-e m-u-r-d-e-r-e-r.*"

Both glanced swiftly at Horst. He was speechless, his face a study in blanched terror.

"*h-e k-n-o-w-s,*" added the raps. There was something indefinably malicious about their sound.

"Stop it!" Horst's voice was strangled, scarcely audible. "Stop it!"

Jensen was unmoved.

"How many of you?" he asked.

Lyngstrand, fascinated by this conversation with the unseen, was grateful for the question.

"*t-h-r-e-e h-u-n-d-r-e-d a-n-d e-i-g-h-t g-l-o-u-c-e-s-t-e-r c-i-t-y h-u-n-d-r-e-d a-n-d f-i-v-e r-e-s-c-u-e-d o-t-h-e-r s-h-i-p-s f-o-u-r h-u-n-d-r-e-d a-n-d t-h-i-r-t-e-e-n i-n a-l-l.*"

"All men?" queried Jensen.

"*t-w-e-n-t-y-f-i-v-e w-o-m-e-n.*"

"My God!" muttered Lyngstrand, in a sudden vivid remembrance that stabbed him like a pain. He glanced at Horst.

Jensen glanced also, and was merciless.

"Are you all here?" he asked:

"*y-e-s.*" There was a little pause. "*h-u-n-d-r-e-d-s m-o-r-e I d-o-n-t k-n-o-w d-r-o-w-n-e-d o-t-h-e-r s-u-n-k s-h-i-p-s a-l-l h-e-r-e.*"

Lyngstrand shivered, looked around him uneasily. Jensen's voice scarcely betrayed a tremor as he pursued:—

"What have you come for?"

"*w-e h-a-v-e c-o-m-e f-o-r h-i-m.*"

"No! No!" screamed Horst, suddenly. "No! *Ach, Gott, schütze mick!*"

Both Lyngstrand and Jensen had a sense of inaudible mocking laughter in the air about them. There was an awful silence.

The raps recommenced spontaneously.

"*t-e-l-l h-i-m t-h-e-y a-r-e f-i-l-i-n-g p-a-s-t h-i-m i-d-e-n-t-i-f-y-i-n-g h-i-m.*"

Jensen turned to Horst.

"You hear?" he asked, grimly.

But Horst, with a blood-curdling scream of terror, had flung himself at the chart-house door, thrown it open. They heard the hiss and sough of the dark seas. He plunged out; blindly, head foremost. Then, just beyond the threshold, he stopped, recoiled, staggered back into the chart-house.

"No!" he gasped, hoarsely. "No! *I can't face them! I can't face them! I dare not jump! I daren't!*"

He shook in a palsy of the faculties. His eyes agonizedly sought their unsympathetic faces. The German submarine commander is a pariah among seafaring men, whatever their nationality. He realized it, hopelessly, as he met their hard eyes. With a sob of self-pity, he stumbled across to a corner of the chart-house, sank down upon the seat, covered his face with his hands.

Lyngstrand's young features were sternly set as he glanced at him. Then he took a long breath, the preparatory oxygen-renewal of the man who dares an experiment that will tax him. He rapped the wireless "callup" upon the table.

"Can the others communicate also?" he asked, loudly, in English. He also was trembling.

The answer came at once.

"*o-n-l-y t-h-r-o-u-g-h m-e.*" There was a slight pause, then the raps recommenced again: "*l-a-d-y h-e-r-e h-a-s a m-e-s-s-a-g-e f-o-r p-e-t-e-r*"—the raps hesitated—"*p-e-t-e-r f-u-n-n-y-n-a-m-e c-a-n-t c-a-t-c-h i-t.*"

Lyngstrand's face went deathly white.

"Yes," he gasped, only, just able to speak, "Peter—yes—go on!" He looked at the table as though expecting to see the hand that was rapping out the message. Tap-tap-tap, it came.

"*p-e-t-e-r l-i-n-g-s-t-r-a-n-d.*"

"Yes—here!" he gasped. "Go on! Who is it?"

"*m-a-r-y t-i-l-l-o-t-s-o-n.*"

He reeled against the table, clutched at it.

"My God!" he murmured, to himself, his eyes closing, his teeth grinding upon one another in an agony of emotion. Then, with a supreme effort of self-control, he asked, loudly: "The message? Give it me!"

"*s-h-e s-a-y-s s-h-e s-u-r-e l-o-v-e-s y-o-u s-t-i-l-l a-n-d i-s w-a-i-t-i-n-g f-o-r y-o-u.*"

"Mary!" The cry burst from him, sobbingly, on a note of poignant anguish. Jensen felt the tears start to his eyes. Horst cowered still, face hidden, in his corner.

There was a long moment in which Lyngstrand failed to bring another sound to utterance. He swayed as though about to faint. Then once more he mastered himself.

"What—what happened?" he asked, unsteadily. "How did she die? Was she torpedoed?"

"*s-h-e s-a-y-s s-t-e-a-m-e-r t-r-o-n-d-h-j-e-m s-u-n-k g-u-n-f-i-r-e r-e-s-c-u-e-d s-m-a-l-l b-o-a-t b-y g-l-o-u-c-e-s-t-e-r c-i-t-y a-f-t-e-r-w-a-r-d-s t-o-r-p-e-d-o-e-d.*"

Lyngstrand reeled with closed eyes. He had a vivid vision of the torn wreck in depths beneath them, carnivorous fish darting where their anchor grappled its untenanted bridge.

"Did—did they have a chance?" he asked.

"n-i-g-h-t w-i-t-h-o-u-t w-a-r-n-i-n-g," came the answer.

Lyngstrand drew another deep breath, glanced at the motionless Horst.

"And—and the man—the man who sank her?"

"k-a-p-i-t-a-n-l-e-u-t-n-a-n-t h-o-r-s-t." There was a terrible precision in those raps.

They ceased. There was a deathly stillness. Through long moments, not one of the three men in the chart-house moved. Then Lyngstrand turned slowly. He took three steps towards Captain Horst, over him. The only sounds were the creaking of gear as the *Upsal* rose and subsided on the swell, the swish and suck of the long waves that ran past her in the darkness beyond the open chart-house door.

Lyngstrand's mouth had set in a thin line. His lips, compressed, opened but slightly he spoke.

"Captain Horst," he said, with grim distinctness, "you are certainly going to die. I give you the privilege of the warning you did not extend to your victims."

Horst looked up suddenly. His eyes, blue still, but crazed with terror, fixed themselves upon the grey eyes that met them pitilessly. His mouth moved under the little red moustache, but no sound came from it.

Lyngstrand continued, an edge of fierce contempt upon his hard voice.

"I even give you a choice. You can, if you like, go out there"—he pointed through the open door to the rayless night—"and throw yourself overboard—"

Horst sprang to his feet, recoiled into the extreme corner of the chart-house.

"No!" he screamed. "No!"

"—or I shall kill you myself," pursued Lyngstrand, evenly.

Horst's face contorted suddenly with demoniac passion. Jensen, who had approached and was watching him closely, saw his hand dart to the pocket of his jacket, and he flung himself forward just as the revolver cracked.

With a red-hot thrust through his shoulder, a sickening faintness in which the floor seemed to rise up to his knees, Jensen tottered back to the chart-house wall Fighting for consciousness, he dimly saw his comrade hurl himself upon Horst—someone's arm high in the air holding a revolver, another arm high with it, clutching at the wrist below the weapon.

Then commenced a terrible silent struggle, the only sounds being the short gasps and sobs of breath of the two men swaying with the motion of the ship. They hugged close, face upon face, in a murderous wrestle where neither dared shift his grip. Both were big-framed, powerful, but Lyngstrand had the advantage of youth. They came, inch by inch, slipping on the floor, past Jensen leaning dizzily against the wall. He saw them through a red mist where the electric lamp glowed vaguely, unmoved like a nebulous star above the tensely locked embrace where life fought for human continuance.

Inch by inch they moved onwards. Jensen, his vision clearing, though impotent to move, saw now that Lyngstrand had the inner berth, that Horst was being gradually, slowly but surely, thrust towards the open door. He saw one of Horst's hands free itself, grip at the door-post, cling to it. He saw the awful terror in the eyes that glared upon his relentless adversary.

Minute after minute the tense and silent struggle at the door continued. Still clutching at the door-post, Horst was gradually borne backward. His feet still in the chart-house, his body, save for that one gripping hand, was bent back out of sight into the darkness.

Suddenly his fingers relaxed their hold. Their feet tripped by the raised threshold of the door, both disappeared headlong in a heavy thud upon the deck outside.

Jensen heard a sharp exclamation, the gasp of bodies that are rolled upon—then the quick scuffling of feet. Agonized for his comrade, he dragged himself painfully towards the door. Just as he reached it one ghastly piercing scream rang through the night.

He gazed out to see two closely-locked bodies disappear over the bulwark.

The dark seas lifted a foaming crest as the *Upsal* rolled.

THE MURDERED SHIPS

James Francis Dwyer

*James Francis Dwyer (1874–1952) was born in Australia of Irish parents
and never lost that ability, inherited from his father, of storytelling. In later
years he reworked some of the Celtic legends, learned from his father, into
his stories and novels. A rebellious youth, he ended up in prison in 1899
for forgery, whilst working for the Post Office. After his release in 1902 he
started to sell stories to Australian papers but found it difficult to make a
living and emigrated first to England, where sales proved just as sparse, and
then to the United States where he was welcomed by the magazine editors.
He was soon selling regularly not only to the pulps and small magazines
but also to the major markets. He won fame with two stories, 'The Bust of
Lincoln' (1912) where a Scrooge-like miser turns philanthropist as a result of
an encounter with a bust of Abraham Lincoln, and 'The Citizen' (1915), a
paean to the American Dream and how two poor immigrants prosper in the
United States and are awarded citizenship. Dwyer was good at making his
readers believe in themselves but he also had the ability to make his readers
hold a mirror up to society and challenge misdeeds. Sometimes he used the
supernatural to achieve that end, as in the following which is in response
to all of the ships sunk by enemy action during the War.*

W E WERE WATCHING FOR SUBMARINES. A SCARED-LOOKING
moon hung over Ireland, a moon that seemed to wonder
whether her watery light was helping decent ships or helping the sea
sharks that waited for them.

The man standing beside me was a lean, sun-tanned Australian—
"Austrileyon" he pronounced it, and he spoke in a whisper.

"You can't murder ships and get away with it," he said. "By gum,
you can't!"

The word "murder" applied to the destruction of a ship interested
me; besides, the Australian uttered the assertion in a manner that told
me that he was willing to prop it up with the stays of logic. I tried to
think of some remark which would act as a bait for the story which
I felt he possessed, but the Australian needed no bait. He had picked
me as his audience, and he went right ahead with his tale without
any encouragement whatsoever.

"When I was a kid," he began, "I shipped on a pearl schooner
out of Broome, Western Australia. If you're trying to keep an
optimistic view of the job the Lord did in making this world don't
go near Broome; I'm a religious man, but I'm inclined to think the
Almighty had something that interested him a lot more on the day
he was building up that stretch of territory. It's a mixture of sand,
camel-thorn, and mosquitoes, the 'skeeters' preponderating.

"It was the 'skeeters' that made me ship on the *Ibid*. That was
the schooner's name. The captain had found a poem that he liked a
lot, and the name at the bottom of the poem was *Ibid*, so he gave it
to the schooner. The Broome folk called those 'skeeters' the Death

Hussars, and they were just about as mean and cowardly and poisonous as these chaps in Germany that are named after them.

"There were six men on the *Ibid* besides the skipper and myself, and my work was to do the work that the six could leave undone without getting into trouble with the skipper. It was most near all the work that was to be done except when we ran into a gale. In between I looked after the skipper, brought him his coffee, made his berth and stood quiet while he talked about the *Ibid*. He was a great conversationalist was Skipper McGee. The moment anyone else spoke he knocked them down."

Someone up near the bows, where the American gunners stood beside their gun, cried out, "Less talking, back there!" And the Australian halted. For a few minutes he remained perfectly quiet, then he continued:

"Old McGee never talked about anything but the *Ibid*. He might have had other themes when he was young, but the schooner had clouded his whole mental area when I shipped with him.

"'Bill,' he would say, 'she's the greatest boat that ever took a bath in the Indian Ocean. She's alive! I've laid awake in this berth on rough nights, and I've listened to her speaking to me with her timbers. She has a song she sings to me, Billy. It goes:

> "'*Don't you worry, Cap McGee,*
> *Keep your big heart light and free,*
> *When we go we'll go together,*
> *But, hell, 'twill be in stormy weather.*'

"And I'd nod my head lest he'd think I didn't believe the *Ibid* was a Melba who sang her own compositions. If he'd told me that the *Ibid* had once walked down the coast to Fremantle because it was too rough to sail down, I wouldn't have contradicted him. No fear! There are some born with authority, some get it given to them, and some earn it for themselves. Cap McGee had earned a chunk of it bigger'n the Peak of Teneriffe, and he was careless as a distributor.

"I'd tell the six loafers what the skipper said about the *Ibid* being alive, and they'd grin. They christened the schooner *Nelly*, because of Nelly Melba, and when the skipper wasn't near they'd sit, with their eyes rolling with delight, pretending that they heard songs coming out of her boards.

"'Don't you hear them, you young fool?' Big Bill Laff, the toughest of the six, would say to me.

"'No, I don't!' I'd snap; and Big Bill would knock me down and keep on pounding my head on the deck till I'd admit that I did hear them.

"'What was she singing?' he'd say. 'Quick, tell me!'

"'I don't know,' I'd snarl.

"'It was the "Swanny River,"' Big Bill would roar. 'Now say it!'

"'The "Swanny River,"' I'd say; and the other five would roll off their berths laughing at me.

"It's a queer thing that the worst people in the world are on the water, where it's so easy for the Almighty to hand them a—"

"*Silence!*" came an order from the bows. "*Silence, there!*"

"It's not me he's shooting his orders at," remarked the Australian. "He's aiming at that honeymooning couple under the stairway. Say, don't you think they got disillusioned about each other when they took a dangerous trip on this boat?"

"He likes her," I answered. "They sit at my table, and he's very attentive to her."

"I wonder what is her opinion about him?" mused the man from Kangarooland. "Of course, if we get one of William's tin fish under our stomach it's 'Ladies first,' so she'd have a chance to shake him off for good."

I discouraged the Australian's speculations, and urged him to proceed with his story of the *Ibid* and Skipper McGee. The yarn, I thought, would keep my mind off submarines.

"Skip McGee sort of prowled around looking for jobs that were a bit risky and where the pay was good. Understand? He had as much respect for the law as a milk snake had for a nice fat frog, and the *Ibid* poked around amongst the islands of the Malay picking up cargoes that other boats didn't like to handle and charging double prices for doing it. No one alive could make Skip McGee mistake a shell game for an orphan's benefit. He'd close one eye and look at the lines on the face of the fellow that was trying to bluff him, then he'd ask a price that would jar the crook's back teeth.

"'This is a straight game,' they'd say; unloosing the kind of talk the Kaiser pulls. 'It's all above-board.'

"'Sure,' Skip McGee would say; 'I know it, lad, I know it. But I've got an agreement with the *Ibid* not to put opium into her unless I got my own price.'

"'It's not opium!' they'd yell.

"'Well, p'r'aps it ain't,' old Skip McGee would say, 'but there's other things that *Ibid* hates as bad as opium. Scores of things, lad. Scores of things. And hemp is that cheap now that they hanged six men at Banjermassin the other day and gave everyone of them a new rope.'

"Fellows that were that smooth you could polish a pearl on their skins would come up against old Skip McGee, and go away sorer than a snake in a shop window.

"We toddled round a bit on that cruise. Karang Buta Lulu, Sumbawa, Pinnunko, Bool, Kuching, Samalanga, and a thousand little Nipa-palm villages that lay between. And we carried most every-thing—spices, wax, opium, rubber, indigo, cinchona, plumbago, and trepang. And once we carried pearls. Pearls! Understand? The little shiny things the oyster sleeps with.

"It was a fellow we met at Palembang who owned the pearls. He wanted to get away from that place in such a hurry that it was good betting to think he didn't get them honestly, and old Skip McGee, who saw he was in a hurry, but who didn't know about the pearls, multiplied his highest rate for a passage by seven, and got it without an argument. The fellow wanted to go to Batavia, and he hustled Skip McGee so hard that we were out of the Musi River an hour after taking him aboard.

"Big Bill Laff and the five other loafers gave that fellow their undivided attention. The chap ate with the skipper, me acting as steward, and the six expected me to bring them back the whole of the conversation—full-points, exclamation-marks, and commas included.

"And then the fellow surprised everybody by catching a fever and dying. The skipper was fool enough to search his body while Big Bill Laff was in the offing. Skip McGee dragged out a canvas bag from inside of his shirt, and he pushed his paw into the bag. There were pearls in that bag. Pearls! Understand? I didn't see them then, but I saw them afterwards."

"*Silence, back there!*" growled a voice.

"Little Willie under the stairs kissed her, and they heard him," whispered the Australian. "He's a fool to tease sailors in that way. All those chaps are miles and miles away from their sweethearts, and—"

"But the pearls?" I interrupted. "Go on and tell me about the pearls."

"Ay, ay, shy," he responded. "Now, you've seen pearls in jewellers' windows and on ladies' throats, haven't you? You've heard people say, 'What wonderful pearls!' haven't you? And you thought they were, too. I bet. Well, friend, if all the pearls you ever saw, or any other man on this boat ever saw, were put down on the deck'longside that bagful of beauties that Skip McGee took off the dead man you wouldn't see the other pile. It would just lose itself in the glory of the heap we had on the *Ibid*. They were from oysters who really understood how to make pearls, cunning old oysters who made it a life hobby to shine them and tint them red and crimson and smoky grey and salmon pink. Talk about art! Why, there was more art shown in the making of one of those pearls than you'd find in the Tate Gallery or the Melbourne Art Museum. We look at the oyster as an uncivilized insect, but let me tell you he's got more art in him than Jimmy Whistler ever had.

"Big Bill Laff looked at Skip McGee when the skipper took a handful of those things out of the bag, and the skipper tore his eyes from the pearls and swung them on to Bill. 'Get on deck!' he yelled. 'On deck at once!'

"Big Bill didn't move, because he couldn't move. At ordinary times he didn't have enough brains to cover a threepenny-piece, and the sight of those pearls stopped that little piece of grey matter from registering news from the outside world, so to speak. William was doing nothing but stare, but he was doing that well.

"Skip McGee didn't like a sailor to stand around and masticate any order he gave him. No fear! He sprang across the cabin and hit Big Bill where his nose humped, and William went through the door. When he found out that it wasn't the mainmast that had hit him, he picked himself up and went up on deck. Twenty minutes later I went on to the deck, and found Big Bill gripping the first joint of his right thumb with the fingers of his left hand, and showing it to three of the crew. He was a liar, because not one of the pearls was as big as that, but it made the others wiggle their eyes a bit.

"'Where's the skip, Snotty?' said one of them to me.

"'In his cabin,' I said.

"'Give him our compliments, Snotty,' he said, 'and tell him that we're just busting for a sight of some oyster buttons.'

"'Tell him yourself,' I said; and the brute caught me by the leg and brought me down flat on the deck, nearly breaking my back.

Skip McGee came up just then, and he asked me what was wrong.

"'I slipped.' I said.

"'Didn't someone throw you down?' he roared.

"'No, sir,' I said; 'I slipped on a piece of fat.'

"It was a mighty good job that I didn't squeak on that fellow. He remembered my action because he was a pretty big coward, and he'd stopped one or two of Skip McGee's punches before.

"That night, just about eight hells, someone gave my leg a jerk, and I sat up to find Big Bill and the others all around me. Big Bill was the leader of the party.

"'We're leaving the schooner, Snotty,' he said. 'She's sinking. To be quite truthful, we were going to let you go down with her, but this big fool Coddy wants to take you along.' Coddy was the fellow who had thrown me down on the deck.

"'And the skipper?' I said. 'Where's the skipper?'

"'Why,' said Big Bill, 'he's elected to stand by the ship. It's his privilege. There's a song written about it. It goes, 'I'll stick to the ship, lads, you save your lives.' Ever heard it? Well, that's his special little hymn.'

"'Where is he?' I yelped. 'I'll see him.'

"'You'll just come along if you want to come right now!' growled Bill. 'You've got two minutes to change your lodgings.'

"Of course, I guessed it was the product of the artistic oysters that had caused trouble, and I guessed about right. We hadn't pulled thirty yards from the *Ibid* before she slipped down into the Java Sea as if she was glad of a rest, and, as I couldn't help Skip McGee by fighting that bunch, I picked up the oar that Big Bill pointed to, and started to pull with three of the others. Big Bill turned the boat towards the coast of Java, which, he thought, was not more than fifty miles away.

"Next morning Big Bill divided the pearls. There were ninety-four of them, and Bill gave each of the five fifteen pearls, while he kept nineteen. And his nineteen weren't the shabbiest of that exhibit.

"That night we saw the lights following us. At least Bill Laff, Coddy, and the form others saw them, but I couldn't. They said they were the riding lights of a ship, and we stopped rowing, and waited for her to overhaul us. Mind you, I didn't see those lights. Couldn't see the glimmer of a red or green on the whole horizon, but they did. I was that prickly with gooseflesh that I was scratching holes in my underwear.

"When we stopped rowing, the ship stopped. That's what they said.

"'How far off is she?' I stammered, turning to Coddy.

"'Why, look at her, you fool! She's not more than half-a-mile astern!'

"Big Bill Laff turned the boat around, and we started to pull back to the lights that those fellows saw, and then the lights started to walk away from us, walk away into the Java Sea. When we'd stop, they'd stop; when we'd go ahead they'd throw in the clutch and come after us; when we started back to them they reversed and kept their distance. The language that went up from our boat was real artistic profanity. Pretty stuff, friend. If there was one thing on which that six could grab ninety-nine points out of a possible one hundred it was language, and that night they were hitting on every cylinder. Every time that ship played the coy lady with us, and that was about two score tunes before the dawn came, their joint vocabulary would have melted an iceberg. They could really swear, I will say that for them. There wasn't a curse word known between Pulo Laut and Tao Shoals that they couldn't handle in the fashion laid down by its inventor."

A sailor came softly down the deck, and the Australian paused.

"Someone's talkin' down here," said the Jacky. "Lieutenant says it's gotter stop."

The Australian took the tar by the arm and pointed to the dark shadows beneath the stairs.

"It comes from there," he whispered. "I'm afraid they're having a row with each other."

The Jacky sprang across the deck, and we heard the indignant whispers of the lovers; then the sailor repeated his injunction and hurried back to the bows. The Australian continued:

"Just before dawn, when I was that tired I couldn't hold an oar, we crept so close to the schooner that some of them saw her name. Coddy was the one to yell it out; then a red-headed fellow who was named Thursday because he worked as a pearler on Thursday Island, also saw it, and yelled it out, too. Do you know what name they yelled out? You don't? They roared out, 'The *Ibid!* The *Ibid!*' And I could see from the look on the faces of the others that they could read it, too. Mind you, I hadn't seen the boat. Hadn't seen her lights even. Funny, wasn't it?

"Coddy and Thursday and a thin, sickly chap named Pannikin wanted to row away from her; but Big Bill Laff, who wasn't afraid of anything, wanted to board her. He knocked Thursday down with an oar, and the rest of them started to pull for the schooner that they had seen sink the night before. I was that scared that my teeth were doing an imitation of a ukulele, and the old Sahara wasn't dryer than my tongue and throat. They were that dry that it would take a camel to carry a yell over them. And I wanted to yell, friend. I did.

"The schooner started to back off, and Big Bill Laff ordered us to stop rowing. From what I could learn they were only fifty yards from her just then. When we stopped, the *Ibid* stopped; at least, I gathered she did, because Big Bill kicked himself out of his shirt and trousers and said: 'I'm going to swim to her! Wait till I get aboard, then I'll yell.'

"'I'm goin' with you,' said a little Englishman named Porky. 'Wait for me.'

"Bill and Porky went overboard together, and we waited. Coddy was near me, and, as I couldn't see her, he kept me posted.

"'She's not moving,' he said. 'Oh, cripes! What a joke! The fellows on her can't see Bill and Porky in the water. I bet they get aboard her.'

"'But she sunk, Coddy!' I stammered. 'She sunk!'

"'She didn't, you fool!' he said. 'She's here right in front of us, furled topsail, and all just as we left her.'

"What do you think of a fellow talking like that, friend? All that bunch of murderous thieves thought the *Ibid* was in front of them, although they had seen her slop right under the waves the night before.

"After a few minutes there came a yell, and Thursday told us to lay into it. We did, but I guess the *Ibid* laid into it, too. We pulled after her till daylight, and when daylight came there wasn't a thing to be seen. I couldn't see anything, neither could those four others. But we had pulled an awful long way out into the Java sea, and we had lost Big Bill and Porky.

"The four divided up the nineteen pearls that were in Big Bill's pocket and the fifteen that Porky left behind him, then we started to pull towards the west. That business put our nerves on the jump. I was more scared of the *Ibid* than I was of a shark, and the four others weren't happy. They tried to sing, but it wasn't what you'd really call singing. Their voices were that shaky that they dropped notes by the hundred, and the loneliness of the Java Sea had any other kind of loneliness beat by eight sighs a minute. It was the kind of loneliness that makes you think of the little dog you had as a boy, of the latch on the back-gate that you could never open when the gander chased you, or the farm paper your father read, and all sorts of things like that. The whole crowd of us were thinking that the *Ibid* was lying just behind the horizon waiting for the dark to pop up and play peek-a-boo with us again.

"And when the night came up she slipped. Played the same game as the night before, at least that's what Coddy told me. Went ahead when we went ahead, stood at neutral when we stopped, and went astern when we came after her. And she with sails only, and not a breath of wind blowing.

"But how can she do it?" I screamed to Coddy. "You say she's getting away from us with her headlights showing. That's impossible!"

"'Well, she's doing it, son,' said Coddy. 'If your optic nerves weren't so badly diseased you could see her.'

"Thursday had taken command of the boat, and Thursday had an idea that Big Bill Laff and Porky were on the *Ibid*. It was hot in that open boat, so you must make a little allowance for Thursday. Under ordinary circumstances he didn't have enough brains to fill a walnut-shell, but I guess you could have packed them carelessly into a child's thimble the night he had us playing tag with the *Ibid*. We hadn't much water on that boat, either, and Thursday said it would be sensible to get on to the schooner if we could. So we played the game of gentle seducer to the *Ibid*; but the *Ibid* wouldn't be seduced.

"That was a worse night than the one before it. Thursday said he heard Big Bill Laff hailing us, and he made us pull like madmen trying to overtake the lights. 'Listen to them!' he'd yell. 'They're aboard her! I bet they've found old McGee's whisky that we went away and forgot. They're yelling again!'

"Did you ever try to catch a care-free calf or a gambolling goat, or any other creature that had acrobatic and wandering tendencies? The *Ibid* was that calf and that goat, and any other animal that you might have tried to put a halter on. Thursday had us larruping the Java Sea into foam all that night, and the *Ibid* didn't seem a whit tired. From what those fools told me about the way she acted, I took it that she thought it the end of a perfect night, but I had blisters on my hands as big as marbles.

"Then just before dawn the *Ibid* let us creep up to her as she did the night before. Thursday kept hailing her, and those four were that crazed that they thought they could hear Big Bill answering them, and telling them to come aboard.

"And over they went! At least, three of them went over, leaving Coddy and me on the boat. We heard them yelling and screaming as they swam towards the place where they thought the *Ibid* was waiting, then after a long while the ocean became silent, the sun came up, and there was nothing on it, no *Ibid*, no swimmers, no nothing!

"Coddy and I were a little dazed. We just sat and stared at the ocean and stared at each other. We were too tired to pull, so we did nothing.

"About midday I picked up a pearl that Thursday had dropped, a beautiful red pearl. Coddy wanted it, so we agreed to gamble, Coddy to take out a handful of his pearls, and I guess odd or even.

"Coddy didn't get the red pearl. We played that game for five hours, and I had nine pearls then, the red one, and eight of Coddy's. It began to get dark, so we stopped playing, and waited for the *Ibid to* come prancing along to keep us company. It was awful lonely there.

"'There she is!' cried Coddy, pointing to the west; and I turned quick. Then I gave a yell. I saw her, saw her for the first time. At least I saw her red and green lights, which I had never been able to see before. Curious, wasn't it?

"'Do you see her?' cried Coddy.

"'Of course I do,' I answered.

"'We'll get to her, Snotty,' he said. 'Get out your sticks and pull.'

"It was the same old game we played the night before, and the night before that. The *Ibid* was just as tricky and some more. We'd paddle softly, paddle madly, and paddle mildly, but it was all the same. She kept her distance like a well-brought-up young lady, and at last Coddy and I gave up.

"'Come on, Snotty, we've got to swim to her like the others did,' he said. 'Come on.'

"Now, I didn't like to hop overboard, and I didn't seem to have the fixed belief that I'd get aboard her like those others had. I wondered why I hadn't seen her on the first two nights, and all of a sudden I knew. I had no pearls then, not a pearl!

"'Coddy!' I yelled. 'Coddy, I want to give you back the pearls! I don't want them. They're not mine, and I don't want anything to do with them!'

"I pushed them into Coddy's hand, and he took them.

"'Ain't you coming, Snotty?' he said.

"'No!' I snapped; and then I turned and looked at where I had seen the lights. They were gone!

"'Do you still see her, Coddy?' I cried.

"'Sure I do,' he shouted. 'Look, we're only a ship's length off her.' And with that he dived overboard. But I couldn't see a light, although I watched till dawn. I saw nothing, and when dawn came I sort of understood. The *Ibid* had come after that crowd, and had sort of fixed them in her own little way. She wanted to go down in a big storm, fighting, and that bunch had scuttled her on a still, quiet night, and she was mad. Clean mad! I was picked up that afternoon and carried up to Batavia."

The Australian finished and toned to the rail.

"You can't get away with ship murder," he said. "These liners and tramps that Kaiser Bill has sunk are all mighty mad about it. They're angry—say, do you see anything over there to port?"

"No, I don't," I answered. "What did you think you saw?"

"Funny," said the Australian. "I suppose it was telling you that story that made me see it, but just for an instant I thought I saw a big liner all white as snow—all white as snow! Just for an instant I saw her. A liner as big as the *Lusitania*."

He thrust his head forward and watched the spot where he thought he had seen the ghost ship, then, with a quick cry, he leaped along the deck and gripped the officer in charge of the gun crew by the arm.

"*Look!*" he shouted. "*See!* Quick, for the love of heaven! Let him have it!"

According to the statement issued by the lieutenant, the first shot carried the periscope of the submarine clean away, while the second struck her black hull squarely. He was a very delighted lieutenant, and when the fuss had died away, he found the Australian and shook hands with him.

"You've got splendid eyesight," he said. "I looked at that spot a moment before and saw nothing. And I had glasses."

"Something else attracted my attention," said the Australian, "then I saw the periscope come up."

"What attracted you first?" asked the officer, a little curious.

The Australian shifted the weight of his body from one leg to the other, looked at me, and then stammered out:

"Oh, I don't know. It was just something—just something on that spot, and when I watched it the sub popped up its head. We were lucky, weren't we?"

"We were," cried the lieutenant. "It was just about this spot that the brutes got the *Lusitania*."

"Is that so?" cried the Australian.

The officer nodded and turned away. For a full minute the Australian stood staring out over the black water, then, with a curious sigh, he turned and made off down the deck.

THE SHIP THAT DIED

John Gilbert

John DeWitt Gilbert (1896–1981) was the editor of a trade journal in Eugene, Oregon, that dealt with the fisheries industry, but at the time this story was written he had just signed up as an artillery officer soon after the United States entered the First World War. It is interesting that the following story, the only one of his that I know, was published in Britain shortly after the previous one by Dwyer, but it had first appeared in the American pulp The Argosy *in May 1917. It shows that the idea of a ship seeking revenge struck a chord with the public.*

THE DERELICT

T HE VOICE OF THE LOOK-OUT BOOMED FROM THE CROW'S NEST:
"An abandoned cutter two miles to the sou'-sou'-east."

The second officer paused in his monotonous pacing of the
bridge, lifted his head and scanned the sea off the starboard bow. He
could not see the drifting boat against the deep-blue of the noon sea,
but binoculars brought it out.

Quietly he ordered the man at the wheel to alter his course and
run toward the discovery. Then he sought the captain, playing quoits
on the after-deck with some of the wounded American officers which
the *Alaska* was taking home.

Unexcitedly the captain looked the derelict over. At a distance
of a quarter of a mile from the cutter the big transport stopped her
engines and lowered a boat. With the second officer in command,
the investigator drew away from the mother ship with eight rough
sailors rowing easily.

From the deck of the *Alaska*, the soldiers watched the two small
boats draw together, and saw the officer board the foundling. Then
a tar semaphored that they were bringing the find back with them.

The *Alaska* steamed to meet them. Over the derelict cutter a
tarpaulin had been lashed by the second officer to hide its contents.
Eager, peering eyes saw nothing but a ship's cutter, badly weather-
worn and storm-beaten, hoisted, with trailing moss and green sea-
growths, into the waist of the *Alaska*, whence all persons but the
captain and his two chief officers were excluded. Throughout a good
part of the afternoon their investigation was continued.

The curiosity of the passengers, to say nothing of the remaining ship's officers, had to go unappeased until dinner. Then, rapping on the table, the captain rose.

"A few of you may be interested in the boat which we picked up this afternoon," he said. "I think that we can tell the world the last chapter of a strange story. If you wish to hear an account of it all, I will meet you in the reading room at seven bells."

THE PHANTOM VESSEL

"You have all heard," began the captain, facing his attentive audience, "of the mysterious case of the *Carnivordshire*, whose disappearance and apparent reappearance has been one of the baffling problems that has thrown a mysticism over the sea. I will tell the story briefly, in case some phases of it have not come to your ears.

"The tramp *Carnivordshire*, A. & A. Company, left Liverpool for San Francisco on February 26th, 1914. From that day to this no word nor message has been received from her. Her wireless call has never stirred the antennæ of ship or coaststation. Her crew numbered thirty-five; the wife of the captain and the captain's children were also aboard.

"The really strange phase of the mystery began six weeks later, when the steamer *Sioux*, a vessel running between Portland and San Francisco, docked at Astoria, and her skipper, David Johnson, filed this affidavit with the port commissioners."

Picking up his scrap-book the captain read from a newspaper cutting:

"'Eighteen hours after leaving the Golden Gate I went on the bridge. It was about two in the morning. The sea was perfectly calm and the night fine. Taking my position, I caught the lights of a vessel some distance ahead and well off to the west.

"'For an hour or more nothing happened. I loitered about the bridge admiring the night, but paying no attention to the other vessel, even though I noted that she was nearing us quite rapidly. Suddenly, however, I realized that she was steaming directly toward us, making much noise. By the beating of her wheel and the thunder of her engines, which were audible even above the sound of my own boat, I knew her to be a tramp.

"'The intruder made no sign or signal as to the course she expected me to take. I waited a moment or two and then gave her my siren—no reply. She was close to us now. I could see her sidelights plainly. Suddenly a word in code lanterns flashed in her rigging. It was *Carnivordshire*. I rang for the first mate.

"'The moon was just setting into the sea. Part of it had already disappeared. I could see that the on-coming vessel would soon obscure it from our view. I shut the *Sioux* down to half speed and whistled again.

"'Because of our slowing speed the stranger had to alter her course in order to head once more directly for us. As she did it, I became convinced that she was trying to run us down.

"'I started a steady whistle and set my engines hard astern. On came the mad ship; she was crossing in front of the moon, but the moon shone on! Her hull was directly in line with it and still the disc remained unhid. My vessel was quivering with the strain of her reversed engines and was drawing back with increasing rapidity. The other ship swung also, but I had the start of her and she was unable to swerve quickly enough to run us down.

"'She crossed our bows with not a dozen feet between our nose and her sidelights. Still no vessel was there.

"'There simply was not a boat in sight, only those lights and the noise of her running. I could see plain water where her hull should have been, could see the waves through her sides. There was no rigging outlined against the moonlit sky. The signals and other lights hung suspended in thin air. No solid thing was near, and yet there was the noise of a ship moving at full speed.

"'She passed—but there was no sign. The waves were undisturbed by any wake save our own.'

"This statement was made over the affidavit of Captain Johnston, the first mate and several passengers who had witnessed the apparition," explained the commander of the transport.

"There are many similar stories here," he added, showing the pages of his book in which were pasted numerous accounts paralleling in general the experience of the *Sioux*. "All of them tell of the appearance of the lights of a vessel which bore down upon them, refusing to answer their whistles and apparently attempting to ram them. All vessels reporting this phenomena seem barely to have escaped when the skipper reversed his engines. Always the lights were suspended in air; always the noise of the vessel was audible.

"There never was a ship. The sea was never disturbed. There were no visible signs of solid matter, but, whenever the incident occurred, there burnt, where the rigging should have been, signal lights that spelled *Carnivordshire*.

"These reports came from all over the ocean," continued the captain. "One ship would put into Pago-Pago saying that she had encountered the phantom the previous night about ten. Later advices would come from Seattle that a tug had gone on a wild goose chase in response to an S.O.S. from the *Carnivordshire* shortly before morning of the same day off the straits of Juan de Fuca. Such reports have been coming in quite regularly down to the present time. This morning we made a real find—the first definite evidence with bearing on the case that has come to hand.

"When the second officer went aboard the cutter which we picked up this morning he found four human skeletons—a woman, two boys and a girl. The bodies had been picked clean by birds. The boat had been drifting for months.

"After the find had been brought aboard we carefully removed the skeletons and made a search of the boat. In a far corner of a food-locker were found some pieces of paper such as are used in wrapping up pilot bread. On them was written a record left by the occupants. It is this that I have here."

THE LAST LOG

There are six of us drifting, we know not where, in a lifeboat. We have food and water enough for our immediate needs but, if help does not come at once, we shall die of thirst and starvation.

I am the wife of the skipper of the *Carnivordshire*. With me are my three children. Something happened to the *Carnivordshire* which I cannot explain and which you will not understand nor believe. Nevertheless, it is true.

One night while Jack, my husband, and I were reading in our cabin, the first mate came in to speak to my husband. They talked together for some time and soon went out, leaving me alone. I was never very much interested in the affairs of the ship, and so had not noticed what they were saying. In half-an-hour Jack returned. He was frowning and seemed troubled. I asked if something was wrong.

"Trouble with the wireless instruments," he said. "The things are affected in some way. Parts of them are kind of rotten. Metal and wood seem to be deteriorating or corroding. I believe they are done for."

I went to bed soon and knew nothing more until I was awakened at about three in the morning by the stopping of the engines. I lay listening for some time. Even at that hour men were moving about everywhere—an unusual thing. It was not long before the machinery started again, but now it seemed to be running unevenly, with jerky, uncertain beatings. Finally they died out altogether and the vessel lay idle in the sweeping swell of the sea. I was astonished at the halt, for we had stopped only the day before to repack some piston boxes. The men had gone swimming for an hour or two.

Without waiting for breakfast I dressed and went on deck. My husband and the engineer were talking just outside the companion way as I came up. Not wishing to disturb them, I stopped before reaching the deck. The engineer was saying:

"The whole thing is corroding. I can gouge the cylinders with a chisel and the boilers are as soft as cheese—"

The men walked away. Something was wrong, that was certain, but I could make nothing of the words I had heard. I went on deck.

Up forward the two mates were bending over something on the deck. As I drew near, I saw to my bewilderment a ragged hole gaping in the iron plates. The men were picking at it with their hands. I drew back and grasped the rail in horror. As I leant my weight against it a great chunk broke off and dropped overboard. I recoiled aghast.

Keeping my eyes on the men about the hole, I backed up to seek the support of the cabin-wall. Groping blindly behind me, I touched the iron house. The cold surface of the metal slipped beneath the palm of my hand. I looked and saw that I had rubbed off a great scale of the steel. My foot splashed into something soft. I was standing in a semi-solid, muddy pile that had melted down from the wall of the cabin.

I gaped about me dumfounded, wildeyed. At the junction of the cabin wall and the deck ran a long crack that narrowed and widened with the strain of the vessels rising and falling in the steady sea. I heard something break and looked up in time to see one of the stays swinging loose and lashing in the air. I slipped, half-fainting, to the deck. I could dent it with my fist. Where I dug my heel, a long rent was made in the iron plating. The metal rubbed up in rolls like freshly baked bread.

I heard my husband call, "All hands aft!"

There was a moment of quiet and the crew began to swarm up from below. I had not noticed their absence. My children sought me out. They were white and wide-eyed. We stood together near the rail.

My husband was never very big, but he was every inch man and master as he stood there, addressing the crew. He looked them over for a minute, and then:

"Men, there is, as you know, something decidedly wrong with this craft. She has been attacked by some mysterious malady which has caused her plates to rot and her engines to slough off and melt away. You could cut the deck beneath your feet with your finger-nail. The trouble started last night with the wireless apparatus. It is an electrolysis or ray of some sort that is corroding wood and metal alike. Now every part of our vessel is decayed. The whole ship is like a mushroom. There is not a solid thing aboard. You could poke your finger through every lifeboat. There is no escape.

"There are a woman and three children aboard. If there were a way for ten people to leave this vessel, would not these four be among them?"

"Ay-e-e-e-e-e," growled the men, assuringly.

"You were swimming yesterday, men. The cutter I lowered for you to use is still being towed astern. It is sound and unaffected by the trouble that has rendered the ship useless. In it there is room for ten persons. Let my wife and the children get in. Six others may be selected from the crew. The two mates and myself waive our chances. Is it all right? The matter is in your hands."

The crew moved to the rail, looking at the boat bobbing a few fathoms away. The line to it was already fraying and rotting with the malady. They looked up.

"Ay-e-e-e-e," they promised.

There was a general murmur and debate for some moments about the men who were to go in the boat. Jack and the mates had come down and they were bidding us goodbye. He was calm and I did not weep.

"You have a chance—a chance. God go with you and save your boat from this plague! Good-bye—"

He was interrupted by one of the sailors who had stepped up above the others.

"Mates," he said, "the line to yonder cutter is about parted. We ain't got no time to argue or cast lots. Mrs. McLelland and the kids are goin' aboard without waitin' for any of us, ain't they?"

"Ay-e-e-e-AYE," first doubtfully and then with conviction.

The boat was drawn up to the side and we were bundled over and told to slide down the rope. The children got safely down, but the rope broke beneath me, throwing me into the water close beside the other craft. The children dragged me aboard. The faces leaning over the rail above looked good-bye. My husband shouted:

"Push clear of the ship and row away. Don't allow any one to get in when we sink. Good-bye. God bless you!"

My eldest boy, Kenneth, and I clumsily rowed our boat off for a few hundred yards and awaited the end. The vessel was going fast. Her masts were bent far over, like candles in summer, and her sides were bulging out with the weight of her decks. The rigging was hanging in tatters. Great, flat chunks from her sides kept up a continuous splashing as they fell into the water. Long cracks appeared in her plates. Widening and gaping, they spread along her sides.

The men could be seen moving about. The sagging deck slowly forced the boat apart and she flattened out upon the water in a great mass of scum. For an acre or more this loathsome coating of rotted ship smeared the surface. What had been left of the *Carnivordshire* rose and fell on the rollers like a blotch of mud. No heads forced their way through the vile scum. We kept close to it till night fell.

Sleep was impossible so we lay there—looking, watching. Suddenly we heard the sound of a vessel and looked to see the lights of a ship where we thought the scum was. She was steaming our way. We screamed and yelled. On she came. Down upon us, never swerving to right or left. She was fully lighted. In her rigging were signal lights that Kenneth, who knows something of nautical matters, said spelt *Carnivordshire*.

We stood up and yelled until I thought I should go mad. Still she made no sign of seeing us. She was upon us now. I bowed my head, expecting the blow. The lights passed over us. The vessel slipped through us. Her flares were all about and still there was no sign of any solid thing. The great phantom continued on her way, leaving us undisturbed by wake or swell.

That was yesterday. We have seen no sign of ship or help and are waiting for the end. I can think calmly of my husband's death for I know we shall be with him soon. He went like a brave man and as the captain of his ship should go. I would rather have him die there than here. The children suffer more than I, for the sun is very hot.

Another day has passed. We are in actual need of water now. To-morrow I may not be able to write. Nothing has happened since yesterday. We have not even seen a bird. All round is blue sea and sky. The sun is maddening. If only a storm would come to kill us before we die of this awful thirst.

The next day. The rest are dead. Kenneth died in my arms but a moment ago. I think I am happy. Last night the lights of the *Carnivordshire* ran us down again. How pink the midnight is! I am coming, Jack. Wait for me. I am coming with the children. Wait—

The captain of the *Alaska* stopped abruptly, picked up his scrap-book, and left the room.

DEVEREUX'S LAST SMOKE

Izola Forrester

Izola Forrester (1878–1944) was the illegitimate daughter of the actress Ogarita Booth who always claimed she was the daughter of John Wilkes Booth, the assassin of Abraham Lincoln. Izola—who usually went by the name Zola—later wrote a book about Booth having survived and not being killed in 1865, This One Mad Act *(1937). Zola acted with her mother as a child but was soon adopted by a family friend, George Forrester, editor of the* Chicago Tribune. *With his encouragement she turned to writing, selling her first story when she was 14, soon after her mother died. She was twice married and bore eight children, yet continued to write and support herself. An enterprising and determined woman, Forrester wrote many books for young girls. She worked with her second husband, Mann Page, on plays and movie scripts. Izola sold several stories and poems to the first specialized pulp magazines,* The Ocean *and* The Railroad Man's Magazine, *both niche markets where it was surprising to find women contributors. The following was the only ghost story to appear in* The Ocean.

"**D**ID YOU EVER HAPPEN TO NOTICE," ASKED BARNABY irrelevantly, "how a man looks smoking a cigar in a fog? You can see the light of the cigar as he draws on it, but not the man behind. Sort of headlight effect, you know. Once, when I was crossing on this same boat four years ago, I saw the light from a cigar, but there wasn't any man behind it.

"It was a ghost cigar."

Reardon laughed from his end of the settee.

"Barnaby, boy, you're liable to see anything, afloat or ashore, given favourable conditions. What had you been smoking yourself?"

Barnaby lighted a cigarette and ignored the speaker. The rest of us in that corner of the smoking-room listened.

It was the fourth day out from Sandy Hook.

The *Königen Teresa* was ploughing an unsteady course through a dense fog, grey-white, like the edge of an August thunder-cloud. It had kept up for a day and a half, so far. On deck it was raw and damp, as only mid-Atlantic can be in March. The waves lurched choppily against the boat. You could hear the steady, monotonous breaking of them, but not an inch of sea was visible in the greyness.

Barnaby had just come in off deck. He was aggressively cheerful and buoyant, under the circumstances. The weather had reduced every one else to a state of limp endurance. The fog had settled on everything, including brains, and when Barnaby came jauntily in we were ready to welcome anything as a diversion, even Barnaby.

Every other minute the fog-horn mourned dismally.

"Wish that thing would hush itself," said Barnaby. "It always makes me think of a cow crying after the calf the butcher has taken away, and I'm awfully sympathetic by nature. And it makes me think, too, of that particular cigar I was speaking of. I don't believe in ghosts. I want to say that, first of all, before I swear I saw one. Any one present remember the late Charlie Devereux?"

"Wasn't that the fellow who married Irene Irving?" Reardon asked lazily.

Reardon's partner at whist looked up at Barnaby for the first time since his entrance from deck and waited for Reardon to play, but the dramatic critic laid down his hand and turned his chair toward Barnaby.

"That's the one," said Barnaby. "Used to be all-around good boy from Union Square up to Times. Not a coupon-cutter, you know, nor a coin-flasher. He had to work once in a while, like the rest of us, but he had a nice little anti-worry sinking-fund planted somewhere, so that when the rainy day happened along he never went out minus an umbrella. And the umbrella was silk at that. Any one else here knew Charlie Devereux?"

Nearly all of us remembered him, although four years is a large cairn to raise over a person's memory along Broadway; but Devereux was different, and the crowd at the card-tables in that end of the smoking-room followed Reardon's suit and laid down their hands. It sounded better than fog-bound whist.

"If there was a man behind that cigar, or, rather, the ghost of a man, that ghost was Charlie Devereux," Barnaby went on. "Who's to the listen?"

"Fire ahead," said Reardon. "But stick to facts, Barnaby. Cold, foggy facts, you know. Never mind local colour in chunks."

"The story tells itself," retorted Barnaby with dignity. "I merely happened to be the phonographic record. I don't believe in it myself, even though I know I saw the whole thing. But for Charlie's sake it should be told, because it shows a degree of sagacity and general long-headed cleverness that no ghost ever let on to before.

"I met Charlie for the first time about a year before he married Miss Irving. One night I found myself cornered up around Forty-Second and Sixth with a crowd of good fellows and only ten dollars left in my own private bank. Charlie Devereux staked me. It was particularly decent because he had only known me about fifteen minutes and the stake was yellow paper. He told me to take it, and said that a man who wasn't good for twenty dollars wasn't good for anything, and it was worth losing twenty dollars to find him out."

"That's like Devereux."

"Why, sure it was. He was simply great in that line. I guess he'd loaned twenty-dollar bills to nearly every new youngster who fell broke along that way for ten years."

"More than that," said Reardon. "And some of the old ones, too."

"But he didn't lose much on the game," Barnaby replied. "The youngsters generally paid up, because it was like lending money to yourself. You could always go after it the next time. Anyway, one day we heard he'd married Irene Irving and they had sailed for Europe in a hurry on the *Königen Teresa*. It was glad news to the little isle that loved him. We wished him well, especially as he had picked out the loveliest girl of that season's Broadway stage."

Barnaby paused to light a fresh cigarette, and Reardon's partner leaned across the table and offered his match-box.

It was a small ivory death's-head with jewelled eyes. Barnaby looked at it with quick interest, and for an instant met the glance of its owner, then went on:

"Nobody along Broadway seemed to know anything special about Irene Irving. She just happened. It was her second season, so she said, and she had a glorious voice, and a face that didn't need any make-up. She got her chance without the asking.

"When they put on 'Fleurette' at the Casino Dunbar he saw a chance, and gave her a song to sing about breaking hearts and sighing waves, and that sort of stuff, with a mermaid mixed up in it, and at the end of the second act Irving sang it dressed in a five-thousand-dollar fish-net hung with real pearls. It was a joyous stunt, and the first-nighters hunted up her name on the program when the curtain fell."

"Devereux found it quick," said Reardon slowly. "They were engaged the next week."

"And married the fifth." Barnaby looked up quizzically at Reardon's partner. "They sailed for Europe on their honeymoon on this very boat, and we all lost track of Charlie except the rumours that floated over of a touring-car and general joy-bell state of affairs. Charlie had to be back in August, and he booked their passage on the same steamer. Point of sentiment, I suppose.

"The rest is left to hearsay and the press-agent, so to speak. Nobody knows how it happened. He was seen walking on deck that evening with Irene, and they seemed to be having trouble, but she left him and went to her stateroom, so that let her out, you understand. But somewhere in the deep sea at that particular point the mermaids are feeding pearls sautés to one good fellow—Charlie Devereux."

"And she wore violet mourning."

"That's correct," said Barnaby. "Lord, I can see her now swinging up Riverside with the neatest team on the path. Didn't seem to take to the gasoline after Charlie's death. Went in for the swell seclusion, and all that. Dressed in violet from head to foot. Violet crape widow's veil, even, and her hair was baby golden. Remember her, Reardon, old chap?

"French crêpon violet gown, elbow gloves in violet suéde, and shoes to match. It didn't do a thing to little Manhattan. Broadway in September is like an impressionable kid at twenty-one. It is ready to worship anything just as long as it is something. And the violet widow of Charlie Devereux dawned on it with the tender pathetic glory of a purple-and-pearl twilight—and took.

"But she declined to mingle with the happy, care-free throng of climbers. Charlie had left her a bully little fortune and not a single restriction to the will except that she wear the violet for at least a year. And just exactly six months and four days after he had been transformed into submarine sauté, aforesaid, I met the widow as a fellow passenger on this boat and she was on her way to marry Jack Beaufort Crane."

"Don't know him," interposed Reardon.

"Hardly any one did, but he was all right. The *Review* had him out in the Orient for about ten years as special correspondent. He missed home comforts, but had the luck to get shut up in Port Arthur at the siege, and the better luck to get out. Charlie helped him, and when the honeymoon was shining brightly on the other side he thought he'd look up Jack."

Reardon's partner tapped softly with the little death's-head match-box on the felt-covered table as Barnaby paused, and again his eyes met those of Barnaby, but he said nothing.

"Crane was connected with the American embassy in Paris, so Mrs. Devereux told me," continued Barnaby deliberately. "I happened to be the only one on board whom she knew, and that means a good deal with a six-day sea trip ahead of one. Before we had passed through the Narrows she had told me how dear and sweet and lovely Charlie had been to her, but that she was going now to the only man she had ever loved.

"Well, anyway, along about the third day we struck this sort of weather and Irene grew reminiscent. Took to walking deck and not eating regularly. I didn't mind it so much, because she usually let me trot along for cheerful company, as it were. Sort of fog antidote, don't you see?

"And she had dropped the violet on New Year's as a good resolution. Used to pace deck in a long dark-blue cloak lined with Stuart plaid, and a cap to match on her blond curls. I rather preferred it to the violet myself. She seemed to dread being alone, and I didn't blame her, as we drew near the probable spot where Charlie had dropped, overboard.

"I was sitting in here smoking, the fourth afternoon, sitting right over where Dillingham is now, when she sent for me to come at once.

"It was so thick on deck you couldn't see your own hand an arm's length from your face. I groped about until I found her standing over the port rail up forward, and the instant she caught sight of me she gave a frightened little cry and caught hold of my arm.

"'Barney,' she exclaimed—'Barney, for the love of Heaven, tell me I am not going out of my mind. Tell me you see something there— there, right in front of us. Oh, Barney, can't you see it?'"

"Stick to facts, Barnaby, boy—cold facts," warned Reardon.

Barnaby did not notice him. He was keeping one eye on the face of Reardon's partner, but this time there was no answering glance. Barnaby threw away a dead cigarette-stub and leaned forward in his chair, his elbows on his knees, his jolly, boyish face a bit moody in its expression.

"I said I didn't believe in ghosts, didn't I? Well, don't forget that as one of the facts in the case. But what I saw was this, and it was daylight, too—about three in the afternoon, I should say.

"Right there in front of us, not four feet away, was the light of a cigar, and I'll swear there was no living man behind it. You could see it as plainly as I can see the light on your cigar-tips now, except for the fog-haze, of course. It glowed steadily there in front of us, every now and then brightening and darkening again, as a lighted cigar does when you draw on it."

"Was there any smoke?" asked Reardon, leaning forward also.

"I couldn't tell, on account of the fog. And while we looked Mrs. Devereux suddenly slipped beside me in a dead faint and the light died away. Not all at once, mind, but as I held her up from the deck in my arms I saw it move slowly in mid-air out beyond the rail and so fade away.

"When she was able, she talked with me down in the cabin.

"She had seen it every time she went on deck, she said, since the boat had reached the open sea. Whether she walked on deck in daylight or at night, it had appeared beside her, and followed her as she walked, as though some one kept her company and smoked as they walked.

"'Just as Charlie always did,' she added to me. 'Sometimes I fancy I can even catch a whiff of the particular tobacco he liked. When you have been with me, though, it has never appeared until now.

"'It is Charlie—I know it is. Why, it follows me from one side of the boat to the other. I have tried walking on both sides, just to test it. I did not dare tell any one but you, for fear they would think I was going out of my mind. If you had not seen it also to-day I should have believed so myself, but you did see it, didn't you, Barney? Tell me you saw it, too, and that it is the light of a cigar.'"

"Maybe you were both crazy," suggested Dillingham pleasantly, as the silence grew oppressive. "Don't lay it on too thick, Barney. The fog may lift."

"It did lift the next morning," said Barnaby. "It was clear and sunny, and we never saw a sign of the ghost cigar all day. Mrs. Devereux did not show up, though, until afternoon, and then she looked mighty bad. I tried to jolly her out of it, and even said I wasn't sure myself that I had seen the light, but it was no good, she only continued to stare out at the water, and would not talk to me.

"'What's the use?' she said. 'It's Charlie. I don't blame him for troubling me if he is able to. I would if I were in his place. We had quarrelled that last night over Jack. He asked me if I wanted to be free, and I said I did, of course, but I didn't mean the freedom he gave me. I didn't want him to die; I only wanted to be free, so that I could marry Jack.'

"'But if he wanted to make you free and happy, and would go so far as to kill himself, why on earth should you suppose he would come back to smoke ghost cigars around you now and set you nearly mad?' I asked her.

"'Oh, but he doesn't mean any harm,' she said. 'I know him so well. He doesn't do it to—to haunt me—that's what they call it, isn't it? If he loved me well enough to die for me, surely he would not harm me now that I am going to Jack.'

"'But the year limit,' I suggested, rather cautiously.

"'I didn't think it mattered, and Jack wanted to be married at Easter. Easter is so pretty in Paris, and we were going to have a violet wedding.'"

"Half-mourning bridal in memory of the late lamented Charlie," suggested Reardon. "I never did care very much for widows."

"But the ghost cigar had settled the violet wedding," Barnaby continued. "She just wouldn't see it any other way but that Charlie wanted her. The fifth day, that was. I tried to cheer her up by saying we would hit Cherbourg the next day, but she couldn't get the old point of view back again. She had lost her grip. After dinner I found her at the same place on deck, leaning over the rail.

"'I want you to do something for me,' she said. 'When you reach Paris I want you to send or give this package to Jack for me. It belonged to Charlie, but it's a gift that Jack sent to him himself from Japan, and I want him to have it back. He will understand how I feel about it.'

"I tried to argue with her, but she persisted, and was so nervous and unstrung that I took the thing to humour her, and promised that Crane should get it on my arrival in Paris. Then, when it grew dark, I coaxed her inside to try and get her mind off the thing, for she was watching all the time for that fool cigar-light to show up any old place at all, and I didn't like the look in her eyes.

"They were having a concert in the saloon, and I found her a good corner, and some jolly talkers to brace her up. It must have been after ten when we missed her.

"Kalman was playing—Kalman Vorga, the Tzigane violinist. You know the sort of stuff he runs to, Reardon. It makes you feel as if you were either crazy or wanted to be—one of the two. I left the crowd and hurried out on deck with that music chasing me. And when I saw Mrs. Devereux I knew it had driven her out, too, to the darkness and the waves, and Devereux's ghost of a smoke."

"And you found her?"

It was the first time that Reardon's partner had opened his lips since the entrance of Barnaby, and everybody turned to look at him. He was bending toward Barnaby, his face white and tense with emotion, his lips set and stern. Even Barnaby was impressed, and the rest of his story was told directly to the man with the match-box, and not to the rest of us.

"Yes, I did find her, but it was too late to do anything. It was late, you see, and everybody was inside listening to the concert. There wasn't a soul at the point where she stood. The light shone near her this time, not an arm's length away. From where I stood you would have sworn a man was beside her, smoking.

"But all at once the light flickered and moved away. She did not stir, but watched it, as though hypnotized, her beautiful eyes wide and staring. There was no fear in her face—nothing but a strange sort of wonder. The light moved, as I say, away from her, and suddenly she followed it, as though obeying an unheard command. Straight ahead it went, steadily, deliberately, like a cigar-light would move smoked by a man walking leisurely.

"But when it reached the rail it did not stop."

Reardon's partner rose abruptly and leaned across the table toward Barnaby. Between them lay the little ivory death's-head.

"And she followed it?" he demanded.

"She followed it," repeated Barnaby. "With her arms outstretched, as though she obeyed a call I could not hear. She was over the rail before I could reach her. I saw her slip down into the darkness, and the light glowed for an instant, then vanished, too, not quickly, but steadily, slowly, just as the last tip of a cigar goes out. I believe that it was Charlie Devereux's last smoke."

No one spoke.

Reardon's partner stood for a minute staring ahead of him with wide, thoughtful eyes; then he suddenly turned on his heel and went out into the fog.

Barnaby bent forward after he had gone and took the little Japanese match-box in his hand to look at it.

"They make those things awfully well, don't they?" asked Reardon, to relieve the strain.

"Yes," answered Barnaby, "indeed they do. I haven't seen this one for four years. Not since I mailed it in Paris back to Jack Crane. They make them extremely well. Won't some one please go and bring him back? We're just about nearing the place where the aforesaid pearls sautés was possibly served, and the fog gets on one's brain. I happen to know."

"You said you didn't believe the story yourself," said Dillingham nervously, as he started to light his cigar and then let the match burn out, staring at the tip of the cigar.

"I don't." Barnaby stood up and slipped into his cravenette. "I don't believe a word of it—that is, on general principles and a certain prejudice I have against ghosts. I don't mind ghosts as long as they mind their own business and keep to the graveyards, but when they come around Atlantic liners and walk deck and smoke ghost cigars, then I am willing to hand them out the benefit of the doubt. I'm going out after Crane."

"Just a minute," called Reardon. "Was there any smoke to that ghost cigar?"

But Barnaby had swung out on deck after Jack Crane.

The rest of us sat about the table with unlighted cigars, staring at the little ivory death-head's match-box before us and thinking of Charlie Devereux's last smoke.

THE BLACK BELL BUOY

Rupert Chesterton

The name Rupert Chesterton was a regular feature of the boys' adventure magazines in the early years of the twentieth century, but details about him are elusive, which makes me suspect the name is a pseudonym. In addition to short stories in magazines he was best known for three novels for boys: The Phantom Battleship *(1911) and its sequel* The Captain of the Phantom *(1921), both rip-roaring naval adventures, plus* The Quest of the Veiled King *(1911), a perilous mission into the Americas. Whoever Chesterton was, once in a while he entered the adult field, as with this story from 1907.*

FORTY YEARS, MAN AND BOY, HAVE I BEEN IN THE AUSTRALIAN pilot service, chiefly on the eastern coast, the waters and ports within the Great Barrier Reef being my special territory.

As you may guess, I have seen some queer things during that time, but the queerest, the most unaccountable, was the Black Bell Buoy affair.

A good many years ago now, the Queensland Government had a monster bell-buoy made, to be anchored over a dangerous rock near the channel leading to the Cardingham River, two miles up which, as I don't need to tell you, lies the busy port of Cardingham.

This nasty lump of coral, which had already taken toll of several fine ships, was called the Black Rock, and so, as a matter of course, the buoy took its name from it. It was a particularly big affair, very heavy and strong—the largest thing of its kind ever turned out in the Government yards, and they were rather proud of it.

When the buoy was finished and ready for work, it was shipped on board the little Marine Board steamer *Rockwell*, which at once set off for the Black Rock. Here the big iron globe was hoisted overboard and anchored to the coral with a special cable. Then, just as the officers thought the job complete, it was discovered that some of the riveting was rather faulty and would have to be seen to if the buoy were to keep afloat.

After some discussion, it was decided to leave two men behind in the gig to attend to it, while the *Rockwell* went a little way further up the coast to drop supplies at a lighthouse. It was summer time, the sea was smooth, and there was not the slightest danger.

Now, the Marine Board was a mighty small affair in those days, very different from the big Government department it has since grown to, and it was quite a job to find two competent men among the *Rockwell's* little company to attend to the defective plates. At last, however, the pair were selected—Danvers, the second engineer, for one, and Pettitt, first-officer of the steamer, for his mate. With the necessary tools they moored on to the buoy, then the *Rockwell* steamed off to visit the lighthouse, promising to pick them up on her way south again.

Before I go any further I ought to tell you that, according to Cardingham gossip, which in this case was pretty correct, Danvers and Pettitt were rivals in love—and keen rivals at that. Old Captain O'Higgins' daughter was the lass both were after, but in each case the same reason—lack of cash—prevented them from proposing, for the old man had vowed that he would have no penniless whippersnappers hanging round the belle of Cardingham.

Little Lucy had many admirers, but it was generally recognized that Danvers and Pettitt held the leading place in her estimation. Which would win the race no one could say, though most people favoured Danvers, Pettitt being a morose, bad-tempered fellow, somewhat given to drinking, if all accounts were true. The pair were not friends, of course, but they had the good sense, being fellow-servants of the Board, not to be open enemies.

And now you know exactly how things stood between those two young men when they were left behind in the *Rockwell's* gig to put in a few hours' work on the Black Bell Buoy.

Exactly twelve hours afterwards, having landed the stores for the lighthouse, the Marine Board steamer ran back to the buoy—to find Pettitt alone, apparently in a state of mortal terror. The tale he had to tell was a remarkable one.

They had practically finished their work, he said, and were just rubbing down the outside of the buoy, when Danvers suddenly gave a cry of alarm. Looking round, Pettitt saw to his amazement that a long tentacle had emerged from the quiet water alongside, and seized his unfortunate comrade round the waist.

Even as Pettitt sprang for the boat to secure an oar wherewith to smash the dreadful-looking thing, poor Danvers gave another shriek and slipped from the buoy. Pettitt got one glimpse of a hideous octopus, or devil-fish, the largest he had ever seen, then man and fish disappeared beneath the waters, leaving the survivor half dead with horror.

Needless to say, when the *Rockwell* got back to Cardingham and the news became known the story created a vast sensation. Most people believed it implicitly, but there were not wanting one or two busybodies who shook their heads sagely and said that it was ill-advised to leave two known enemies together on a buoy.

Wasn't it possible, they suggested furtively, that Pettitt, overcome by jealousy, might have murdered his rival and then trumped up the octopus yarn? But proof was lacking, and the scandalmongers were in the minority, so that Pettitt's version of the sad affair was generally accepted. Little Lucy O'Higgins seemed very much distressed at Danvers' death, but as time went on she appeared to recover her former spirits.

Curiously enough, Pettitt never seemed quite the same after the accident. Whether it was the suspicion that had been cast upon him by the gossips, or the horror of his meeting with the octopus, it was impossible to say, but he grew moody and irritable, so that his superiors began to look upon him as half crazy. He gave way more than ever to drink, too, and at last someone or other told him that the Government service would be better without him.

The loss of his comfortable billet on the *Rockwell* seemed to make him more queer than ever; but it was not long before he got a berth as mate of the schooner *Bertha*, running between various East Coast ports.

Some months went by, and then, to the disgust of the Marine Board, it was discovered that the Black Bell Buoy, which had been doing useful work, had somehow or other got adrift. Even while the Government steamer was on her way to look for it and fix up a temporary buoy, a French brig went and piled herself up on the Black Rock, and the officials' disgust changed to active annoyance.

The *Rockwell* failed to find the wanderer, whereupon the Marine Board issued a "Notice to Mariners," wherein they offered a reward of fifty pounds for the recovery of the big globe, which was supposed to be drifting alternately north and south within the Barrier Reef, according to the set of the tides.

The prospect of earning fifty pounds for a simple towing job set every skipper between Rockhampton and Cape York on his mettle, but for some time the bell-buoy eluded them altogether. Then one day a tramp steamer put into Cardingham and reported that she had heard a bell ringing the previous night, and had seen a large sphere drift past her in the gloom.

A week after, a brigantine put into Rockhampton with extensive damage to her bows, caused by running into a globular object with a bell on top.

The Marine Board grew still more annoyed; not only was their buoy a deserter, but it was rapidly becoming a danger to navigation. So they increased the reward to a hundred pounds, and every man jack on the coasters kept his eyes peeled night and day for an iron globe with a melancholy bell clang-clanging away on top.

At last, about a month later, a steamer came into port and announced that she had actually captured the derelict, and had taken it in tow, but, a swell springing up, the buoy had got under her stern, smashing two blades of her propeller, whereupon the anxious skipper had cut his prize adrift.

That captain's tale of woe proved to be the forerunner of several. Two schooners, several steamers, and one or two smaller craft all sighted the bell-buoy at different points and took it in tow, but not a solitary one of them succeeded in getting it into port. Either it broke adrift, bobbed alongside and stove in a plate, or else it made a vicious dart at the towing vessel's stern and damaged her steering-gear.

From a standing joke among seafarers the bell-buoy progressed till it became an emblem of bad luck; most of the skippers—reward or no reward—would as soon have thought of hooking on to it as of taking Davy Jones for a messmate.

A year went by, and the buoy was sighted only once, so that at last people began to think that it had been cast ashore at some lonely spot or got stove in and sent to the bottom. A smaller substitute had been moored in its place, and the general public forgot all about it. Curiously enough, though the Marine Board people had given it up as lost, they omitted to withdraw the reward.

Meanwhile Pettitt, late of the *Rockwell*, had been jogging along fairly well in his new billet on the *Bertha*. He was still as gloomy and preoccupied as ever, and given to drinking more than was good for him, but he was a good navigator and officer, and so kept his job—till after what happened one squally night. The facts of the affair, I should explain, were given to me afterwards by the bo'sun of the *Bertha*.

The schooner was running up the coast, bound for Cooktown, when the look-out man reported a bell ringing some way ahead.

"You must be mistaken, man," said Pettitt gruffly. "We're out of Soundings, and there's no ship near."

"It wasn't a ship's bell, sir," answered the sailor. "My colonial oath! Perhaps it might be the old Black Bell Buoy, sir!"

At that Pettitt seemed to stagger, and told him not to be a fool. All the same, however, he got his glasses and had a look round forward. Soon everyone on deck could hear the irregular strokes of the bell, and they began to talk about the buoy and the hundred pounds reward hanging on to it.

Presently the mate came back aft, looking very pale.

"It's the buoy right enough," he said. "I thought the cursed thing was at the bottom long ago. Put your helm down a couple of points"—to the man at the wheel—"we want nothing to do with that lump of ill-luck."

Just as the schooner's head was paying off, with the bell clanging away to port, the captain came on deck. Directly he heard what was a foot he bristled up.

"Put the ship back on her course," he said, "and clear away the boat. I'm going to get that hundred pounds, or know the reason why!"

Pettitt flared up at that, and put all sorts of objections in the way, but the skipper laughed at him for a superstitious old woman and ordered the boat away. They soon picked up the bell-buoy, made a line fast to it, and started to tow.

"You'll repent it, sir," cried the mate, looking like death himself. "There's some curse on that buoy; we shall fail like all the other ships."

"To blazes with your nonsense!" answered the captain angrily. "Do you think I'm afraid of a lump of iron? I'd tow Old Nick himself for a hundred pounds!"

Pettitt went off in a huff, and the schooner went on her way, with the buoy bobbing and yawing about astern, clanging away till the din got on everyone's nerves. As the night went on the wind rose to half-a-gale, and the sea got up with it, till at last the *Bertha* was making precious bad weather of it, sometimes with the buoy half under her stern, sometimes with the tow-rope twanging like a harp-string.

At last, seemingly, Pettitt could stand it no longer; he went aft to the captain with several of the more timid hands behind him, and asked that the buoy should be cut adrift, as it was no longer safe to attempt to tow it.

Accounts differ somewhat as to exactly what happened; but there was a pretty lively argument, the captain losing his temper and swearing he'd stick to the globe till the line parted. While they were all jabbering, as luck would have it, a big sea got up behind the schooner, and before anything could be done the buoy came rushing along in the crest of it and crashed full tilt into the *Bertha's* stern, starting pretty nearly all the timbers.

"We're sinking!" yelled someone. "It's the working of the curse!"

Pettitt cut the line; but the mischief was done, and in less than ten minutes the schooner sank like a stone. The crew got away just in time in their boat, but rowing ashore through the surf the craft got broken up, and only Pettitt and two men reached the beach alive.

After their tale was told, of course, the buoy got a worse name than ever, and so strong was the feeling about the mischievous thing among shipmasters and owners that the Marine Board sent the *Rockwell* off on a special cruise just to locate the sphere and sink it. But the buoy dodged its would-be destroyer with the same uncanny persistency with which it got in the way of other craft, and the Government steamer returned to Cardingham with her errand unaccomplished.

As the months went by and nothing more was heard of the buoy, everyone agreed that it must finally have perished from sheer old age and rough usage.

And now I'm getting near my own little part in the story. It was about a year after the loss of the *Bertha*, when I was cruising up and down in my cutter looking for inward-bound ships. Late one evening we sighted a fine-looking 2000-ton steamer. She made a signal for a pilot, and I went on board. Judge of my surprise when, as the captain came forward, I recognized him as Jim Pettitt, whom I had known in his Marine Board days, but had more or less lost sight of afterwards. He was looking very old and grey for so young a man, I thought, and there was a queer light in his eyes that I didn't like.

"I daresay you're surprised to see me here, old man," he said, as we paced the bridge together, after I had set a course for Cardingham. "To tell you the truth, I'm a bit surprised myself. I had a long spell ashore after the old *Bertha* went down, and it was the greatest luck that gave me the command of this new steamer. She's new and I'm new, old man—this is my maiden voyage and hers. Come into the chart-room and drink luck to us!"

I did as he wished, but in my heart I decided that he would have to lock up his bottles if he meant to keep the *Hippolyte*.

Back on the bridge again he went, rambling on in the same odd, excited fashion.

"Ah!" he said. "It seems too good to be true, pilot—here am I steering for Cardingham, skipper of a ship! I shall be able to marry Lucy O'Higgins now, if she'll have me. Her father won't refuse her to a full-fledged captain, will he?"

"I suppose not," said I, and then I made a blunder.

"I always thought poor Danvers was her favourite," I added unthinkingly. "She seemed to pine after—"

Pettitt turned upon me furiously.

"He wasn't!" he growled angrily. "He boasted as though he were, but it was all lies. I'd have asked her to marry me long ago, but the luck's always been against me. Now it's turned, I'll go and see her directly we tie up. Jove, but I'm anxious to get into port!"

"You find this a contrast to your Marine Board days, don't you?" I asked presently, staring ahead through the darkness.

"Yes," returned Pettitt thoughtfully, "you're right."

"You'll be pleased to hear that the old bell-buoy seems to have finally disappeared," I told him.

The captain started as though I had struck him.

"Ah, that cursed buoy!" he gritted through his teeth. "The thing seemed to haunt me; I think it would have driven me mad if it had stayed afloat much longer. And yet—ha, ha!—it brought me luck. But for it sinking the *Bertha* and losing me my job I should never have drifted to Melbourne and picked up the *Hippolyte*. But I'm glad the wretched thing has gone—more than glad. I hope by this time it's red rust, a hundred fathoms deep."

He spoke so savagely that I glanced at him in surprise, but without another word he strode to the starboard side of the bridge and leant over the rail, muttering to himself.

As for me, I kept my eyes lifting ahead for the first twinkle of the Cross Reef light, while I listened intently for the warning note of the Black Bell Buoy—the smaller globe which had taken the place of the unlucky wanderer.

It was a fine, calm night, but very dark, and prudence dictated that till I picked up the light or the bell-signal I should reduce speed. I was just moving towards the telegraph when Pettitt intercepted me with an impatient gesture.

"Let her alone, pilot," he said. "She's all right. Jove! Surely you're not nervous, man? I ought to know this bit of coast by the very smell of the water, seeing the things I've gone through hereabouts.

238 FROM THE DEPTHS

We shan't hear the buoy, it's too calm, but I'm willing to wager we pick up the light within the next five minutes. How excited I feel! There'll be a wedding in Cardingham before the month's out, or I'll never go to sea again."

He broke off abruptly, and stood gazing ahead, apparently listening intently, with the strangest look on his face, as revealed by the binnacle lamp, that I have ever seen.

I let him have his way about the ship's speed for another five minutes, then, as no light hove in sight, I moved to the telegraph. Pettitt's hand closed over mine as I seized the lever.

"Heavens, are you trying to annoy me?" he demanded fiercely. "She's all right, I tell you; I know the waters. I only took a pilot because—"

"I'm in charge here for the present," I said firmly. "My judgment tells me—"

"Hang your judgment!" cried Pettitt. "I'm going to take the ship into Cardingham to-night, or—"

Crash!

As he spoke there came a dull, thudding sound forward, followed by the wild clanging of a bell. The steamer seemed to recoil, flinging us this way and that; then her bows sagged downwards, and affrighted cries rose from the forecastle.

"We've struck the Black Rock!" I cried, thinking of the bell I had heard.

"You lie!" shouted a voice beside me, and, turning in amazement, I beheld Pettitt, his face distorted with fury and his eyes ablaze, pointing a degree or two to starboard of the steamer's bows. There, drifting slowly through the gloom, I beheld a huge black sphere, with a bell on its top, still tolling out an occasional melancholy note as it topped the wavelets.

"It's the old Black Bell Buoy!" shrieked the captain, while I stared aghast. "It's been my ruin all along, curse it! But I've—"

The mate sprang up the bridge three steps at a time.

"It's all up with us," he cried hoarsely. "Our bows are completely stove in, and the water's pouring in like a mill-race! Shall I order the boats out, sir? I don't think she'll float a quarter of an hour."

"Aye, do what you like," answered Pettitt dully, then he turned and gripped me by the arm.

"See," he cried, pointing ahead, "there is the light, we are two miles at least from the Black Rock. It was the old Bell Buoy we struck—that wandering curse! I have, lost my ship, I have lost Lucy—and all through that. And yet I deserve it all, mark you—I deserve it all!"

"Never mind that now," I told him, for the ship was settling fast, and the frightened men needed some sharp talking to if the boats were to be got out properly. "It's all—"

"I say I deserve it," Pettitt almost shrieked, and one look into his blazing eyes, as he gripped my arm and held me there power-less, showed me that the man's brain had been turned by his misfortune. "I was a villain, a cold-blooded murderer. The gos-sips were right—it was I that killed Danvers! He boasted, as we worked together on the buoy, that Lucy O'Higgins preferred him to me. I hated him, and when he got through the manhole to the inside of the globe my temper got the better of me. Something whispered to me that he was in my power, and I threw the cover back and screwed it up. Do you hear? I buried him there alive, inside the buoy!"

I tried to shake him off, but he clung to me the tighter, while the stricken steamer settled lower and lower and the panic at the davits grew worse.

"When I had shut him in," continued the madman, with his lips almost at my ear, "I saw my blunder—the buoy would be inspected sooner or later and my crime discovered. But it was too late to bring him back to life—the lack of air had suffocated him—and so I filed through the cable-chain, so that the buoy might soon go adrift, and be lost for ever. But the luck was against me—the cursed thing haunted the coast, and drove me well-nigh frantic, while the memory of Danvers was always with me. And now—do you hear me?—now the curse has worked itself out. I wrecked his life—his spirit, inside that iron tomb, has wrecked mine! Ha, ha! It is fate, pilot. If I—"

Savagely I flung off his vice-like grip, for the boats were in the water and the mate was calling to us to come at once if we would save our lives.

"Come, sir!" I cried to Pettitt, still babbling furiously to himself. "She'll be under in another minute."

"I'm going to take her into Cardingham," he shouted fiercely. "Get off my ship, you coward! The Black Bell Buoy, ahoy! Ah, Danvers, you've paid me out at last! That cursed bell!"

The deck heaved under my feet, and I dived headlong over the side just as the *Hippolyte* flung her battered bows high in air, rolled slowly to port, and sank like a stone, with a shrieking, cursing figure still clinging to her high bridge.

There was an inquiry, of course, but I was fully exonerated on the evidence of the quartermaster at the wheel, who proved that the captain had forcibly prevented me from reducing speed.

It was also demonstrated indisputably that the *Hippolyte* had not struck the Black Rock, her shattered hull being discovered some three miles to the westward. Captain Pettitt's body was never recovered.

For a long time I kept the terrible story he had revealed to me in his frenzy strictly to myself, doubtful as to whether it were not merely some hideous phantasm of his overwrought brain, unbalanced by the suddenness of catastrophe which had overwhelmed him.

But two months afterwards, the old Black Bell Buoy, sadly battered and red with rust, was washed ashore not many miles from Cocktown. Inside it they found a skeleton and some shreds of mouldering cloth still bearing the uniform brass buttons of the Marine Board. The last link of the short length of cable which still hung from the bottom of the globe bore traces of having been filed nearly through, the remaining portion having been fractured, probably by strain.

And then I knew that Captain Pettitt, madman as he was, had told me the dreadful truth that night when he stood face to face with the workings of an inscrutable Fate on the bridge of the sinking *Hippolyte*, with the strokes of the Black Bell Buoy ringing out his funeral knell.

THE HIGH SEAS

Elinor Mordaunt

Elinor Mordaunt (1872–1942) was the pen name of Evelyn May Clowes who later changed her name by deed-poll to Evelyn May Mordaunt, although her married name after 1897 was Evelyn May Wiehe. Mordaunt was married twice, neither happily, and was only at her happiest when travelling. She visited and often lived in a variety of places including Mauritius, Australia, the Canary Islands, Morocco, Singapore, Fiji—there was barely an island or continent she missed. She supported herself and her one son entirely by writing, producing on average two books a year between 1909 and her death. Mordaunt's skill was in her power of observation blended with her own personal experiences and the result is often a story of tension and the unexpected, as the following reveals.

THE YELD BOYS WERE TWINS. IT WAS AN ODD LAYOUT ALTOgether, so every one said; for twins are supposed to be alike, and Agar,—"rantin' roarin' Agar," as they called him—and his brother Bran were as different as any two could well be. They are supposed to love each other, too, these twins, and it would be difficult to find in any port from Bombay to Riga, from Funchal to Frisco, from Canton to Surrey Docks, two men who hated each other worse. Agar looked on his brother with a bragging, loud-voiced contempt. When they were both boys he bullied him unmercifully, beat him, took all he had. Yes, always that; took everything that he had or might have had, so that Bran hated him with a righteous hatred, if a personal hate can ever be righteous, feared him, brooded over him so continually that his swaggering, broad-shouldered figure, his high-coloured face and flaming hair, blocked out everything else, even the girl, Ivy Dene.

Night after night Bran lay awake planning what he would do, what he would say, to Agar; but he did nothing, and it was seldom indeed that he said anything.

Both men were bred to the sea, living, when at home, in that slip of a village, Rye Harbour, with its tall, pitched, weather-board houses, edging the tidal basin of the River Rother.

The village lay flat on the shingle. To one side of it was the river, little save mud at low tide; to the other the grey flats and the grey Camber Castle. To the front of it were mounds of shingle, alive at midsummer with vivid patches of Madonna-blue borage and yellow sea poppy—grey shingle and dike and grey mud and slimed herbage stretching for a full mile to the sea.

Back of it were more dikes, pastures a trifle greener, scattered flocks; and then Rye itself, hung in a sort of maze upon the hill, forever agape, like the old woman in the ballad; looking down at her shorn skirts, at the place where the sea had once frothed about her feet, like lace and lawn, where galleons and great ships had laid their offering upon her quays—fine laces, gin, and other liquors from Holland; silks and wine from France, oranges and dried figs from Spain.

Always—well, almost always—the two boys had been enemies. At the very beginning, perhaps, Bran had been ready to adore his brother; a gentle word would have won him. If he was weak, his brother was strong; if he was slender and timid, his brother was broad and fearless, or so it seemed: for when you are able to make other people fear you, personal cowardice is apt to go unnoticed. Bran would have been willing to admire in his brother what he lacked in himself, to feel these traits were, indeed, almost his own, since they were twins. A feeling like this might have led to that lifelong and beautiful affection which may at times be found among brothers. In place of this it led to a bitter hatred, that hatred which a little thought will show us may become almost beyond words between twins. Agar could not bear the sight of Bran, could scarcely pass him without a kick, and yet sought him just for that—to kick and gibe and twist. If Bran was near, his colour grew even higher than ever; he swore he could have nothing in common with such a "runt." Bran on his side felt that he had been cruelly robbed. If there was not enough of Agar to make two men, there was enough to make one man and a half; and that half, if God had only been fair, would have gone to swell his own slender shape, to lengthen his right leg, an inch shorter than the other, to provide muscle, blood, some of the flamboyant, arresting colour of his brother.

Look what Agar robbed him of—one half of the flesh and bone that should have been his; his belief in God. For if there were a God, how could He have looked on, seen him defrauded in the very womb, and of all that made life worth living—lastly of Ivy Dene?

During the boys' childhood there was no school nearer than Rye, and they walked to and fro each day, taking their dinners with them. Between leaving in the morning—his mother's good-by kiss, the last sight of her waving her hand—and the return during the late afternoon, there passed every day a long, complete, and most dreadful lifetime for Bran Yeld. He left home a child, afraid, but refreshed by sleep; he returned every evening old—old and grey-faced with misery.

The walk to school was not so bad. The bigger boys—always, as it seemed, Agar was one of the bigger boys—larked along the side of the dikes, chasing the sheep, throwing stones at the water-rats and moor-hens, seeking for birds' eggs, for pignuts, for water-cress.

The first hours at school were not so bad. There had been Ivy Dene walking by his side, and now she was there in the same class. They went up and up together, while Agar remained stationary, sullen, scowling. "I'd darned well lick the kid if I'd a mind to such flimsy goody goodying," he said. But he never did lick him; not in class, anyhow. He took it out of him on the asphalt playground at the mid-morning break, behind some rick or hedge at the dinner-hour. It was not only that he bullied Bran; he shamed him, forcing him to kiss his big toe, as though he were the pope, to eat food that he had spat upon, and in front of Ivy Dene, too. Worse than that, on the way home he would twist his fingers in the girl's lint-white hair, while she screamed to Bran to deliver her—Bran who could do little more than kick at Agar's shins and scratch, toppling sidewise upon his one weak leg, weeping with rage and hatred and the heartbreaking weariness of the day, but suffering for Ivy's little hurt far more than he suffered for his own great one. Yet always Agar had only to look around, with a jerk of the thumb, and Ivy would follow him.

Often Bran would creep out after tea, along the hollows between wind-driven mounds of shingle, find Ivy, and sit with his arm around her neck, comforting her, crooning over her like a mother; while she lay her head upon his shoulder and sighed, saying:

"I am always happy with yer, Bran; oh, how I love yer, Bran! Don't let Agar come a-nigh me! don't yer! Don't yer, now! He's ugsome, ugsome."

"An' yet yer follow him."

"I din na follow him 'cause I'm lief, but 'cause I must. I'm freet of him, Bran Yeld—freet of him as my teeth are all freet o' lemon."

"Yet yer go with him." It was hard for Bran to be hard to her, and yet he persisted; it seemed as though there was something that he must get at.

"But I'm not lief ter go with him. O Bran, I'm not lief ter go with him; strike me dead if I am." She would draw a little back and look at Bran, and he would know that she was speaking the truth. She paled at the very thought of Agar. "'E tied up a puppy as 'e found wandering," she breathed one day close into Bran's ears, "an' set un o' them there fightin' cocks o' Squire Tasker's ter peck un's eyes out." Her own large, pale-blue eyes were strained with terror.

"Yer shun na 'a' looked," said Bran, hardly; upon which she wept.

"I'd liefer not looked, but I cun na not look when he bade me look," she would wail; while Bran kissed her and comforted her, kneeling at her feet, holding her slender little hands to his face.

Bran brought her forget-me-nots from the dikes, wove her wreaths of pink convolvulus. He made a little poem to her and sang it:

She is very pink and white;
She is not eight, not quite.
I'd like her for my wife,
And I'll love her all my life.

He also made her a bead ring, with beads as blue as her eyes,—all true-blue beads,—and they were betrothed.

Then one day she appeared at school so late that Bran had gone on thinking she was not coming, so shamefaced that she could scarcely sidle into the door, wearing a barbaric trophy—a dead shrew, hung round her neck with a piece of twine.

"'E bade me wear it, an' I mun, though I'd liefer 'a' died first." That was what she said.

By the time she was thirteen and the twins fifteen, she was tall and slender, and as faintly coloured as the pale sands, save for her eyes, which had darkened to the same tint as the borage; and timid, sweet, kind, and good as any girl could well be.

Agar had already gone to sea. Bran would follow soon; he was not so strong as his brother and would be as well with the fishing-nets and lines for a while.

When his brother was away he was intensely happy, so happy that he felt no one in the world had ever known such a rapture of life, had such a girl to love, found such beauty in the sea and sky, the redbrown sails, the grey and purple shingle.

From the moment his brother returned, however, he was possessed; he could think of nothing else. He hated Agar for himself; but even more he hated him for the way in which he absorbed his every thought, pushed his way in between him and everything which was beautiful and sweet and tender.

The first time Agar boasted of having kissed Ivy on her lips, so faintly red and smooth and finely curved, Bran could have killed him; would have killed him had it not been that the divers pictures of the way in which it should be accomplished, each more terrible than the first, followed one another so quickly that his decision became blurred. Besides, it seemed that whenever he saw Agar he was facing him, high-coloured, swaggering, contemptuous.

Still, he would kill him some day. He told himself that again and again; he, Bran Yeld, with his long, clearly pale face and soft, fine, dark hair; his brown eyes, as timid and appealing as a fawn's; with his gentle wistfulness—Bran, who, if it had not been for his brother, forcing him to hatred, might have well stood for a type of saint.

When Agar was away on his voyages he forgot about him; once he was back again there was no forgetting. Agar boasted of his light loves in every port; but when he was at home at Rye Harbour he divided his attentions between the sloe-eyed girl at the inn and pale Ivy Dene.

Bran's idea of love was all giving; Agar's all taking. Bran gave flowers and books, plants which he had set himself, such fruit as he could gather or buy; but when Agar gave at all, he was wiser in his generation.

One day Bran came to Ivy's house toward evening carrying a basket of blackberries decked with crimson leaves, more leaves than blackberries. When he entered the kitchen Mrs. Dene was standing at the table skinning a hare. Ivy sat in one corner, her hands in her lap; it seemed to Bran that there was the light of a past, complacent smile in her eyes.

Mrs. Dene drew off the skin of the hare as one might draw the glove from one's hand, and held up the faintly grinning, bloody thing by one leg.

"There," she said—"there's a love-gift as is worth the havin'. Yer brother Agar brought 'un fer a present fer our Ivy there. A fine present, too; four full days' dinner in it fer us two lonely 'omen, I go bail. A love-gift worth the 'avin'. Come, now, out o' this, Bran Yeld, you an' yer rubbish. I'll 'ave no more of it, cluttering up the 'ouse. Agar, now, that's different. Only last week 'e brought 'er a boco o' fish." She paused for breath, then took up her tale again shrilly: "Eh, come, now, don't yer stand there all o' a goggle, Bran Yeld, fer I'll not 'ave yer an' yer muck litterin' the 'ouse, sawying arter my gel. What 'u'd yer give 'er if she married yer, tell me that, yer an' yer rubbish—three jumps at the pantry door an' a glass o' cold water!" She laughed loudly, coarsely. "Come, now, an' done with it."

She caught roughly at his little basket as she spoke, and flung it and its contents out of the window. Bran glanced at Ivy. She had covered her mouth with one hand, but her eyes were laughing.

He had it out with her afterward.

"I was na laughin' at yer, Bran Yeld; only—only yer did look so sort o' cobobbled."

She glanced at him piteously.

"It's not as how I like Agar; I'm freet o' him, with his hair all a-gleed. It's yer, Bran Yeld, as I love," she cried. And Bran held her in his arms; kissed her, comforted her.

But the next night she was out among the shingle banks with Agar. Bran, in a sweating agony, could hear how Agar laughed, and kissed her great smacking kisses.

It was after this that Bran, eighteen now, took his first long voyage, round the Cape of Good Hope to Australia and on to Frisco, then down by the Horn and so home.

When he got back he found that Ivy was married to his brother, who boasted openly in his cups that he had married her only to larrup her and 'cause she could cook well. Partly this and partly to spite that snivelling young brother of his, younger by three minutes than himself, or so the midwife had said.

After this the two brothers came and went, sometimes on long, sometimes on short voyages, though always, by some chance, as it seemed, the one went east while the other west, and never once did they strike the same port or the same ship at the same time.

Both alike they kept clear of the dawdling coastal traffic, for the blood of deep-sea sailors ran in their veins; it was the one point in which they resembled each other. Agar was the stronger, the tougher, but Bran's seamanship was by far the best. As for steam, they regarded it with scorn; would speak of "knockin' off goin' to sea and goin' in a steamer."

In between their voyages they returned to the harbour, the one man to his mother, the other to his wife.

A child was coming to Ivy.

"I will wait to kill the man until it is born, for fear the fright should harm her," thought Bran. Then when the child was born dead, it seemed that Ivy was too broken to stand any further shock; that all their lives had settled to a changeless, dreary dusk as grey as the dunes.

Then Bran met her among the sand hills at the farther side of the harbour one evening, and she was weeping.

She was frightened, frightened, she said.

"He allus freeted me with his gleed hair and his yaller eyes, allus, allus! Ugsome, that's what he is, that brother o' yourn, Bran Yeld."

"What did yer want fer to go an' marry him, then?"

"I'd a liefer not, but I did," the woman's voice dragged tonelessly between weariness and despair. "Aye, yer are right there; I did, though I'd 'a' liefer not."

"Yer loved him?"

"Not me. It's yer I loved, Bran Yeld; but while yer was goin' on with yer flowers and verses, 'e took me, though I'd 'a' liefer not. An' now it's hell that I'm in, Bran Yeld, day and night, whensumever he's at 'ome."

She pulled down the neck of her torn, faded dress—poor Ivy, with all the fine smoothness of her dragged, discoloured, faded—and showed her bruise.

"Thank God as he's away on a long voyage to Australia come next week, and maybe afore he's back again I'll be dead. Please God, I'll be dead," she cried.

Bran himself had only a week more at home. He watched Agar, his comings and goings, followed his drunken footsteps home at night; but he was never alone, he was never drunk enough to be helpless. The week past, and he was still alive when Bran went up to Scotland to join his ship at Glasgow. He had sailed on her before and knew her. He had friends in the town, and out of his heart sickness, feeling that there was nothing more to be done, he joined up a day sooner than he need have done.

When the rest of the crew came on board next day, behold! Agar was among them.

Now, thought Bran. Never once had it crossed his mind that it would be wrong to kill his brother. Wherever he went Agar carried unhappiness; he had broken his mother's heart, he was killing his wife. And yet in a way Bran was glad that the thing was being done in order; that the man had been, as it appeared, delivered into his hands.

Once again, however, luck seemed against him, for the brothers were put in different watches, and it seemed as though they were never in the same place at the same time.

From the beginning it was a bad voyage. Some one had given the old man a small porker just before he started, and he brought it aboard with him, killed it while they were yet off the west coast of Ireland, endangering their lives in that wind-driven spot, when he might well have waited till they reached the belt of calms, all for a bit of fresh pork, and not yet two weeks at sea. No wonder the men grumbled; for there's not a deep-sea sailor who does not know that killing a pig at sea brings wind.

One stormy midnight the watch below was called up to trim the main yards, and Bran and his brother worked together at the capstan. But Agar was behind Bran, maliciously treading on his heels, and there was no chance to get at him.

They trimmed the yards to

Yo-ho, Piper, watch her how she goes.

He was near him again when the fore yards were trimmed, but great seas were washing them both alike, and neither had a hand to spare.

If ever the winds had a spite against a special ship, they had it against the *Catherine* that voyage. All down the west coast of Ireland she was torn and buffeted, until she should have been close upon the track of the northeast trades. Here she dropped into a heavy swell, worse than any dead calm, fretting and wearing the lank sails against the rigging, fretting and wearing the hearts out of her crew.

To keep them employed, the old man set the men to holystoning decks and touching up the paintwork.

Bran, a neat hand with a brush, was set to grain the break of the poop a fine, streaky yellow like oak.

Agar was holystoning decks; again and again Bran looked at the broad back in the blue shirt and thought, "There's the place for a knife"; but for some time the two men were never alone on deck. Besides, Bran had a feeling that his time would come. God—once more he believed in God—had brought his enemy to him there on the same ship. The rest would follow.

One day when he had finished the break of the poop and was busied with the rail, leaning well over it, he saw Agar below him, down on his hands and knees. No one else was in sight.

"This may be my time," thought Bran, and dropped his heavy seaman's knife point downward directly above his brother. But at that moment Agar, raising one arm to wipe the sweat from his forehead, turned a little sidewise, so that the knife stuck in the deck.

Next day the finely grained break of the poop was all smeared and spoiled.

From that moment the brothers watched each other constantly. When one was asleep in his bunk, the other would make some excuse of seeking oilskins or knife in the forecastle to make sure that his enemy was there, not lurking behind the midship-house, a knife in his hand.

Agar had no desire to put an end to Bran. Your really cruel man seldom kills save in an access of zeal; it spoils sport. But whenever they passed each other, coming on or going off watch, he would turn aside to jump upon Bran's bare feet; he stole his blanket, fouled his clothes, upset his tar-pot when he was tarring down, bringing the mate about his ears. At the wheel one day, when Bran had been sent aloft to clinch a new crossjack leech-line, he spilled the wind from the sail, shouted with laughter to see his brother cling to the slackly flapping canvas. And always, without ceasing, he held Bran up to brutal ridicule before the other men; told how he had stolen the girl his brother wanted from under his very nose. Not that she had been worth the having; he would toss any man aboard for her.

Another bark, a barkentine, and a schooner hung near them. Now and then it seemed as though the four vessels drew a little closer under pressure of that mysterious attraction which draws ships together in midocean, but that was all. The three others had their noses pointing homeward, and not one of the men but would have given a month's pay to be safe aboard one of them, free from the *Catherine*, which struck them as ill omened.

For two weeks they hung there. Then the wind came, blowing aft; at first small and fitful, freshening to half a gale, and the *Catherine* wallowed forward, rolling both rails awash.

Thence onward there were forever changing winds. It seemed impossible to make the trades, for which they sighed as landsmen for land.

Neither of the watches could count on a quiet spell below; it was trimming yards, taking in and making sail, morning, noon, and night.

At last,—and it was as though Nature had been playing like a cat with a mouse, then pounced,—just southwest of the Azores, the bark was caught in such a run of storms as no one aboard her had ever known.

It was impossible to keep the galley fire alight for the seas she took. The forecastle and deck-house were swamped; the men were never dry; there was sleet in the rain.

The first day of the storm the royals carried away before the old man, mad proud of his carrying on, would have them taken in. Then the main upper-topsail split from head to foot; and as there could be no question of bending another in that gale, the lower topgallant-sail was made fast, so that they ran under the lower topsails and foresail.

The water poured in an avalanche over the weather bulwarks and back over the lee bulwarks. Day and night the maindeck was a maelstrom of yellow water; the men worked in it up to their waists; half the cook's pots and pans were gone from his galley.

A man, sent aloft, fell and was killed. The first officer, making his way to the poop, was caught on the companion-ladder, which was torn from its hooks and carried away, he with it. On his way to relieve the wheel one morning another of the crew was washed overboard. There were three more men sick in their bunks, and thus both port and starboard watches were so weakened that it was difficult to make any move without calling up the men below.

The vessel was pooped again and again; more than twenty feet of the taffrail was torn away, and a couple of boats were lost. The ends of the running gear were washed through the ports. Drinking water began to run short. The men went in a body to the old man, haggard, drenched, red-eyed spectres of men, and begged him to put about. But he would not heed them, and Bran Yeld laughed in his heart. Sometimes it seemed to him that the captain, mad with vanity, half-drunkard, half-fanatic, was in reality God Himself.

There was no rest possible either on deck or below; any moment an extra big sea might break in the forecastle doors and the men be drowned like rats in their bunks, if they happened to be there, which was seldom enough.

Then one forenoon came a sea which rose high above the bark, poised, and dropped.

The ship gave an awful sickly roll under the weight of water, swung a good five points out of her course, then recovered just as a second sea struck her amidships.

With a roar it poured across the poop and clear over the top of the midshiphouse. The door of the forecastle gave way, and the men there, including the three invalids, were killed.

Once more the bark was righting herself, shuddering, when a third wave launched itself upon her. The old man was lying in the scuppers with a fractured skull; the decks were swept clear, for six men, caught at the braces, were gone; the galley, and the cook with it.

This left five whole men, the second mate, the carpenter, one A. B., and the two brothers.

That evening the old man died. He had been mad to carry on as he did, but now there was no stopping the *Catherine*; for how was it possible to heave to with only five men to steer, trim the yards, attend the braces, haul the spanker-boom amidships, let go the sheets?

That was what they said. Then in desperation they had a try at it.

The two brothers and the other A. B. went aloft. The A. B., stupid with cold, his fingers so numb that they were without feeling, fell from the shrouds and was killed.

Bran and Agar were left aloft. Fighting with the fore upper-topsail, toiling savagely, shoulder to shoulder, the blood spurted from the tips of their hooked fingers as they wrestled with the ice-stiffened sail.

Between them they got the bunt up and the bunt gaskets made fast. The sail was like an immense wild bird, savagely fighting for its life, tearing at their hands, striking them in the face.

Then by some superhuman effort Bran wriggled his way upon the yard and lay across it, picked up the leech of the sail and held it down, hugging it with chest and belly.

An immense sense of exhilaration swept over him. Suddenly it seemed that he was master of his brother on the swinging footrope below him, and he cursed him, yelling through the wind for him to pass the gaskets.

Agar's head was thrown back, his eyes wild with fear, his face grey. It seemed that he was too numbed and dazed to do as he was bid, though he tried obediently again and again with great fumbling hands to pass the gaskets round the sail; while the man above shrieked at him:

"You sodger, you! You gory fool! You landlubber, you! You white-livered Turk! Dutchman! Dog!"

The words came in gasps, for it needed a fierce pressure of Bran's lean body to keep the heaving sail close to the spar.

There was something almost comic in Agar's face, with its wide stretch of cheekbone, its flaming beard, staring up at him.

"If I took a knife to him now it 'u'd be both of us," Bran was thinking, when a dreadful, grinding wrench ran through the bark from stem to stern, so that she writhed like some wounded animal with a knife in its belly, heeling over until the two men hung far out above the tumult of grey waters, clinging like drenched flies to the yard.

"My God! he's let 'er run off!" shrieked Agar. Bran caught sight of his brother's eyes. They were rolling with fear, his face ashen. "My God! he's let 'er run off!" His shrieks dropped to a muttering, he shivered, showing his teeth like a dog. "The sticks 'ull be out o' 'er. O God! the sticks 'ull be out o' 'er—eh! eh!"

He glanced down at the decks, lost in a turmoil of water, then sidewise at Bran, half appealingly. It was clear that the man who had set others trembling was himself half wild with fear.

There was another tearing crack. The foremast shuddered and shook like a little tree in a great storm; it seemed certain that the men must be shaken from the rigging. Their teeth chattered, and they clung with hands and knees. The mainmast had gone, snapped off at two thirds of its height from the deck, breaking down the lee taffrail. How the bark kept afloat was a wonder, for her lee was rail-deep under water, her deck like the side of a house.

The loosened sail, which had torn itself away from under Bran's body, flapped wildly, with bangings and shriekings.

Right at the back of his throat Bran began a hoarse shanty, "Shenandoah," beloved of all deep-sea men:

The sails set free, a gale is blowing—
Away my rolling river!
The braces taut, the sheets a-flowing—
       Aye, Ah; Aye, Ah!

He had never been frightened of anything or any one in his life save his brother, and he was no longer frightened of him, for he had seen his very soul naked, indecent with fear.

Somehow or other he made his way down to the main-deck, clambered along the starboard taffrail, and so to the poop, with its chart-house flattened like matchboard.

The carpenter, whom they had left at the wheel, was lying across it with a broken arm.

"No one man livin' could 'a' 'eld 'er," he moaned as Bran touched him, his ruling passion—a pride in his belief that no man could steer as he steered, that he could humour a ship, holding her alone against any storm—still strong within him.

The rudder had broken loose. The mate, who had stood to the braces, was overboard with the mast.

Thus there were only three left to man the *Catherine*.

The wind had dropped a little. After a while the carpenter got to his tools, and they set to work to try to get the broken top of the mast clear away, so that the vessel might have a chance of righting herself. Presently Agar joined them, and they worked like men possessed, running like flies up the steep deck at each fresh onslaught of the waves.

As dusk thickened to darkness they got the mast clear. But the carpenter, clumsy with his one arm, caught his foot in a trailing rope and went overboard with it. The two brothers were left alone.

Low down on the horizon, beneath the dead pall of greenish black sky, ran a fine strip of red, outlining the horizon like blood-stained sword.

It struck across Agar's face. His red hair and beard were all "a-gleed," as Ivy would have said. His eyes ran to and fro over Bran, anxious, ingratiating.

"Well, old man, there's only us two left," he said, and gave an awful half-grin of propitiation; then he muttered something about making the best "o' a hellish bad job," and whisky in the lazarette, if only they could get at it.

Bran did not answer, but he looked at him and smiled, an odd one-sided, half-crazed smile. He was singing again amid all that beat of sullen water, that roaring, shrieking, grinding which is the voice of a wind-jammer in labour for her life:

> *For we're bound to Rio Grande,*
> *And away, Rio! aye, Rio!*

The laugh and the song frightened Agar even more than the curses which had sounded so strangely from Bran's lips. Suppose he should go mad and jump overboard! The sweat pricked out upon Agar's forehead at the thought, for he had an awful dread of loneliness.

For five days the hulk of the *Catherine* drifted before the wind, which on the sixth day dropped to a calm, fifteen degrees north of the line.

Here in the doldrums, region of stifling heat, of oily seas, of vast depression, they hung for another week, then slowly drifted up close to the line, and lay there.

The cutting away of the mast had eased the ship, but the cargo had shifted, and she still wallowed with one rail to the water's-edge.

Sharks swam round and round her; the sea grew thick and foul with the debris which was thrown overboard or had slid from the steep deck—hen-coops, casks, gaping barrels.

Bran went about his work with no spoken word, though he sang continually, easing the ship all he knew, keeping her in some sort of order; while Agar followed him like a cur-dog close to heel. It seemed that he could not be quiet; he talked incessantly. There was nothing that he would not do for his brother; he fetched, carried, cooked for him, fawned upon him in a state of misery and fear beyond all words.

The horizonless sea; the pall of mist, like some dank, greasy dish-cover dropped above them; the rotting, stinking ship; the silence,—above all the silence,—terrified him beyond words. Yet when Bran sang, it was even worse; for he sang not to Agar, but as though there was no living soul aboard save himself; sang with a high triumph in his note. Within him was the serene strength of the man who feels that he can afford to wait.

Then one day he set his brother—still without words, pointing—to help him repair the lee taffrail. It was reasonable; any day the wind might rise with the sea, and both of them be swept overboard.

Together they collected spars, Agar carrying them, for by this time Bran was very weak. The bigger man could have felled the other with one hand, and yet, out of the very terror of loneliness, his one desire was to propitiate him, to keep him alive. Often Agar would hear his own voice talking, talking, and seeing Bran with no sign of hearing, he would grow wild with the terror of madness.

Then the appointed time came to Bran; quite suddenly and yet unmistakably. For as they made the spars fast in the place of the broken taffrail Bran saw that his brother, driving a nail, was leaning far over the edge of the ship. Throwing his weight on the opposite end of the heavy beam on which Agar leaned, Bran tipped it sharply, so that Agar fell overboard.

Agar could swim a little, and the lee rail was low in the water, and he would have caught it or some trailing rope had not Bran thrown tools and fragments of wood at him, driving him down. Once he actually touched the broken rail, clung there; but Bran struck at his hands with an axe, and with a loud cry Agar fell back into the water, sank, rose, and sank again. His flaming beard, his flaming mop of hair, his livid face, and his despairing eyes were dreadful to see; there was blood over the woodwork where he had caught it with his hands. But Bran felt no compunction; the world was well rid of such vermin.

He moved aft, singing as he went.

> *Royals free, royals free,*
> *Studding-sails aloft, boys, royals free;*
> *Clew up th' to'ga'sails, and take 'em in again;*
> *Bear a hand, jolly tar, at the mizzen, fore, and main.*

Once again Agar rose, but Bran did not see him; for he was on his knees in the little shelter which he had rigged up amid the wreckage of the deck-house, offering praise and thanks to the God Whom he believed to have delivered his brother into his hands. The life was out of the drowned man by now; but there was an awful grin on his face, as though he had just learned that even this was not the end.

That night Bran was sleeping like a child, when a wild white squall swept down upon the *Catherine*. Bran was washed from his shelter before he was yet well awakened. He scrambled out of the scuppers, made the fife-rail, and turned, true sailor as he was, to face the next.

As he turned he was unafraid. But at the first glance upward he trembled, withered with fear.

It was a brilliant moonlit night, as clear as day, the sea white with racing breakers. High above Bran Yeld's head curved the immense bulk of the oncoming wave, with its foaming edge. It was like the hand of God outstretching above him, dropping to snatch.

And yet it was not the wave which scared Bran. It was what he seemed to see in the wave, hung high in the curve of it, which held him rigid with terror—Agar's livid face and flaming beard; Agar's awful head dressed in all the panoply of foam, like a king in his plumes.

The remnants of the old lower-topsails were shrieking in the wind. A block broke loose and fell, striking Bran fair between the eyes as he stood staring upward.

When he saw light once more the day was clear and sunny, the maimed ship was halting before a steady wind.

Bran had been washed, wedged tight, between the deck-house and the flag-locker; both his legs were broken. But he was not alone. The passenger whom he had seen coming aboard on that high, curving wave lay close, packed as tight as he was, snug and close beside him; close as they had both lain in their mother's womb—Agar with his flaming beard all a-gleed in the morning sun.

They were in the track of passing vessels now, and a homeward-bound steamer, sighting the *Catherine*, sent a boat's crew to board her. They took Bran Yeld back with them, and their doctor mended his legs none so badly. To the feet of his brother they tied a load of shot done up in sacking, and sank him then and there, close on the line.

At least so they said, but Bran denied it; for the sea is deep by the line, and if they had sunk Agar fairly, as they swore they did, how was it that Bran found him already there, upon any ship he happened to sign on to? Always, always, with never a miss, getting round the crew first, swearing them to secrecy and denial, try as Bran might to dodge him, across the Atlantic, through the Pacific, round the Horn, into the China Sea, the Black Sea, the Baltic, there was Agar.

The only place he never came—and it was ten good years before the white-haired man with the scarred forehead dared to venture there—was in the little tarred weatherboard shanty at Rye Harbour, with Ivy Dene's arm around him.

Even then he did not dare to linger. Agar was not there, but he might come at any day, any minute. Bran's brown eyes, timid, wild, were forever from this side to that. He had feared Agar when he was alive; he feared him more now that he was dead. Ivy alone, withered and prematurely old, colourless save for her eyes, gave him peace and courage; and even then he dared not stay.

"I'm freet ter go with yer," she said, "but I'd be a deal more freet to have you trapsing the country without me, Bran."

Thus, with pedlars' baskets hung upon their backs, the two traipsed—oh, again, and again you must have met them—up and down, across and across England, Scotland, Wales; so long as it was far from the sea, until at last they were happy, most happy in forgetting, the tired, faded woman, the half-daft man with scarred forehead, forever passing to and fro upon the earth, fugitive and vagabond.

THE SOUL-SAVER

Morgan Burke

Morgan Burke (1886–1964) started his career as a civil engineer but from 1916 on became something of a drifter, turning his hand to writing, painting and even writing a stage play Siesta *(1934), labelled a melodrama about the discovery of hidden gold. He was an occasional contributor to various American magazines, notably* Blue Book, Munsey's *and* Liberty *in the 1920s, but he doesn't seem to have left a mark. Yet I think the following is the most unusual story in this volume.*

I CURSED MYSELF A GOOD MANY TIMES FOR SAILING WITH CAPTAIN Morbond. I cursed myself—still I sailed. For years I'd had my master's papers. Twice I'd refused a ship—I don't know just why, unless it was that curious confused look in his eyes when I spoke of leaving him.

"I wouldn't stand in your way, Roberts. You know that. But somehow you understand me. We hitch. You have your own way here with me as much as if the ship was yours."

He'd sort of paw his charts when he said it, not nervous exactly, but disturbed—with that look in his eyes that got you. Not affection, you understand, because I think he hated all men. His body and heart and soul were iron, and his vitals were blued steel. Not exactly vicious, either, too impersonal for that, but cruel... God, how cruel!

I'd watch him and just wonder. But I never interfered, and perhaps that's why he tied to me. It wasn't because I was afraid to interfere— at least I don't think it was. I felt like it plenty of times, you can bet your sweet life.

You see, in the ten years I'd been with Captain Morbond, I'd never seen him gentle with anything, not a single thing—except that damn' white mouse. Pink eyes it had, and its tail was pink. And it would cuddle in the hollow of his big hand while he talked to it till I thought he must be crazy.

The first time I saw it was a couple of hours after we'd put a line aboard the *Woosterman* about four hundred miles off Halifax. We'd just come through a blowy three days' blizzard, the bitterest, cold-est, most terrible days I ever heard tell of at sea, and I've seen and heard tell of some bad ones. Well, it turns off calm as a dead snake's tail after sunset, and we're rolling easy the third day after when the crow's nest quartermaster sings out a ship off the port bow. I makes her with my glass and there's something queer about her. I'm on the bridge at the time and I throws us off our course to take a look at this lubber, rolling like she had the colic or something.

And she sure had it. I called the second officer to take the bridge and lowered away the launch to board her when there's no answer to our hail. She's abandoned all right—lying in the trough with a spinning helm and the decks awash; and it's a ticklish job all through.

But this isn't a story of salvage, except that the salvage from the *Woosterman* which was the Skipper's share was a small fortune, enough for him to make good his threat to quit the sea. And this in turn was what made it possible for things to happen as they did.

As I said before, our tow was riding easy with a small crew aboard her under the second officer. I would have taken her myself as was right and regular, except that the Skipper, in one of his contrary fits, insisted otherwise. And so there I was standing in his cabin, amazed into stuttering silence to see him petting that damn' white mouse.

"What in hell's the idea?" came out of me suddenly. You see, I had known him a long time and wasn't so respectful in private as I might have been.

With a kind of grin shoved over his shoulder he lifts up the repulsive white thing in the palm of his hand.

"That, Mr. Roberts, is a man's soul!"

"Soul—what do you mean, a man's soul?"

"You're a practical man, Mr. Roberts, very practical. Because of that, sir, you wouldn't understand—you *couldn't*."

Well, I'm not so practical that I can tell for certain whether a man's crazy or not. But I went out of there cursing him and the mouse that was a dead man's soul; cursing all the years I'd sailed with such a diabolical fool; swearing that this voyage would be my last with him.

At first I couldn't make out what it was all about, but I'd hardly reached my own cabin before the third officer is knocking at my door. He's a young fellow and a nice fellow with a heart in him as big as his biceps. And he comes in with his face white, talking in a whisper.

"He's dead!" he says.

"Who's dead?"

"That cockney sailor hophead the Skipper beat up this morning."

Now I hadn't heard that the Skipper had beaten up anybody that morning. Those things are usually kept sort of dark, you understand. But I did know that the Skipper had taken one of his violent abstract dislikes to one of the crew, a wan-faced cockney on his first voyage with us, a fellow that seemed to be in a dope-daze most of the time.

It was a customary thing for Captain Morbond to do this, to select some weakling of the crew to browbeat and taunt and abuse. It seemed to be a cruel and chronic method of his, either to work off his own rotten temper or to put the fear of God in the rest of them as a matter of discipline. More than once I'd seen him beat a man half to death for no reason at all, and it seems that this time he'd gone too far.

We talked it over there, the young third officer and I. Some of the crew were making vague threats, he said, but he thought he could handle it. Besides we were convinced, as was the ship's doctor who joined us, that the man had really died from shock and his own weakened dope-full condition, and not actually from any definite blow he had received.

*

As we sat there, the three of us, recalling instances of similar occur-rences we had seen and heard of, I was remembering vague rumours and unsavoury tales that had come to me down through the years about this Captain of ours. Men on his ships had died before. Years ago as third mate his brutality had been forecastle talk in half the ports of the world. He was young then and mighty in his strength, they said. He was older now, but his temper was even quicker, and there certainly was no difference in the power of his wicked fist.

And yet, even as I despised the man, there was something about him that held me to him. Not loyalty. It was something else, some-thing weird—and evil. Then suddenly the significance of the whole thing slammed me between the eyes. He had said it was a man's soul—that damn' white mouse! A man's soul—*a dead man's soul*—and *a man had just died*! A poor weakling cockney sailor's soul! Where in hell did that white mouse come from, anyway?

Well, I didn't think he'd do it, but he did—quit the sea just like he said-he would. Took his big gob of salvage money from the good old *Woosterman*, went up on the New England coast and bought him a place he knew of, at the edge of a small fishing town. He'd told me about that place, a small estate built years before by an old sea-captain whose family had petered out.

Anyway, I was finished and done with him. *Through*—and thank God for it! I hung around shore for about three months. I had a nice little wad of salvage money myself, and I went out to visit some of my folks in Indiana. But the itch of the saltwater is on my hide and always will be, I guess. I stood it as long as I could, then when I went to sea again I had my own ship, and bygones were bygones.

Now maybe some people think that seeing the world from the bridge is a changeful, exciting life. But it isn't so. In the early days when you're jumping from ship to ship—that's all right. There's adventure, then. You're giving the world a few eyewashes, you're fighting and gambling and loving, maybe, in this port or that. You're running into lads you've shipped with before at queer times and in odd places—and that's Life.

But this was over for me. I'd done all that. I'd gone up in the world as far as the sea was concerned, and there's nothing very exciting about having your own ship even if it *is* a good ship with a good line: just jogging back and forth across the old Atlantic about as regular as Sunday comes after Saturday. It's monotonous, really. Monotonous as hell, and I guess I'm not old enough yet to relish it. I kept thinking of things I'd been in on,—little fracases of one kind or another here and there over the earth,—and in eight months' time the thing kind of got me. So I wasn't disappointed when the Company decided to stick the old girl in dry dock for some repairs.

I was free again for a few weeks, but not free either. All the time something had been feeding on me. Maybe it *wasn't* the monotony of being a respectable skipper on a respectable ship—maybe it was something else. You remember, Captain Morbond had said to me that I was too practical to understand about that white mouse of his being a dead man's soul. Maybe I am! But I'm not so damn' practical that the infernal idea didn't slosh around in my bilge!

The thing I'm getting at is that I'd been away from my old Skipper for about eight months. I had my own ship and was glad to be quit of him. I'd said bygones were bygones and thought I meant it. But I didn't, apparently, because the very first thing I did when I was free was to get on a train and go up to see him.

Well, I got into his town late in the afternoon, an old-fashioned no-good kind of a town with a lot of fishing boats huddled up in a naked little cove, and a couple of hotels that were full of fool city people for the town to graft on in the summer. I took a bus over from the station and got off in front of the general store, that was down close to the water. There I went inside to make inquiries about my friend the Captain. The proprietor of the place was a sailor-man himself, soaked in the brine of the sea for so many generations his name should have been "Dill" but it wasn't. And if I thought to make friends with him by announcing myself as a friend of Captain Morbond, I was mistaken.

Old Man Sabin just sat there on the far side of an iceberg, as he directed me to the house on the hill. I tried to be friendly, but the encouragement was not at all, and as I walked up the street that was the main street of the town, I wondered what devilish thing Captain Morbond had been up to in this quiet uneventful village to turn men against him so.

As a man who has taken and given directions all his life I had no difficulty finding the place nearly two miles from the store. The ramshackle old house, of somewhat imposing proportions, sat well back from the road on the side of a hill overlooking the town and the cove, with the sea beyond. It was a sightly place. I kept looking over my shoulder out at the sea as I strolled slowly up from the road. I almost envied him the detached quietude that must be his in a place like this.

There was no answer to my knocks at first, till I'd nearly beaten the door down. And then finally a great roaring voice, that I'd heard bellowing orders in storm and calm, ordered me blasphemously to enter. I turned the knob and shoved open the heavy door with my shoulder. It was the front entrance, and the door swung wide into a long room that swept clear across the front of the house. Behind a huge flat-topped table covered with maps and charts, sat the Captain.

*

He greeted me with an affable, glowering grin of surprise and behind his eyes was that strange confused look which I have spoken of. I could see he was glad to see me, glad that I had come—but suspicious, too. I found a chair and pulled up alongside the table opposite him, there in that great room that was like a ship's museum.

The place was full of all kinds of junk from God knows where. Things of the sea of all shapes and description: souvenirs and curios— compasses, clocks and sextants. Funny place, that room—and on the table before him were spread those charts of his. There he sat day after day plotting courses, and making voyages. Indoor, *paper* voyages,—with a scale,—marking his positions with needles that had red sealing-wax heads on them. It was pathetic—it was tragic. His enemies should have seen him then. But when he got up and led the way back to the kitchen, I saw that his stride was as powerful as ever, that he had lost no single bit of that great physical force which had driven him and with which he had driven men.

He lived alone, it seemed, attended to his domestic needs himself. I was not to learn why till afterward. But, together there with many a reminiscence, we had a full and satisfying supper. At this time, I was even expecting to stay the night. Then after we had eaten and laid the clean dishes away we returned to the large room and sat ourselves again at the table in the centre. Here we smoked and he told me of his paper voyages. He was tracing old voyages he had made and improvising others.

Not once did I see even a sign of his old testy irritation, and I thought that perhaps his being alone for so long a time had worked a miracle. But naturally there kept recurring to my unspoken thought the attitude of the old sailor storekeeper down in the town in whose eyes I had seen hate at the very mention of Captain Morbond's name. There was a reason for that, and I was going to find it out.

You may think that all this time I was not remembering about the white mouse that was supposed to be a man's soul. But I was, just the same. I kept looking for it out of the tail of my eye, and wondering if he still had it. I kept wondering a lot of things that I'm still wondering about, for that matter. For, you see, Captain Morbond was no fool. He may have been crazy in spots, but he was not a fool and don't forget it.

He must have thought I was, though. I can see now that he thought so all the time. Maybe that's why he liked to have me with him. Maybe I was—maybe I still am. But what I saw, I *saw*—and I'm telling it just like that.

We'd been talking for perhaps three hours, and between us had put away less than a pint of rum, so you see it wasn't that. But along about the time I was going to mention something about turning in, I suddenly saw the white mouse scamper across his shoulders and down his sleeve onto the table in front of him. He looked over at me curiously—amused at my startled look, I suppose.

"Remember this little fellow?" he asked stroking the soft pink and white thing with his big finger.

"Yes, I remember it," I said none too pleasantly.

"You didn't believe it when I told you it was a dead man's soul I'd saved for him," he grinned.

"Most men have their fancies," I said, thinking to humour him.

"Fancies, hell! A man's got a soul, hasn't he? No matter what kind of a lousy piece of corruption he is, a man's got a soul. And it's alive and clean and white and pretty just like this bit of thing *you* call a white mouse!"

"It's as good an idea as any." I didn't want to get into any argument. According to my experience, arguments, especially about souls, never get anywhere, anyway.

"'*Tisn't* just an idea. It's a fact. I've proved it. A man dies and the instant he does it, out of the air, out of nowhere, comes this white mouse and sits on the corner of my desk, way out there at sea in my cabin. *You* saw it. You know there wasn't any white mice aboard that ship. Talk about your ideas, jabber about your fancies all you like—but this is a *fact*—and I've proved it!"

He reached down in a half-open drawer at his side and blast his heathen heart if he didn't have *another* one!

"Two men's souls!" he mused, gently cuddling those damn' white mice between his two hands. *"Dead men's souls!"* And he laughed.

I just looked at him. I couldn't say anything—didn't, in fact, know *what* to say, but let me tell you the whole thing was weirdly repellent—terrible and horrible, too. I went kind of sick and reached over and took another drink.

"I got this other one since I saw you last." As he said it he went through me with a look that wondered suspiciously if I'd heard about it.

Of course I hadn't. But I managed to evade his invitation to remain the night, and somehow got out of there, away from that tight, heart-stifling atmosphere that sort of plugged my breathing—away from him and his white-mice souls of men that had died.

When I got back into the town it was dark and quiet as the inside of a dead fish, but in the rear of the store was a dim light, so I rattled the bolted door till the old-salt proprietor came peering to see who it was.

"I been expectin' you," was what he said. And he looked at me curiously with a kind of knowing leer that was none too friendly.

"Look here," I said. "This Captain Morbond, what's he been up to around this town? You don't seem to like him none too well and I want to know why."

"Well, for one thing," said the old fellow deliberately, "he killed a friend of mine about six months ago."

You see, my hunch was right. I just *knew* it, knew it before he told me. Didn't the Skipper have another white mouse?

"You mean *murder?*" I said.

"I wouldn't call it nothin' else."

"How'd it happen? And how'd he get out of it?"

I sat down and made myself comfortable, as it was likely I'd be spending the night right there. And the thing was just about as I thought: the Skipper had come into that town, big and brutal and domineering. He bought the place up on the hill and if he'd been halfway decent, the dignity that went with the traditions around the old house would have made him a popular figure. As it was, he hadn't been there three weeks before the town feared and hated him to a man. It was not only his eccentricities of temper and manner, but certain of his actions had antagonized the town mind.

At first he'd had one of the old Haskin sisters for a housekeeper. It was from her that the story had spread over town about the Skipper's white mouse. The next thing the town heard was that she had been thrown off the place bodily one day when the Skipper had caught her setting a trap for it. In all her fishing village life she'd never before known what real blasphemy was—nor *fear*.

He'd told her he'd make a white mouse out of *her*. He'd warm her withered virgin soul on the flames of hell... Well, she'd passed it on to the town, without making it any less, you can probably guess—and some of the women had even seen her black-and-blue marks, according to Old Man Sabin.

Now, down by the dock not far from his store, Old Man Sabin said, was a place that was supposed to be a boat-house, but was mostly something else. It was run by a man named Galloway and had a bar in it. Here "the boys" hung out nights. It was just one of those more or less harmless village dives where there is booze and checkers and a mangy pool table. Also there were sea yarns there, much reminiscence—and a great deal of blatant lying.

Captain Morbond was received here with not too much friendliness but he had plenty of money to spend on himself, and his custom could not be discouraged. Galloway insisted on that. His truculence, however, aroused plenty of resentment, and out-and-out hostilities had been on the verge of occurring many times. The story of the white mouse and her own narrow escape as reported by the hysterical Miss Haskin came to Galloway's with swiftness and stirring interest. Possibly the Skipper knew this would be so. Anyway, the next day, or night rather, he dropped in casually with that everlasting arrogance of his right on the tail-end of a remark made by Billy Wescott, who was Old Man Sabin's particular friend.

The boys had been speculating about Miss Haskin's story curiously, hardly able to believe all its weird details concerning so insignificant a thing as a white mouse. Billy Wescott had just said with a sceptical chuckle:

"They say he claims it's a dead man's soul—"

And right there's where the Skipper walked in! He glares around as usual, walks over to the bar and asks for rum. Now maybe he heard that last remark and maybe he didn't, but anyway he pours out a drink from the bottle Galloway sets in front of him—with every eye in the room on him as he does it. Then every eye sees him deliberately reach down in his pocket and bring out the white mouse they'd been hearing about!

He put it on the bar beside that bottle of rum and stroked it gentle with his big forefinger, then with glass lifted he bows toward it and says so that everybody can hear: "Here's to a dead man's soul!"

Now at Galloway's it was the custom to listen politely to a bare-faced lie without too much scepticism. But from the first the sceptics had been wide open with doubt about the fantasy of the white mouse and everything else included with it. Already the Captain had made himself one against many, and the many were feeling strong that night. Unfortunately for Billy Wescott, his tongue was the crowd's tongue—and there was rum on it.

Nobody knows just how it happened, or just what it was he said beyond that first statement. Maybe it wasn't so much what he said as how he said it… Anyway the next thing anybody knew the Captain started for him and Billy Wescott picked up a chair. It was a fatal mistake. Billy was not an old man, but neither was he young, and never in his greatest strength would he have been a match for the Skipper. He made one feeble lunge with the chair and that was all. The next instant the Skipper had him, a whirling centre of crunching, smashing blows. Whenever he went down the Captain picked him up and beat him down again, then eventually flung him the length of the room and himself sat back against a table with an ugly grin on him, alert that the attack might be renewed by some one else.

But it wasn't. Old Man Sabin said that, with some of the rest, he went over to poor Billy Wescott and poured some rum into him to bring him to, but the Skipper, from where he sat against the table, laughed at them with brutal scorn.

"Hell, you fools... he's *dead!* Can't you *see* he's dead? *Look!*"

He was pointing toward the bar where he'd left the white mouse playing beside the bottle of rum—and by the living gods, there were *two* mice there, where *one* had been before!

"But that was *murder!*" I said. "Do you mean to say the town let *that* pass?"

"Hell!" said Old Man Sabin. "It was a fight, wasn't it? Billy jumped on him with a chair, didn't he? Besides there's too much hooch being run into this town to start anything like that. Anyway, the coroner is Galloway's brother—so they called it 'accidental homicide in self-defence.'"

So that was how he'd come to get the *second* white mouse! It was hard to believe but there sat Old Man Sabin and he had seen it happen!

Well, the next day I went back to my ship, and as soon as she was ready for the sea again I took up my regular job seesawing back and forth across the Atlantic. I'd given my address to Old Man Sabin in case of an emergency, but I didn't hear anything from him for more than a year. Then finally, at the end of a particularly quiet voyage, I went up to the office for my orders, and there was a letter from him, asking me to come up there.

I didn't like to go but I had to, and I'm here to tell you it wasn't a pleasant trip. Gives me the shivers every time I think of it. But I went, and this time Old Man Sabin was glad to see me. Somewhat furtively, he led me back into the rear of the store.

"Well," I said, pretending to be cheerful, "—what's the latest?"

He was a bit nervous, and kept leaning back on his stool to look over his shoulder out the window.

"That's just the trouble, there isn't any latest. But the thing is gettin' me and I couldn't stand it any longer. Now maybe there isn't anything wrong at all, understand? Maybe I oughtn't of sent for you. But I aint seen him for about three months and I been thinkin' you'd better know. Of course I ought to have gone up there myself, I suppose, but I was scared to. *Everybody's* scared to.

"You see, after you left, he kept gettin' worse and worse. And we kept seein' less and less of him. But let me tell you—there's been funny goin's on up there. Jack Bascom was comin' by there with his girl one night and he hears a lot of shots all in a bunch. There was a *couple* of bunches of 'em. Well, Jack just steps on the gas and comes hell-bent into town, thinkin' the Skipper'd let fly at him for some reason or other. But then in a day or two somebody else hears the very same thing, and begins to talk about it.

"The next time the Captain comes down for supplies he doesn't seem any different. But every now and then somebody's hearin' those shots all in a bunch. Funny about that shootin'! Maybe six or a dozen shots at a time. What do you suppose he's shootin' at?"

Well, of course I don't know what he was shooting at, but I'm pretty sure he wouldn't shoot at *me*. However, it's late in the afternoon and I think it's just as well I get up there before dark. So up the road I went, and in at the gate. Everything looks quiet enough, neglected to the point of desertion. It's still and peaceful there looking down over the town and the sea beyond.

I kept wondering why in hell the man insisted on eternally fighting himself and the world, when such calm and quietude might have been his. I knocked at the door but there was no answer, and it was locked tight. I went around to the side of the house and stepped up on the porch, but that door gave no answer either. There was a many-paned window on that porch and I noticed that it had no latch

on it. I hesitated a moment, thinking of the shots, then softly raised
the sash and straddled over the sill.

Before I was entirely inside, I knew there was something terrible
there. The air of the hall was thick and heavy with a strange sick-
ish odour. I stepped noiselessly down the hall to the half-open door
of the big front room. The low sun shot through the window and
illuminated a scene of horror.

Seated at the table covered with maps and charts was the Skipper,
bent forward with one arm outstretched, as if his hand were plotting one of his paper voyages. At first I thought he must be asleep
all hunched up there and I started across the threshold, but stopped
suddenly at an astounding and horrible thing.

I *saw* it—heard it too! It sounded like the dry sliding rustle of
grain flowing down the great wooden chutes into the bins of an
elevator. God, the thing was terrific! Down from his body, out of
his clothes, across the table and over the floor there poured with
that ghostly, scrambling, rustling sound, a sudden startled stream
of horror—hundreds of white mice—*thousands* of them! A silvery-
white devastating horde!

Then I knew—I saw the outstretched hand lying there on the chart
was stripped to the bones, of its flesh. I knew then that these souls
of men, dead from that bone-naked hand, had multiplied again and
again to feed on his rotting flesh. The whole story was there, in that
fetid room tricked out like a ship's museum. Those repeated fusillades
of shots—frantic shots, heard from time to time!

Beside his chair was an empty automatic. In a corner was another.
The crossed cutlasses over the fireplace had been torn down frantically—one lay with broken blade on the floor. And all over the

place were strewn the withered little bodies of the white mice he had killed.

Down to defeat had gone the Skipper in the choleric apoplectic passion of fear, fighting with pistol and cutlass the ever-increasing myriads of white mice that were dead men's souls. Voracious souls that had emptied his clothes of the body they had fed on, leaving only the mockery of his bones!

I may be too practical to understand it all—I may even be the fool he thought I was—but I saw what I saw...

NO SHIPS PASS

Lady Eleanor Smith

Lady Eleanor Smith (1902–1945) was the daughter of the barrister and politician Frederick Edwin Smith who was made Earl of Birkenhead in 1919 when he became Lord Chancellor. Father and daughter both shared an immense zest for life, even though both died tragically young, the father of cirrhosis of the liver and the daughter of heart failure. Lady Eleanor was sure that she had inherited gypsy blood and researched deeply into the Romany culture, writing about it in Tzigane *(1935). By association she was also fascinated with circus life and became the first president of the Circus Fans Association in 1934. She even performed in a circus, on horseback. She threw herself with great vigour into everything that interested her and when she turned to writing she produced a book or two a year for the last half of her life. The volume* Satan's Circus *(1932) includes most of her strange stories, though not the following, which was published in* The Story-teller *in May 1932. It seems to me that this story could have been the inspiration for the TV series* Lost.*

"I AM GLAD," THOUGHT PATTERSON, "THAT I'VE ALWAYS BEEN a damned good swimmer..." and he continued to plough his way grimly through the churning tumbled argent of the breakers.

It seemed hours, although it was actually moments, since the yacht had disappeared in one brief flash of huge and bluish flame; now the seas tossed, untroubled, as though the yacht had never been; and the boat containing his comrades had vanished, too, he noticed, glancing over his shoulder—had vanished with such swiftness as to make him think that it must have been smudged by some gigantic sponge from the flat, greenish expanse of the ocean.

The strange part was that he was able, as he swam, to think with a complete, detached coherence; he was conscious of no panic; on the contrary, as he strove with all his might to gain the strip of land dancing before his eyes, his mind worked with a calm and resolute competence.

"I always thought we'd have a fire with all that petrol about... Curse all motor-yachts... I wonder if the others have been drowned?... Good job I gave the boat a miss..."

He was not even conscious of much regret as he thought of the probable fate of his comrades—his employer, his employer's son, the members of the crew. Already, as he swam on and on through gently-lapping waves, the yacht and those who belonged to it had become part of the past, remote and half-forgotten. The present and the future lay ahead, where a long line of sand shimmered like silver before his eyes.

Yet it was funny, he mused; there had been no sign of land seen from aboard the yacht, and it was not until the actual panic of the fire that he had noticed the dim shape of this island, "near enough to swim to," as he had cried to the others, but they swarmed into the boat, taking no notice of his cries. And so he had embarked alone upon this perilous adventure.

He was a strong swimmer, but he was growing tired. Were his limbs suddenly heavier, or had the sea become less buoyant? He clenched his teeth, striking out desperately, then floated for a while, lying on his back, the huge arch of the sky towering a million miles above him like some gigantic bowl, all fierce hydrangea-blue. When he turned to swim again, he was refreshed, but more sensible of the terrors of his situation.

And yet, was it his fancy, or had the shores of the island loomed nearer during the moments of this brief rest? At first he believed himself to be suffering from hallucination, then, as he looked again, he realized that he was making remarkable progress... He was now so near that the beach glittered like snow in the tropical sunshine before his eyes, and the sands dazzled him, yet he could perceive, lapping against them, a line of softly-creaming surf, and above the sands there blazed the vivid jewel-green of dense foliage. The gulls wheeled bright-winged against the brighter silver of sea and sand. Then he was prepared to swear that his ears distinguished, sounding from the shore, a harsh and murmurous cry that might have been— for he was very weary—something in the nature of a welcome for the creature trying so desperately to gain this sparkling and gaudy sanctuary.

And then exhaustion descended upon him like a numbing cloak, and his ears sang and his brain whirled. His limbs seemed weighted, and his heart pumped violently and he thought he must drown, and groaned, for at that moment life seemed sweet and vivid, since life was represented by the island, and the seas were death.

"Well, now for death," he thought, and as he sank, his foot touched bottom.

He realized afterwards that he must have sobbed aloud as he staggered ashore. For a moment, as he stood ankle-deep in warm, powdery sand, with the sun pouring fiercely upon his drenched body, the surf curdling at his feet and the cool greenness of a thickly matted forest cresting the slope above his head, he still thought that he must be drowning, and that this land was mirage. Then the silence was shattered by a shrill scream; and a glowing parrot, rainbow-bright, flew suddenly from amidst the blood-red shower of a tall hibiscus-bush, to wheel, gorgeous and discordant, above his head. Beating wings of ruby and emerald and sapphire. Dripping fire-coloured blossom. Loud, jangling, piercing cries. The island was real.

Patterson fainted, flopping like a heap of old clothes upon the smooth, hard silver of the sand…

When he came to himself, the sun was lower and the air fragrant with a scented coolness that seemed the very perfume of dusk itself. For a moment he lay motionless, his mind blank, then, as complete consciousness returned to him and he rolled over on his face, he became aware of a black, human shadow splashed across the sands within a few inches of where he lay. The island, then, must obviously be inhabited. He raised his eyes defiantly.

He could not have explained what he had expected to see—some grinning, paint-raddled savage, perhaps, or else the prim, concerned face of a missionary in white ducks, or, perhaps, a dark-skinned native girl in a wreath of flowers. He saw actually none of these, his gaze encountering a shorter, stranger form—that of an elderly, dwarfish man in what he at first supposed to be some sort of fancy dress. Comical clothes! He gaped at the short, jaunty jacket, the nankeen trousers, the hard, round hat, and, most singular of all, a thin and ratty pigtail protruding from beneath the brim of this same hat. The little man returned his scrutiny calmly, with an air of complete nonchalance; he revealed a turnip face blotched thick with freckles, a loose mouth that twitched mechanically from time to time, and little piggish, filmy blue eyes.

"Good God," said Patterson at length, "who are you, and where did you appear from?"

The little man asked in a rusty voice proceeding from deep in his throat:

"Have you tobacco?"

"If I had it'd be no use to you. Do you realize I swam here?"

"You swam? From where?"

There was silence for a moment, a silence broken only by the breaking of the surf and by the harsh cry of birds, as Patterson, more exhausted than he had first supposed, tried idiotically to remember to what strange port the yacht *Seagull* had been bound.

He said at length:

"I—we were on our way to Madeira. The Southern Atlantic. The yacht—a petrol-boat—caught fire. And so I swam ashore."

"Petrol? "the man replied, puzzled. "I know nothing of that. As for the Southern Atlantic, I myself was marooned on these shores deliberate, many and many a year ago, when bound for Kingston, Jamaica."

"Rather out of your course, weren't you?"

The little man was silent, staring reflectively out to sea. Patterson, naturally observant, was immediately struck by the look in those small, filmy blue eyes—a singular, fixed immobility of regard, at once empty and menacing, a glassy, almost dead expression in which was reflected all the vast space of the ocean on which he gazed, and something else, too, more elusive, harder to define, some curious quality of concentration that, refusing to be classified, nevertheless repelled. He asked:

"What's your name?"

"Heywood. And yours?"

"Patterson. Are you alone here?"

The narrow blue eyes shifted, slipped from the sea to Patterson's face, and then dropped.

"Alone? No; there are four of us."

"And were they also marooned?"

As he uttered this last word he was conscious that it reflected the twentieth century even less than did the costume of his companion. Perhaps he was still lightheaded after his ordeal. He added quickly:

"Were they also bound for Jamaica?"

"No," Heywood answered briefly.

"And how long," Patterson pursued laboriously," have you been on the island?"

"That," said his companion, after a pause, "is a mighty big question. Best wait before you ask it. Or, better still, ask it, not of me, but of the Captain."

"You're damned uncivil. Who's the Captain?"

"Another castaway, like ourselves. And yet not, perhaps, so much alike. Yonder, behind the palms on the cliff, is his hut."

"I wouldn't mind going there. Will you take me?"

"No," said Heywood in a surly tone.

"Good God!" exclaimed Patterson. "I shall believe you if you tell me they marooned you for your ill-manners. I've swum about eight miles, and need rest and sleep. If you've a hut, then take me to it."

"The Captain'll bide no one in his hut but himself and one other person. That person is not myself."

"Then where do you sleep? In the trees, like the baboons I hear chattering on the hill?"

"No," Heywood answered, still looking out to sea. "I've a comrade in my hut, which is small, since I built it for myself. A comrade who was flung ashore here when a great ship struck an iceberg."

"An iceberg?" Patterson's attention was suddenly arrested. "An iceberg in these regions? Are you trying to make a fool of me, or have you been here so long that your wits are going? And, by the way, tell me this: how do you try to attract the attention of passing ships? Do you light bonfires, or wave flags?"

"No ships pass," said Heywood.

There was another silence. It was almost dark; already the deep iris of the sky was pierced by stars, and it was as though a silver veil had been dragged across the glitter of the ocean. Behind them, on the cliffs, two lights winked steadily; Patterson judged these to proceed from the huts mentioned by his companion. Then came the sound of soft footsteps, and they were no longer two shadows there on the dusky sands, but three.

"Hallo, stranger!" said a casual voice.

Patterson turned abruptly to distinguish in the greyness a sharp, pale face with a shock of tousled hair. A young man, gaunt-looking and eager, clad normally enough in a dark sweater and trousers.

"And this is a hell of a nice island, I don't think," the stranger pursued, thrusting his hands into his pockets. He had a strong Cockney accent. Patterson was enchanted by the very prosaicness of his appearance; he brought with him sanity; walking as he did on faery, moon-drenched shores he was blessed, being the essence of the common place.

"Name of Judd. Dicky Judd. I suppose you're all in. Been swimming, ain't you?"

"Yes. And this fellow Heywood won't take me to his hut. Says it's full. Can you do anything about it?"

"You bet," said Judd. "Follow me, and I'll give you a bite of supper and a doss for the night. This way—the path up the cliff. We'll leave Heywood to the moon, Come on."

Ten minutes later, Patterson was eating fried fish and yams in a log-hut, with an open fireplace and two hammocks swung near the rude doorway. He had noticed, as they climbed the slope together, a grander, more commodious hut built a few hundred yards away amongst some shady palms. This, he surmised, must be the home of the elusive Captain. No sound came from it, but a light burned in the narrow window. As he ate his food he speedily forgot the existence of these fellow-castaways. He asked instead, gulping down water and wishing it were brandy:

"How did you come here, Judd? With the others?"

Judd eyed him swiftly. For one second Patterson imagined that he detected in the merry greenish eyes of his companion the fixed, almost petrified expression that had so much perplexed him in the gaze of Heywood. If he was right, this expression vanished in a flash, yet Judd seemed to withdraw himself, to become curiously remote, as he answered coolly:

"Not I. I came here after them—some time after."

"Do you mean that, like me, you were the only survivor from your ship?"

"That's about it," Judd answered, with his mouth full.

"Tell me about it."

*

"Oh… there's nothing much to tell. She was a great liner—I had a berth aboard her—and she struck an iceberg in mid-Atlantic. There wasn't room for me in the boats, so I jumped… But she was a lovely ship, and big as a city. *Titanic*, they called her."

"You're pulling my leg. And for Heaven's sake chuck it—I've had about enough for one day."

"S'trewth, I'm not!" Judd told him energetically. "But no matter. You don't have to believe it."

And he whistled, picking his teeth.

Patterson asked with a shiver:

"Look here, joking apart, do you mean to tell me that you honestly believe you were cast ashore here from the wreck of the *Titanic*?"

"On my oath," said Judd. He added, jumping up: "Bugs is bad here to-night. Wait while I swat a few."

"Just answer this," Patterson interrupted." Why in Heaven's name, when you think you were wrecked in mid-Atlantic, should you have landed here on a tropical island off the African coast? Bit of a miracle that, wasn't it?"

Judd was silent for a moment, flicking at the mosquitoes with a palm-leaf fan. He said at length, sucking his teeth:

"Not being a sea-faring man I take it, you don't happen to have heard a fairy-story told among sailor-boys all the world over—story of a mirage island that floats about the seas near wrecks bent on collecting castaways?"

Patterson thought desperately.

"This man's as mad as Heywood, and that's saying a lot… And I've got to live with them…" Aloud he said: "No, I've never heard that one. But there's one other thing I want to ask you… Who's this Captain that Heywood was talking about? Has he been here for many years?"

"I'll give you this goatskin for a blanket," said Judd," and you can doss near the doorway, where it's cooler. So you know about the Captain?"

"I've only heard his name. I asked you has he been here for very long?"

"Many years," answered Judd, with a peculiar inflection.

"Tell me more about him."

Judd laughed.

"You don't half want to know much, do you? You'll clap eyes to-morrow on Captain Thunder, late of the barque, *Black Joke*, well-known (he's always boasting) from Barbados to Trinidad and back again. But you may whistle for the Captain to-night!"

Patterson was sleepy.

"Sounds like a buccaneer," he muttered into the goatskin, and was soon unconscious, oblivious even of Heywood's noisy entry.

By early morning the island's beauty seemed more exotic even than the radiant plumage of the parakeets darting to and fro in the dim green light of airy tree-tops. Patterson was refreshed after a good night's sleep, and consequently less depressed. He bathed with Judd, leaving Heywood snoring in his hammock. The beach was a shining snowdrift, the sea a vast tapestry of hyacinth veined and streaked with foam, glowing, glittering in the brilliant sunlight.

They swam for twenty minutes and then lay basking on the sands.

"Hungry?" Judd inquired.

So delicious was the morning that Patterson had quite forgotten the eccentricity manifested by his comrades the previous evening. Rolling over on his stomach, he was about to reply in an enthusiastic affirmative, when he surprised once more in his companion's gaze that bleak, fey look that had already disconcerted him. He could not understand it, yet it was as though a sombre shadow fled across the beach, obscuring this gay and vivid world of amber sunshine, creaming surf, tossing sea and glowing, brilliant blossom. Beauty was blotted out when Judd, the commonplace, looked like that; he felt suddenly lonely, humble and scared.

"Judd," he said suddenly, and Judd wrenched away his eyes from the horizon.

"Judd, listen, and please tell me the truth. Just what are our chances of getting away from here?"

Judd eyed him thoughtfully.

"'If you want the truth, we haven't any. Sorry, and all that, but there it is."

"Rubbish!" said Patterson. "A ship will surely pass one day. Just because you've had bad luck…"

"No ships pass," Judd told him.

"Rubbish again! Look how close mine came yesterday. The trouble with you, Judd, is that you've been here too long, and got into a rut. I don't believe you care much whether you're rescued or not. Now, I do. And I'll tell you my plans—"

"Listen a minute," said Judd. He propped himself up on his elbow, avoided his companion's eyes, and resumed: "You might as well hear it now. No sense in keeping it from you, although you'll think I'm nutty. Listen, then, Patterson. We're here for keeps. Get that? Look at the Captain and his friend; look at Heywood. If I told you how long they'd been here you wouldn't swallow it, and I'd not blame you. But you've got to know some time—we're here *for ever*. Now I feel better."

Patterson shuddered in the blazing sunlight.

"Do you really think we've got to stick this until we die?"

Judd flung a pebble at a pearly cloud of seagulls.

"Worse than that, Patterson. Worse by a long chalk. I told you last night this island was mirage, magic. Stands to reason it is, floating round the world picking survivors from shipwrecks in all the Seven Seas. Well, there's something worse than that—much worse—and I'm going to tell you what it is. There's no death on this island. Death forgets us. We're here for all eternity."

Patterson laughed nervously.

"You should be in Bedlam, Judd. I suppose a few years' desert-island does that to one. But look here, now I've come to join you, we'll get away somehow, I promise you that."

Judd slipped on his trousers."

"You don't believe me, and small blame to you. I was like that once. But it's true. I swear to God it is. There's no death here. For the animals and birds, yes, or we should starve. But not for us. We're here for all eternity, and you may as well make the best of it."

Patterson, trying to dress himself, found that his hands were trembling. Yet he tried to be reasonable.

"Look here, Judd, what put this crazy idea into your head?"

"Do you know," Judd replied," how long Heywood's been here? Of course you don't; I'll tell you. He was marooned in eighteen twenty-five. Add that up for yourself. As for the Captain, he's had a longer spell. He was a pirate, one of those Spanish Main fellows I read about when I was a kid. His crew mutinied in July, seventeen ninety-five. Another sum for you, if you're quick at figures."

"Very interesting," Patterson commented idiotically.

"Don't you imagine," Judd continued, "that we haven't all of us tried to escape in the past. We've built rafts and boats—they've always been chucked back here on the beach by mysterious tidal waves or tempests. Then we've tried to kill ourselves and one another—we've been wounded and lain sick for weeks with mosquitoes battening on our wounds, and our wounds have festered, but we've pulled through. Now we don't do that any more. Too much pain for nothing. You always pull through in the end. We've tried to drown, and swallowed quarts of water, but always we've been flung back on the sands here. Death's not for us—we've jolly well found that out. And so we make the best of it. It's all right after a time. You live for eating and sleeping and you blooming well don't think. Sometimes you go mad, but in the long run you get sane again. And you kowtow to the Captain, who's got twice the guts of anyone. And, oh, yes, your clothes last just as you last. Funny, isn't it?"

"What about breakfast?" suggested Patterson.

"I knew you'd think me loopy," said Judd. "All right, come on back to the hut."

They scrambled to their feet, and there was an awkward constraint between them. Then Patterson pulled Judd's arm.

"What's that? Look over there! Is that another confounded mirage?"

Judd screwed up his eyes. Beside the rocks, where seaweed flourished like green moss, a woman stood, skirts kilted in her hand. She was barefoot, and sprang from one rock to another with the grace and agility of a deer. She was gathering mussels. As she worked she sang, and the drowsy, bell-like sweetness of her voice was wafted faintly to their ears all mingled with the cry of seagulls.

"Oh, that," said Judd. "Well, you'd better remember to act respectful when she's about. That's Doña Inés, the Captain's girl. She was his prisoner; he had her with him on his boat when the crew of the *Black Joke* mutinied, and they were cast up here together. At least, they both say so. First she hated him, then loved him for forty years or so, and since then, for about a hundred years, she's been fed up, but he's still keen on her. So keep away, that's my advice. Once Heywood went snooping after her, and the Captain cut his throat. He'd have died elsewhere, of course, and he suffered the tortures of hell, he told me. He'll show you the scar if you're interested."

Wait," said Patterson, "you've given me a turn with your crazy talk, and she's coming towards us. There's no harm, I suppose, in speaking to her?"

"None, as long as you're respectful."

They waited there on the beach while the woman approached them. She was young, about twenty, and extremely handsome. She wore a stiff, flowing skirt of burning crimson, and a little jacket of orange. Her dark, rippling hair hung like a black plume down her back, and her oval, vivid face was delicately modelled with high cheek-bones, a mouth like red blossom, and immense velvety-brown eyes. She was Spanish, of course, and well bred; her wrists were fragile, exquisite, her bare feet slender and arched. Her body was lithe, graceful and voluptuous; she moved swiftly, as though she danced, and as she drew near to the two men, a sudden soft breeze blew a lock of floating ebon hair across the fire and sweetness of her mouth.

Patterson was dazed; he had encountered much superstition during the course of the morning, his stomach was empty, and he was but ill-prepared for such beauty. Doña Inés said gaily, speaking fluent, attractive English:

"Good morning to you, *señor*. I heard last night of your arrival, but was not allowed to greet you, as I so much desired.

"Please forgive my execrable manners. We shall see so much of one another that it would be as well to start our acquaintance on friendly terms."

Patterson pulled himself together and kissed her hand, a long, delicate hand all dusky-tanned with the sun. A huge diamond glared from the third finger.

"Morning, Inés," said Judd, casually. "Where's the Captain?"

"Micah?" She became suddenly indifferent. "Waiting for his breakfast, I suppose. I must go to him. Shall we walk up the hill together?"

And so they went, and the Doña Inés moved lightly between them, all bright and flaming in her gaudy clothes, and told Patterson that he must accustom himself to this idea of eternity. After the first hundred years these things mattered little enough.

"As well be here, laughing and walking in the sunshine, as in our graves. Don't you think so, *señor*? And I, who am talking to you, have so much experience of these things. Why, haven't I lived here with Micah Thunder for near on a hundred and forty years? And it might be yesterday that he sacked Santa Ana, he and his fleet, and took me prisoner when I was on my knees at Mass, and swore that I should be his woman. And so I was, both here and on his ship. But I have almost forgot the ship, and Santa Ana, too. Now there is only the island, and yet I am not a stricken woman, am I, nor yet a day older than when cast up on these shores?"

And so she prattled, her dark eyes flashing like jewels, until she and the two men came to the clearing where were the two huts, and there, in front of the smaller one, sat Heywood, surly as ever, eating.

"Good-bye, *señor*," said Doña Inés. "We will meet later, when I have fed my Captain."

Patterson sat down on the ground and said nothing.

"Here's orange-juice," said Judd, "and custard-apples, and some combread I baked myself. No butter—we don't rise to that—but, all the same, we'll dine on oysters."

Patterson ate in silence. He supposed himself to be hungry. And he thought that he was in a nightmare, and would wake soon with the steward shaking him, and find himself once more in a gay, chintz-hung cabin of the *Seagull*, with bacon and eggs waiting in the dining-saloon. But he did not waive.

"I'll help you rig up a tent after breakfast," said Judd. "I've got some sailcloth. It'll last for a few days, and then you can build a hut for yourself."

Heywood, eating ravenously, said nothing, but eyed him in silence.

"I wish," he thought desperately, "they wouldn't stare like that."

And suddenly he knew of what their fixed eyes reminded him. They were like dead men in the way they gazed. Glassy and vacant, their eyes were as the eyes of corpses. Perhaps their fantastic stories were true, and he had in reality been cast for all eternity upon a mirage island.

"Oh, Lord," he thought, "I'm getting as crazy as the rest of them. And yet the woman, the Spanish woman, seemed sane enough, and she believes their tales."

After breakfast he worked at putting up his tent, sweating in the copper glare of the sun, while Heywood went fishing and Judd vanished into the woods with a bow and arrows. No sound came from the other hut. When he had finished erecting his tent, Patterson lay down in the shade inside it, and found himself craving for a cigarette with a passionate, abnormal longing. It was stuffy in the tent, and mosquitoes clustered round his hot face. He shut his eyes and tried to sleep, but sleep evaded him. And then, as he lay quietly in the oppressive darkness, his instincts, already sharpened by twenty-four hours' adventure, warned him that someone was watching him. He opened his eyes.

Outside, regarding him impassively, stood a small, slim man in dainty, dandified clothes of green-blue shot taffeta. These garments, consisting of a full-skirted, mincing coat and close-fitting breeches, were smeared with dirt, and seemed to Patterson highly unsuited to desert-island life. The little man wore cascades of grubby lace dripping from his wrists, and rusty buckles on his pointed shoes. He bore himself like a dancing-master, and had no wig, which seemed odd to Patterson, who gaped at a gingery, close-shaven head reveal-ing glimpses of bare skull like pinkish silk. The face of this man was long and narrow and candle-pale, with thin, dry lips and pointed ears. His flickering, expressionless eyes were green as flames; he blinked them constantly, showing whitish, sandy lashes. His hands were long, blanched, and delicate, more beautiful than a woman's, and he wore on one finger a huge diamond ring, the twin to that other stone blazing upon the finger of Doña Inés. Patterson, disconcerted by the cold, unwavering eyes, scrambled to his feet and held out his hand. It was ignored, but the Captain bowed gracefully.

"Captain Micah Thunder, late of the *Black Joke*, and at your service."

He spoke in a high, affected, mincing voice.

"I have already," Patterson told him, "heard talk of you, Captain Thunder, and am, therefore, delighted to have this opportunity of meeting you."

"You're a damned liar," replied Captain Thunder, with a giggle. "My fame, I understand, has not, through some absurd mischance, been handed down throughout the ages, or so Judd informs me. They talk, I hear, of Flint and Kidd—even of Blackbeard, most clumsy bungler of all—but not of Thunder. And that, you know, is mighty odd, for without any desire to boast, I can only assure you, my young friend, that in the three years preceding the mutiny of my crew I was dreaded in all ports as the Avenger of the Main, and, indeed, I recollect taking during that period more than thirty merchantmen."

He sighed, giggled once more, and shook out the lace ruffles of his cuffs.

"Indeed, sir?" said Patterson, respectfully. To himself he thought, in a sudden panic: "I must humour this man; he's worse than any of them."

For the Captain, with his conical, shaven head, his long, pale face, his deprecating giggle, his cold, greenish eyes and high, affected voice, seemed, as he minced there in the sunshine, most terribly like an animated corpse coquetting, grotesquely enough, in all the parrot-sheen of silken taffetas and frothing lace. This creature, this little strutting jackanapes, so bleached and frozen and emasculated, looked, indeed, as though a hundred and more years of living on the island had drained away his very life-blood, leaving a dummy, a vindictive, posturing dummy, clad in fine raiment, staring perpetually out to sea with greenish, fishy eyes. And something, perhaps the very essence of evil itself, a breath of cold and effortless vice, emanated from him to stink in Patterson's nostrils like a rank and putrid smell. The odour of decay, perhaps; the very spirit of decay, for surely, in spite of sanity and commonsense, this man should long ago have rotted, not in a coffin, but rather from a gibbet on Execution Dock.

And Doña Inés, creeping up softly behind him, seemed brighter, gayer than a humming-bird, in contrast to her pale pirate. Receiving a signal from her eye, he knew that he must make no mention of an earlier meeting.

"My mistress, Doña Inés Samaniegos, of Santa Ana," announced the Captain, with a flourish.

"Your servant, madam," said Patterson, formally.

And the lady, very grave and beautiful, ran her hand lightly over the Captain's sleeve and swept a curtsy, deep and billowing. She was not merry now, neither was she barefoot; she seemed haughty, and had shod herself in high-heeled, red shoes.

"This flower," said Captain Thunder, casually, indicating his paramour with a flick of white finger, "springs from a proud and splendid Casilian family. Is it not so, my heart? I took her when my fleet sacked Santa Ana, finding her myself, when my hands were steeped in blood above the wrists, praying in terror before a waxen, tinselled image of the Virgin. She was sixteen, and very timid, being fresh from convent. Before I wooed I was forced to tame her. When I had tamed her, I was still enamoured, and for four years she sailed the Main as queen of my fleet. The *Black Joke*, my ship, and the Black Lady, as they called my woman (being accustomed to flaxen peasant maids from Devon), those were all I prized in life. My ship they took, my woman I have kept, and will continue to keep whilst we remain here."

The drawling voice was icy now, and the light eyes had become green stones. Patterson realized that he was being warned. He answered lightly:

"And may I congratulate you, Captain, upon a lovely and most glorious prize?"

"Do you mind," said the Captain to Doña Inés, "when that little ape, Heywood, tried to take you, and I slit his throat?"

She nodded, her eyes very dark and lustrous.

The Captain turned to Patterson.

"There is no death on this island, sir, as you will discover for yourself, but it is possible to fight, and, fighting, to inflict wounds. A sorry business, very, I declare I regretted it, when I saw the poor creature gurgling in mortal agony. He was sick for many days. But, sooner or later, we all heal. However, I'm soft-hearted, once my rage is appeased. And now you will pray excuse me, while I seek the shade. I'll leave madam here to entertain you for ten minutes. A change for her, a pleasant interlude for yourself. In ten minutes, then, my dove?"

Bowing, he retreated, walking away with pointed toes, more like a dancing-master than ever.

When he was out of earshot Patterson said impulsively:

"I'm not enamoured of your Captain!"

"And I," she said thoughtfully, "was once enamoured of him for forty years."

"And now?" Patterson wanted to know.

"Now? "She scooped up some sand and let it sift through her fingers." Oh, my poor young man, does anyone remain in love for all eternity? Do you really believe that pretty legend?"

"Then you hate him?"

"Hate? No. You can neither hate nor love for a hundred years. I have suffered both, so I know, and tried to kill myself three times. Oh yes, there is not much that I cannot tell you about love. One does not live as long as I have lived without learning wisdom."

"And please tell me, Doña Inés," begged Patterson, "what you have learned about life in a hundred and forty years."

"A hundred and sixty," she corrected. "I was twenty when cast up here. What have I learned? One thing above all—to live without emotion. Love, hate, tedium—those are all words, very unimportant words. They are nothing. I like to eat when I am hungry, sleep when I am tired, swim, when the sun is hot. All that is good, because it is just enough. I used to think—I never think now. I was mad, you know, for a little time, five years or so, because I thought too much. But soon I was cured. That was when, having loved Micah and hated him, at last he sickened me. I imagined I could not bear that. But you see I was wrong."

She laughed, shaking back a tress of hair, and he knew that, with death, she had also lost her soul and her humanity. She was, as she had said, empty, drained of all emotion; she was as sterile mentally, this lovely lady, as the parakeets chattering above her head. But she was very beautiful.

"And the Captain?" he inquired. "Is it rude to ask what are his feelings towards you?"

"Indeed, no!" And she laughed again. "The Captain is still a man, although he should have been dead long ago. Being a man, he has need of a woman sometimes. Being a man, he is determined that other men shall not take that woman. That is all. Apart from that, like us all, he is petrified."

And then, although the ten minutes were not up, she heard Judd coming up the hill, and slipped like a bright shadow to her own hut.

Days passed slowly on the island. One day was like another. Always the sun poured brilliantly upon sapphire seas, gleaming sands, jewelled foliage. Macaws flashed like darting rainbows through the dusky green of jungle arches, the fruit hung coral-bright from trees whose blossoms flung out trailing creepers gayer, more gaudy, than the patterns of vivid Spanish shawls. And yet it seemed to Patterson after two months that all this radiant beauty was evil and poisoned, like a sweet fruit rotten at the core. What should have been paradise was only a pretty hell. Slowly, reluctantly, he had been forced to accept the island for what it was according to his comrades. He now believed, although shamefacedly, that Thunder and Doña Inés had lived there since the mutiny of the *Black Joke*, that Heywood had been marooned in the last century for insubordination, that Judd had emerged from the wreck of the *Titanic*. And yet, obstinately, he still clung to the idea of escape. One day he would escape. And then, once away from the island's shores, he would regain mortality, he would wrap mortality about him like a cloak.

Meanwhile, he noticed one or two curious facts. His clothes, after eight weeks' rough living, were almost as good as new. It was no longer necessary for him to shave more than once a week. And, once, Judd, climbing a palm in search of coconuts, had slipped, crashing on his head to what seemed certain death fifty feet below and had been picked up suffering from nothing worse than slight concussion. This accident shook his faith more than anything else that he saw.

They lived comfortably enough on fish, home-baked bread, fruit, coco-nuts, and the flesh of young pigs found in the jungle. Patterson learned to shoot with a bow-and-arrow, and to tell the time by the sun and stars. He learned to be patient with Heywood, who was half-witted, and he learned to search for turtles' eggs in a temperature of ninety-nine in the shade. He learned, too, to treat Captain Thunder with respect and Doña Inés with formality.

Sometimes, the Captain, a reserved, sour-tempered man, would unbend, and, fingering his cutlass, tell stories of his life as a buccaneer on the Spanish Main. Terrible stories, these, vile, filthy, sadistic stories of murder and vice, plunder and torture, and fiendish, cold blooded, ferocious revenge. Told in his drawling, affected voice, they became nauseous, and yet Doña Inés listened peacefully enough, her dark eyes soft and Velvety, her red, silken mouth calmer than an angel's. Sometimes she would look up and nod, and say:

"Oh, yes, Micah; I remember that, don't I? I was with you then, wasn't I?"

"You were, my dove, my heart. If you remember, I burnt your hand in the flame of my candle until you swooned, because you affronted me by asking mercy for those dogs."

And she would laugh.

"I was foolish, was I not, Micah? For what did it matter?"

Patterson, loathing these conversations, was, nevertheless, forced to listen because at night there was really nothing else to do. Always before in his life he had accepted books without question as being quite naturally part of his life; now that he had none, the lack of them appalled him. He tried to write, scratching a diary on strips of bark, but the effort was not successful. Nor did his companions do much to ameliorate the loneliness of his situation. He preferred Judd to the others because Judd was young and gay, and comparatively untouched by the sinister, dragging life of the island, yet there were times when even Judd seemed to withdraw himself, to become watchful, remote, secretive. Patterson learned to recognize these as the interludes when his friend, pitifully afraid, thought in a panic of the future that lay ahead for him.

Heywood was sulky and monosyllabic. The Captain, so cynical and depraved, with his vicious mind, his giggle, and his will of iron, had revolted Patterson from the first. Only Doña Inés, with her vivid face and her beautiful, empty, animal mind, seemed to him restful and gracious, like some handsome, well-behaved child, in this crazy world of sunshine and plenty and despair. For this reason she began to haunt him at night, so that he was unable to sleep, and he longed, not so much to make love to her as to rest his head against her and to feel her cool hand upon his forehead, soothing him, that he might forget for a few hours. But Doña Inés was watched so carefully that it seemed impossible to speak to her alone.

And then one day, when he had been on the island for more than three months and was in a mood of black depression, he encountered her in the woods.

*

He had wandered there in search of shade, aimless, solitary, and discontented. She was gathering moss, on her knees, her bright skirts kilted. Stars of sunlight dripped through the green and matted tent of foliage, cast flickering, dappled shadows upon the amber of her neck and arms. When she heard his footsteps, she turned to look at him, smiling very wisely, her head turned to one side.

"May I speak to you," he asked her, "without being snarled at by the Captain?"

"But of course," she said. "Micah and Heywood went out an hour ago to fish on the other side of the island."

He sat down beside her on the green froth of the moss.

"Inés," he began, and he had never called her by her name before, "I wonder if you will be patient and listen to me for a moment?"

She nodded, saying nothing; she was never very glib of words.

"It's this," he said encouraged; "perhaps, being so much wiser, you can help me... It's a bad day with me; I've got the horrors. To-day I believe all your crazy stories, and, try as I will, I can't escape from them... to-day I feel the island shutting me in, and I want to run away from the island. What am I to do?"

"You must begin," she told him, "by making yourself more stupid than you are. Oh, it was easy for Heywood, more easy even for Judd. For you it is very difficult. Can you not think only of to-day? Must you let your mind race on ahead?"

Her voice was murmurous and very soft. He said, after a pause:

"It would be easier, I think, if I might talk to you more often. Time, the time of the island, has touched you scarcely at all. With you one almost ceases to feel the horror."

"If it were not for Micah I would talk to you, yes, whenever you want. But you know how I am situated."

"Oh, don't think I'm trying to make love to you," he told her impatiently, "it's not that. It's only that you bring me peace—you're so beautiful, so restful."

Doña Inés was silent. He said, after another pause:

"Perhaps that wasn't very polite of me. In fact, it was clumsily expressed. Let me try once more—listen, Inés, you're sanity, loneliness, a bright angel in a mad world. I respect you as I would respect a saint. But I want to be with you, I want to talk to you. I'm lonely when you're not there—I need your protection."

Doña Inés looked away from him towards the green twilight of the trees. His eyes devoured her dark, clear-cut profile. She said at length, speaking very slowly in her grave, beautiful voice:

"*Mi querido*, I can't grant your request. I am too afraid of Micah, and perhaps I am afraid of something else… Listen, if I saw much of you I might forget that I should be a dead woman. I might forget that my heart is cold and my mind empty. I might wake up again, and I don't want to wake up. I am afraid of life, after so many years. And already you are making my sleep a little restless."

She turned her face towards him and he saw that the red flower of her mouth was trembling. A bright drop, that might have been a tear, save that she never wept, hung like a jewel upon the shadow of her lashes. Yet her face was radiant, transfigured, more sparkling than the sunshine.

Straightway, Patterson forgot about respect and saints and Captain Thunder, and kissed her on the lips.

For one enchanted moment she was acquiescent, then pushed him away, hiding her face in her hands. And he, realizing the horror that lay ahead for both, felt more like weeping than rejoicing.

"Go away," she whispered, "go away before you make me hate you for what you are doing. A moment ago you talked of peace: do you realize that you are stealing mine?"

He stammered, scarcely knowing what he said:

"Perhaps there are better dreams."

"Not here," she told him; "here there are no dreams but bad ones, and so it is safer not to dream at all. Please, please, go away."

"Inés," he said eagerly," I *will* go away—we'll both go away. If I build a boat, or a raft, and provision her, will you trust yourself to me? We'll escape—we may drown, but I promise you—"

He stopped. In her tired yet vivid eyes he had suddenly surprised, for the first lime, the dead, haunted look that so much disconcerted him when he glimpsed it in the others' gaze. It was as if she retreated very far away, drawing down a blind.

She said, patiently, as one speaking to a child:

"Oh, my friend, please don't be so foolish... I have tried, we have all tried, so many times. And it hurts, to fail so often."

"Then you won't come?"

She climbed slowly to her feet, brushing moss from her bright skirts. Then she shook her black, silken head twice, very emphatically.

"No. I will not come with you."

"Then," said Patterson, "since I can't stay here to watch you with the Captain, I shall escape alone. Won't you change your mind?"

She came near to him and put her hand for one moment upon his shoulder.

"No. I will never change my mind."

And with a swishing of silk, that sounded strange enough in that tropical, emerald glade, she left him to his thoughts, and his thoughts were agony.

For weeks he slaved in secret to build a great rakish-looking solid raft that grew slowly into shape as it lay concealed amid the dusky green of overhanging branches. He had told no one save Doña Inés of his resolution to escape. The reason was simple; in his heart of hearts he dreaded their bitter mockery, their cynical disbelief in any possible salvation from the trap of the island. Yet he still had faith; once aboard his raft and he would be for ever borne away from those perilous and beckoning shores; he might find death, but this he did not really mind, although he much preferred the thought of life, human life, life with Inés. And then he had to remind himself that the Spanish woman was a thing of dust, to crumble away at the first contact with normal humanity, and that he would, in any event, be better without her, since she meant another mouth to feed.

But he still desired her, and it was as though the Captain knew, for she was very seldom left alone. And so he toiled in secret, and in his spare time nursed Judd, who lay sick of a poisonous snake-bite that swelled his foot, and turned it black, and would have meant death in any other land.

Once, when his raft was nearly completed, he caught Inés alone on the beach, where, against a background of golden rock, she fed a swirling silver mass of seagulls. The birds wheeled, crying harshly, and Doña Inés smiled. She wore a knot of scarlet passion-flower in the dark satin of her hair. Patterson, determined not to miss a second alone with her, advanced triumphantly across the sands. The seagulls scattered.

"Look, you've frightened my birds," she complained indignantly.

"Never mind the birds—they can see you whenever they want. I can't. Inés, haven't you changed your mind about coming with me?"

She shook her head.

"Inés, please, *please* listen! Even if we drown out there together, wouldn't it be better than this?"

"Oh, yes, if we drowned. But we should not drown. We should come back here—to Micah—and then our lives would not be worth living."

"My life," he said, "isn't worth living now, not while I have to see you with that creature night and day."

"Be quiet," she warned in a low voice.

Patterson turned, following her eyes. Behind, only just out of earshot, stood the Captain, watching them sardonically. The breeze lifted the skirts of his green taffeta coat, ballooning them about his slender body. The green, too, seemed reflected in his face, so pale was it; paler, more waxen, even than a corpse-candle.

"Are you also feeding the birds, Patterson?" inquired the Captain, softly.

"No. I am looking for turtles' eggs."

"How many have you found?" the Captain wanted to know.

Patterson felt rather foolish.

"None—yet."

"Then you had better make haste, unless you wish to fast for dinner. Come, my rose."

And Captain Thunder turned away indifferently, followed by Doña Inés, who walked behind him obediently, her head bent, with no backward look.

That night Patterson thought he heard weeping in the hut that lay only a few hundred yards from his own, and he crouched, perspiring, sleepless, for many hours, until it was dark no longer, and bars of rose and lemon streaked the sky. Then he got up and went forth to the woods to complete his preparations for escape.

He had rigged up a sail upon his raft and had already floated her on a narrow lagoon that led towards the sea. He was taking with him three barrels of water, a barrel of bread, his fishing-tackle, a blanket, and a flint and tinder. He knew he would not starve, since fish were plentiful, but he was aware that he would, probably, unless he were

fortunate enough to end in a shark's belly, die of a thirst that must
endure for many days of torment in a pitiless and scorching heat.

Yet he could not wait; he must start at once, before the sun
was up, before the first sign of life from that hut nestling on
the cliffs behind him. And so, at a moment's notice, he took his
departure, nervous and weary and taut with anxiety, drifting with
his raft like some dark bird against the misty violet-blue of the
lagoon at dawn.

Everything was silent; trees and cliff and sky, the limpid reflection
of these in the glassy waters of the lagoon; even the monkeys and
the chattering parakeets, all were frozen into a breathless silence
that seemed to watch, aghast, the reckless departure of this creature
determined at all costs to break away from their sorrowful eternity.

Soon it was daylight, and the sun beat gilded wings, and Patterson
drew near to the sea. A curve in the lagoon showed him the tawny
cliff, and above it the huts. From the Captain's hut came a finger of
blue smoke that climbed, very straight, into the bright clearness of
the air.

"Good-bye, Inés."

And he was surprised to find how little pain there was for him in
this parting. He reminded himself once more that she was a ghost,
a creature of dust.

He passed the rocks and was soon outside, away from the island,
on the sea itself. The ripples danced, white-crested as though laced
with silver. Patterson fished with success. He tried to fry his breakfast and, failing, devoured it half-raw, with a hunch of bread. It was
very appetizing. After breakfast he lay watching, with ecstasy, a stiff
breeze swell his sail.

Already the island seemed to have receded. Patterson gazed with
exultation at the coral-whiteness of its strand, the radiant green

foliage of its trees. An hour before, and these, had been loathsome
to him; now that they belonged to the past, he grimaced at them
and waved his hand.

The raft drifted on.

The sea was kind to him that day, he thought, so innocent and
gay and tinted like forget-me-nots. Despite himself, despite his almost
certain death, he found his mind flitting towards England, and his
life there, as though he were fated to be saved.

He turned towards the island, gleaming in the distance.

"Farewell!"

It was a cry of defiance.

And then, in a moment, like thunder splintering from the sky,
came sudden and shattering catastrophe. He was never very clear
as to what actually occurred. All he knew was that from peace and
beauty there emerged swift chaos. A wall of water, all towering
solid green and ribbed with foam, reared suddenly from the tranquil
seas to bar his path like some great ogre's castle arisen by magic,
huge, destructive, carven of emerald. Then there was darkness and
a tremendous roaring sound, and the raft seemed to buck like a
frightened horse. He heard the ripping of his sail and then he was
pitched through the air and something seemed to split his head and
he knew no more.

When he awoke, the sun beat hot upon his temples. He felt sick,
his limbs ached, and he groaned. He lay still, his eyes closed, and
tried to remember what had happened. And then he heard a sound
that might have been some dirge sighed by the breeze, a soft murmuring music that seemed to him familiar. The song of the island.
He knew, then, that he was back upon the island. He had no need
to open his eyes.

"Oh, God," he sighed.

And the sweat trickled down his face.

And then, inevitably, sounding close in his ear, the sneering, hateful voice of Captain Thunder.

"Home so soon, my young friend? No, you would not believe, would you? You knew too much…"

Patterson made no sign of life. Back once more on the island. For all eternity… the island… and then the murmuring song swelled louder, louder, mocking him, laughing a little, as Inés had laughed when he had told her he was going to escape. The song of the island! And he must hear it for ever! He opened his eyes to find the Captain looking at him cynically.

"Now that you understand there is no escape," said the Captain, "perhaps you will not take it amiss if I venture to criticize your manner towards Madam Inés…"

But Patterson was not listening.

STORY SOURCES

The following list the stories in order of publication with original sources.

Barham C. N. "Tracked", *Cassell's Family Magazine*, May 1891.

Chesterton, Rupert, "The Black Bell Buoy", *The Novel Magazine*, February 1907.

Forrester, Izola, "Devereux's Last Smoke", *The Ocean*, March 1907. Text taken from *The Ocean. 100th Anniversary Collection*, edited by John Locke (Castroville, CA: Offtrail Publications, 2008).

Muir, Ward, "Sargasso", *Pearson's Magazine*, October 1908.

Shaw, Frank H., "Held by the Sargasso", *The Story-teller*, October 1908.

Scheffauer, Herman, "The Floating Forest", *Pall Mall Magazine*, August 1909.

Hodgson, William Hope, "The Mystery of the Waterlogged Ship", *The Grand Magazine*, May 1911.

Robertson, Morgan, "From the Darkness and the Depths", *New Story Magazine*, January 1913.

Gilbert, John, "The Ship That Died", *The Argosy*, May 1917. Text taken from *The Novel Magazine*, July 1919.

Dwyer, James Francis, "The Murdered Ships", *The Premier Magazine*, June 1918.

Mordaunt, Elinor, "The High Seas", *The Century Magazine*, October 1918.

Austin, F. Britten, "From the Depths", *The Strand Magazine*, February 1920.

Burke, Morgan, "The Soul-Saver", *The Blue Book Magazine*, February 1926.

Smith, Lady Eleanor, "No Ships Pass", *The Story-teller*, May 1932.

Wetjen, Albert R., "Ship of Silence", *The Blue Book Magazine*, July 1932.

BRITISH LIBRARY TALES OF THE WEIRD

*Haunted Houses: Two
Novels by Charlotte Riddell*
Edited by Andrew Smith

*Glimpses of the Unknown:
Lost Ghost Stories*
Edited by Mike Ashley

*Mortal Echoes:
Encounters with the End*
Edited by Greg Buzwell

*Spirits of the Season:
Christmas Hauntings*
Edited by Tanya Kirk

British Library Tales of the Weird collects a thrilling array of uncanny story-telling, from the realms of gothic, supernatural and horror fiction. With stories ranging from the 19th century to the present day, this series revives long-lost material from the Library's vaults to thrill again alongside beloved classics of the weird fiction genre.

FROM THE DEPTHS

And Other Strange Tales of the Sea